UNEXPECTED LOVE AT SILVER RIDGE

CLAIRE CAIN

To all my fellow mountainfolk.

CHAPTER ONE

Wells

The mountain air felt crisper, fresher up here than it had been in Aspen, somehow.

Not that I should have been surprised by that—this air was something precious. It filled my lungs completely, my chest rising and falling in great gusts, just to be obnoxious. In some ways, these felt like the first cognizant breaths I'd taken in months. Maybe years.

Preston had been irritated if I sighed too loudly—*sighed too loudly*.

Tears pricked my eyes, making me squint into the bluebird sky. Not a cloud in sight on this gorgeous late-August morning. Since Utah had so far proven to be so much like Colorado in terms of seasons, the chill of fall would be here in a matter of weeks, especially this high up in the secluded little hamlet of Silverton.

Hamlet. Wasn't that a word people only used in British

historical romance novels? It applied well enough here, though. Silverton was a small town, population eighteen hundred in the incorporated part of the city, with another thousand or so out in the wilds of the unincorporated land of the county.

To get here from the Salt Lake City airport, drive North. Take the Weber Canyon in South Ogden and drive and drive and drive until you feel like you should be in another state. Then, skirt the reservoir built to help control the spring run-off of the Spruce River, which winds its way through the valley that leads to the arching peaks of the Silver Ridge mountains, tucked deep within the Wasatch mountain range.

The thing about Silverton is, it takes nearly three hours to get here from the airport. No wonder the townspeople are struggling, though somehow, my great-aunt had made the Silver Ridge Inn a success, even in off-seasons.

Once here, I researched the area and discovered a faster way—across the dam that formed the reservoir, but the state had closed that road to civilian access for some unknown reason until 2012. They had finally opened that passage, and it cut a solid hour and twenty minutes off the drive. I'd missed that as an option when driving in, so the scenic route had kept me company.

And scenic, it was. I loved the quaking aspens of Colorado, but this land looked incredible. There remained something wild and untouched in the craggy cliffs of Silver Ridge, which overlooked the valley floor and the reservoir like an Alpine overlord. It was intimidating, awe-inspiring, and home to some of the best skiing in the West—or so said the Silver Ridge Lodge and Ski Area's brochure. I'd sifted through every piece of marketing swag Aunt Tilda kept in her Reception area, and along with the handful of menus for local fare and business cards, had found brochures for the lodge.

Another breath gave me space in my lungs, in my mind. With this quiet bliss permeating my system—maybe for the first time ever—I closed my eyes and sipped coffee in a green-glazed pottery mug from the collection of stoneware Tilda had used for her coffee and tea service in the mornings. Like so many things here, it had been made by a local artisan.

A pang of regret hit then, like it had over and over again in the last few months—one of few emotions I'd felt fully, letting the surprising loss carve its way inside and then drag back up, a quiet burn like ashes in its wake. Why hadn't I bothered to come visit? Why hadn't I come and seen what she'd been doing here, how she'd made it a success?

The inn had been all but closed these last few months. Tilda had died in late March. Someone had sent notification that she'd listed me as the beneficiary of the inn and a small sum of money in early April.

At first, it had felt like a nuisance once past the initial surprise. Still sleep-walking through life, I thought I'd sell it off, or see if my cousins wanted it.

But then, Preston told me he'd lost all my money.

Then I found out he'd cheated.

Then I woke the hell up after a nearly two-year-long sleep and got out of there before we tied the knot and I shackled myself into a life of keeping my hair long and never in a pony tail, of being fit but not *too* fit so that my breasts got small, of being manicured and unemployed just to suit a man I did not, in the end, know at all, and his diabolical mother, who might have been even more controlling than her son.

So. About that...

Preston Umbridge plucked me from my paid internship at a fancy Aspen resort and made me his pet project—I hadn't realized it at the time, of course. I'd only seen him as an attractive, wealthy man interested in *little old* me, and sadly enough, my parents had done everything to encourage that mindset.

In fact, when my mother found out he'd taken me out, which she'd heard long before I ever told her because the gossip channels in the echelons of wealth my parents and Preston's family ran in were small, she told me to do whatever I must to marry him because I had no hope of doing better.

I'd thought it an unusually kind complement to Preston, and not a put-down of me. Since then, I'd often wondered if she knew exactly who and what Preston was and had made that statement precisely because she'd meant to be hurtful.

Preston and I were supposed to marry over a spring weekend mid-April, about two years after our first "chance" encounter. By then, I was long gone. The lawyer I'd hired with the inheritance Tilda had left me notified Preston that he'd been removed from all of my accounts and any signing authority, my will had been changed, and he could go jump off a cliff.

Okay, maybe not that last part. But frankly, I smiled when I thought that, every single time—what a huge improvement on the utter despair and self-loathing I'd been sorting through the last few months. I'd gone from sleep-walking to awake, but the reentry into real life had been brutal. Something about the chilly mornings of the last few days had vaulted me soundly from *wallowing and depressed* into *angry as Medusa*, and honestly? It felt fantastic.

I felt more like myself every day. Not that my usual self was angry, because at this point, I could admit that I didn't *know* myself anymore. I had to rebuild and rediscover, and that was one part of what I was doing up here, tucked away in this piddly, adorable, maddening town.

My coffee had cooled down unacceptably, so I went inside, letting the white bordered screen door slam with a *clack* behind me. We had no occupants booked until this weekend, so I could be as obnoxious as I wanted. We'd only had a small handful of guests over the summer, which I'd been told wasn't a huge surprise with Tilda's passing and the handover—the usual visitors in summer likely giving me time to get things going.

Time I absolutely needed, to be honest.

My coffee now refilled and warm, I stalked back to the porch where I'd review the accounts and the schedule and wrack my brain for how to get people through the doors in September and October before the snow came and the mountain opened for skiing. The shoulder seasons here were fall and spring, and even though they were utterly gorgeous, people were far less likely to travel up this way for anything other than the snow. Even then, I'd gathered that the town needed a resurgence in a bad way.

"Pardon me."

The sound of the deep voice made me jump back, sloshing hot coffee on my wrist and feeling it slop onto the toe of my boot.

"Oh, hi."

"I'm sorry. I didn't mean to startle you. I was just coming to the door—"

"No, please don't apologize. I was in my own head. Let me just set this down," I said, leaning to deposit my dripping mug on the painted white wood table to my left.

I righted myself and looked up just as the man offered his hand.

"Liam Morrison."

His smiling mouth and eyes looked more than a little charming, I had to admit.

Charming. Ha. Not quite that simple.

This guy... *wow.* Wow. They grow 'em well here in Silverton.

I scrubbed my palms on my jean shorts, wishing there was a little more to them now that I had a guest, and extended a hand to meet his—even as the fact that I hadn't voluntarily touched another person in months flashed through my mind.

"Wells Bryant. Nice to meet you."

Annoyingly, I detected a bit of breathlessness. Had to be from surprise, the coffee spill, and the short shorts seeming even shorter, and not from meeting Silverton's golden boy in the flesh at seven in the morning.

"I've been meaning to get over here and welcome you. I'm sorry for your loss—Ms. Tilda was a pillar of the community."

He let his hand drop from mine, and I glanced down to see a six-pack of bottles in his hand.

"Thank you. Unfortunately, we weren't close, but I wish we had been." I cocked my head to one side. "How can I help you, Mr. Morrison?"

"Liam, please."

"Okay, Liam. How can I help?"

"Well, Ms. Bryant, I'm here to welcome you, formally. I know it's months overdue, and for that, I sincerely apologize. Do you drink beer?" he asked, like welcoming me and my beer drinking were at all related.

"Uh, yes, on occasion, I enjoy a good beer."

His eyes were startlingly bright blue, especially set against his dark brown hair.

I hadn't noticed things like that—eye color, hair—in months. Maybe since I'd first met Preston, who'd made it clear even recognizing there were other men in the room would result in his brooding displeasure.

"Good. That's good. I've brought you a sampler pack of beer as a small token of welcome. It's, uh, it's from my brewery. And I'd like to offer to show you around town, at some point, when you have time, if you want."

To my surprise, little streaks of red rose above the line of the beard on his cheeks.

"Thanks for the beer." I smiled and... waited.

Then it occurred to me maybe he wanted a response to the invitation.

"And... sure, that's... nice. Even though I've been here a few months, I haven't gotten away from the inn much at all, and I'm sure you'd be able to help me get the lay of the land."

I resisted the urge to roll my eyes. The town consisted of no more than a main street and a few small side streets. I'd walked its entirety hundreds of times by now. Why was I pretending I needed his help to acclimate to a place I'd lived in for a quarter of the year already?

"I'd be glad to."

A bright smile appeared.

"I can't today, though. I'm meeting with my cook, and I hate to reschedule. She's about to take some time off, and I don't want to make her delay."

And maybe, if we put it off, I could avoid this. How could I so easily slip back into the accommodating version of myself?

"I understand. Here's my card. Just call... or text, or... you know, whatever works best for you. We'll do it soon."

"Sure. Thanks."

Relief whooshed in at the sight of him backing down the porch steps.

"Have a good day, Ms. Bryant." The half-smile on his face looked somehow triumphant even as he backed away from me.

"Just Wells—just call me Wells."

"Ok. See you again soon, Wells."

Wells. Hearing my name—my chosen name—from that man's lips reminded me I could breathe. I'd broken with the old life, and the choice to reclaim my name and abandon the one my parents had given me—*Serene Wellington Bryant*—was a moment-by-moment reminder.

I'd always thought of myself as Wells, ever since my cousins, Great-Aunt Tilda's grandkids, had adopted it on the only visit I remember making as a child. But my parents had insisted on Serene. It would be a lovely name for someone, but the Serene I knew was passive, placating, and ultimately deeply wounded. She'd been coerced and controlled for too long—by her parents, and then after just a brief spat of freedom thanks to college and the ensuing independence, she'd let herself be tied right back to someone who wanted to make all the decisions about everything in her life.

But not anymore. Here, Wells existed, and she would thrive.

I watched Liam walk down the winding stone path to the sidewalk. He turned right, evidently heading back to the lodge where he likely lived since it was the only thing in that direction. It took ten minutes to walk to the lodge's first parking lot, but in the winter, I'd been told, guests at the inn could easily ski over there and buy tickets at the ski-up window, then load the gondola and be at the top of the mountain in a matter of twenty minutes.

As Liam Morrison disappeared out of sight, I sat down

and swirled my cold coffee. I never would have guessed he'd be so... like this. He belonged to the town's beloved family, essentially royalty around here, both because they owned the biggest business and the biggest draw to the town, and because they were reportedly excellent people.

I'd pictured him being pushy, or maybe even just more gregarious—man about town and ready to charm. Maybe I'd gotten too used to Preston's passive-aggressive pushiness, the ever-present demand to do as he asked or suggested without ever really saying so. Rationally, I knew not everyone would be like that, but it'd been too long since I'd even spoken to a man near my age.

Liam had seemed shy, a little embarrassed, and polite. That paired with his mountain man look—broad shoulders, towering height, dark, short beard, and hair long overdue for a cut... he surprised me.

I met with the cook, Marcella, who'd held down the fort along with the skeleton crew of staff over the summer, but then we'd closed for August, both because we had no bookings, and because it'd always been tradition for Tilda. Marcella was taking maternity leave and planned to come back in November when the mountain opened, so I'd be truly on my own aside from the maid and Reception staff for a while. They were great, but it didn't stop me feeling even more nerves.

At one time, Tilda had planned to open a restaurant and feature full-service lunch and dinner along with the breakfast she provided. But the growth the town had projected after the dam road opened never came, much to the dismay of everyone.

Fortunately for me, I only had to deal with breakfast. Marcella said I could easily set up a standing order for a few items at *Rise and Shine*, the local bakery and coffee shop, and they'd deliver them so we didn't have to hire temporary kitchen help. That suited me, so I went to meet with the manager and set up a system for ordering.

I tucked flyaways behind my ears, pulled my long blond ponytail tighter, and settled my hat closer down on my eyes. I surveyed my outfit—olive green tank top, jeans shorts (I'd changed out of the short version for my meeting with Marcella), bunchy socks, and hiking boots. I grinned in pleasure at the knowledge that in this little mountain town, I was entirely appropriately dressed for a meeting with a fellow small business owner.

The fact that this was the polar opposite of my experience the last few years wasn't lost on me—it was the source of half the pleasure. I didn't even really like hiking boots, but Preston had said they made my feet look too big, so I hadn't worn them in years. He'd hated my hair in ponytails, so it had always been down, usually with perfectly crafted waves and glossy finishing spray added. Certainly, I hadn't worn a hat in more than two years either.

Miraculously, and as a show of the modicum of progress I'd made thanks to time and my therapist, I didn't cringe at the thought of even those small things I'd given up.

So no wonder then that I'd adopted this uniform of ponytail, sometimes with a hat, sometimes without, and casual clothes and boots.

The walk into town took only about three minutes from the front porch of the inn. I wandered along a beaten path until the sidewalk started and took in the quiet street.

Silverton was nothing short of quaintly picturesque. Thanks to the stillness that set in during the afternoons, you might think this place a movie set. But mornings and evenings were busy while at midday, at least during summer when hottest, people kept to themselves. Add to that the low tourism numbers for the year—not surprising that a low hum of nervous energy filled the gaps of the day.

I pushed open the door to the *Rise and Shine* and took in the adorable inside. If the inn didn't keep me so busy, I would have come here every day. The walls and window trim were all painted sunshine yellow, with big display windows in the front so passers-by could see how busy the place was. The tables and chairs were white, all of their dishes robin's egg blue.

They had only six tables, two pulled together and occupied by the afternoon crew—a group of older men who congregated daily, or close, because they were almost always there when I came in the afternoon. Whenever I happened across them in here, they seemed like they were having the time of their lives.

I stepped to the counter, which hit about at my ribcage. The surface held big display cases on either side of the digital register, a small jar that had a hand-drawn elk with a speech bubble that said *jerks don't tip*, and a bell. I hesitated, peering back into the kitchen as much as I could, which wasn't much, and then tapped the bell lightly.

From behind me wafted the sounds of the group talking.

"So I said, 'listen, L-T. If we're getting out of here, we're doing it *now*.' And do you know what he said to me?"

The man speaking had a Vietnam Vets hat on, riddled with patches and pins. He swung his head from side to side, surveying the other four faces, each with his own hat and insignia, one hand gripping his pretty blue coffee mug. All the men smiled as he continued.

"He says, 'well, I suppose I didn't want to live forever anyway.'"

The speaker slapped the table, and the men laughed heartily for a moment before another story began.

"Miss?" A small voice came from behind the counter.

I swung around and smiled at her. "Hi. I'm here to meet with the manager."

"Oh, hi. That's me," the woman said, raising a delicate hand in a disarming wave. "Give me just a sec to refill these guys and we'll meet at the table in front, if that's okay? Can I get you anything?"

She turned to grab a carafe of coffee from a drip machine behind her and moved to the swinging doors at the far left of the counter.

"I'd take some coffee too, if that's all right."

She nodded as she approached the men who greeted her with boisterous welcome.

"There she is, the prettiest girl in all the land," one said.

"You boys need anything else? I've got a meeting here with Ms. Bryant."

The men all turned to me where I'd just taken a seat in a sunny spot at the front table.

"Bryant, is it?" one man, who looked to be the oldest of the crew, asked.

I stood and walked to them, though they sat only about ten feet from me as things stood. "Yes sir, Wells Bryant. I've just arrived in town after my aunt Tilda's passing."

A flurry of sympathies passed around simultaneously, then died down.

"She was a lovely woman, a real asset to the community. She'll be missed," the man said. He stood, more agile than I might have expected, particularly since his hat featured a

WW2 patch. "William Morrison. Pleased to meet you, Ms. Bryant."

He held out a gnarled hand, and I took it.

"The pleasure's mine, sir. I'm glad to meet you."

"So you're taking the inn, then? It sat empty a while, seemed like," Mr. Morrison said.

"Yes sir. My aunt left it to me, and it came at a perfect time. I have a lot to learn, I know, but—"

"You'll do fine. I can tell it about you. My da used to say you could tell about a person by their eyes, and I can tell with you. You'll do fine," he said, a light lilt entering his voice as he spoke.

I smiled, charmed. "Thank you. I hope you're right."

"Morrison men are always right," he responded as a bell jingled behind us.

"Morrison men may always be right, but that's because the women told them what to say and do," someone said.

I angled myself to see the door and noticed a strikingly pretty woman walking in front of none other than Liam Morrison. I hadn't heard he was married, but it only made sense he was.

"Ah, granddaughter. Of course you're right," Mr. Morrison said and welcomed a hug from the woman, who then leveled me with an expectant look.

"*Finally.* I've been wanting to meet you. I'm Leo Morrison," she said, thrusting a hand out to me, which I took without a second thought.

I knew her by reputation, now that I realized who she was—not Liam's wife, but his sister. She looked young— younger than me, I'd guess, though not by much. She had long blond hair, and those bright blue eyes that I could now see were a family trait based on Mr. Morrison, Leo, and Liam, and fair, lightly freckled skin.

"Wells Bryant."

"Nice to see you again, Wells," Liam said as he stepped closer.

Leo shot him a look of surprise. "You two already met?"

"Just this morning," he explained.

"Well, there you have it. You've met nearly a third of the family just today. All we need is Dan, that vagrant Jamie, and my son and daughter-in-law, and you'll have met the whole crew," Mr. Morrison said. He looked at Liam and Leo affectionately.

The store manager piped in. "Can I get you two anything? Ms. Bryant and I have a meeting, but I'll be off in about an hour."

Leo raised her eyebrows. "You have a meeting with her and you didn't tell me?"

The manager rolled her eyes.

"I don't report to you. Plus I would have told you after. Now go settle down and listen to these wise men tell their stories while I have my meeting," she said, a sweet smile on her face.

"Yes, dear," Leo said, a wry smile on her face. "But you," she said to me as she pulled out a chair next to her grandfather. "I want to talk to you soon."

I resisted the urge to look over my shoulder and see if she was talking to someone else. I knew no one stood behind me. She *was* talking to me, and I had no idea why. But she was direct, and I liked that, and so far, the Morrison family had been genuine and charming, so I nodded. "Okay. Noted."

Half an hour later, I'd worked out an ordering system with the bakery's manager, Bel, and had discovered that she, too, was extremely likeable. Before I left the shop, Bel and Leo demanded I meet them for dinner the next night, and only because I'd left behind despair and stopped being a recluse, I said yes.

I waved goodbye to the group of veterans still sipping coffee and chatting, then Bel and Leo, and made my way to the street where the sun still burned bright and warm, though this half had fallen into shadow.

"Hey, Wells!" came a shout behind me, and before I could turn all the way, Liam Morrison jogged to me. "Sorry to shout. I wanted to see if you might want to take that tour tomorrow?"

I bit the inside of my cheek, not sure what to say. I'd made the mistake of saying I was free all day tomorrow earlier, at which point Bel and Leo had waylaid me for dinner. If he'd overheard me from his seat at the vets' table, only a few feet away from the one I shared with the girls, then the chances were good he'd know if I made an excuse.

I scuffed my boots across some fallen bright red geranium petals that must have fluttered from the hanging pots out front of *Odds*, the shop neighboring *Rise and Shine* on this side. It was full of odds and ends, thus perfectly named.

"Uh, sure. I think I'm free," I said, squinting at him through the shade under my hat.

I could feel myself resisting looking directly at him—he was just too appealing. Some primal part of me seemed to know I shouldn't give him my full attention or I'd be doomed, and I didn't have time for that nonsense.

One side of his mouth quirked up, and I dipped my head, eyes back on those tiny petals.

"All right. Meet you out front of the inn?" he asked.

I nodded. "What time?"

"How about eight? We can grab coffee from Bel and then wander around with it."

"See you then," I said, and nearly ran away.

Surely, it must seem odd to him, but the exchange had left my throat tight and my breath short. I wasn't ready to interact with someone like this—not anyone, and especially not someone like him. I'd never seen Preston coming—never could have imagined where we'd end up, but I could see Liam Morrison and the caution sign above his head flashing red at me.

I was just waking up—hovering just below the surface of feeling fully conscious and being able to function without the numb sensation that clung so close, nagging me. I couldn't risk anything that would push me back into that space. Limiting exposure to risks like Liam would be essential to finishing the climb out of that pit.

All I wanted was to hear the *clack* of the inn's screen door behind me.

CHAPTER TWO

Liam

I'd been working up the courage to introduce myself to Wells Bryant for months. *Literally.* And as much as it pained me to admit it, it hadn't gone all that well when I did.

It wouldn't be an exaggeration to say the first time I saw her, I thought I was hallucinating. With me just back from a three-day hike, short on water, she came around the corner downtown looking exactly like something my imagination would cook up, but better.

Long legs, long blond hair, bill of her hat pulled low over her eyes so I could see just a shadow there, thus adding to the mystery. Her skin looked smooth, her body fit, her clothes at that time much as they'd been today—jean shorts, a tank top, hiking boots.

It'd felt a little bit like God was saying *I told you I exist.* If I hadn't just been in the mountains where such things were announced with clarity to every fiber of my soul, I might have been more stunned.

Even still, he'd made his point.

Braggart.

Before I could make a fool of myself, my no-good little brother Danny had pulled my attention away, and by the time I'd looked back, she was gone. For more than two weeks, I'd thought she might actually be a figment of my imagination, until I saw her again hauling garbage bins out to the curb in front of the inn.

So that's where she was staying—good to know.

I'd been too far away to call out to her, and then, something about her posture hadn't been open—her shoulders hunched just a bit, her arms wrapping around her waist as she hurried back down the path to the inn's porch.

But then it hit—if she was taking out the trash, she wasn't just visiting there. She worked there. She must have been someone to Tilda Saint, and she must be someone I'd need to get to know if I wanted the place. I'd been planning to approach Tilda about it this summer, but she'd passed away before summer came. I'd been busy enough working out financial reports and preparing our information for the lodge's audit that I hadn't gotten around to figuring out who'd taken the thing over.

It went on like that—me seeing her, wondering what exactly her role at the inn was, and wondering what her name was—for another eight weeks before Danny harassed me so much about the crush I had on "the new girl" that I marched down there, six-pack in hand, and bumbled around like a school boy to welcome her.

She'd clearly been reluctant to join me today for a tour, but I'd pushed it after hearing her say she was free all day. I shouldn't have been eavesdropping, but after seeing her from afar for so long and then finally being near her, hearing her voice, getting a small peek under the rim of that hat—I was barely able to control my desire to stare.

Because up close, she looked even better.

But here's the thing—I was self-aware, smart enough to know she wasn't exactly clamoring to spend time with me. And I hated to say it, but that was new to me.

I'd always been popular, a big fish in a tiny pond, and even as I moved to Salt Lake City for college and then did a stint in the Army, friends came easily. Maybe on account of my glowing personality, or maybe I had a tendency to want the attention and take it, but either way, it was unusual to have someone, and forgive me for saying it, a woman, react the way she did.

Really, she'd had a non-reaction. She'd been courteous, calm, direct... no stumbling over words or blushing or *anything* that might give away what she thought of me.

I was flying blind—not a place I wanted to be. Add to that my need to broach the subject about whether she was open to a buy-out, which left me feeling less than confident.

I'd woken early, gotten in a decent run, cleaned up, and was ready to walk out of the house at seven. The problem was, we were meeting at eight. By the time quarter 'til rolled around, I'd paced myself through a few laps around the lodge. If Dan had been awake, he likely would have made fun of me, but at least I had a real job.

He'd counter that with something cute about how I had a job but not a life, blah blah blah, little jerk, but on that note, I couldn't fault him.

Maybe that's why I was so damn nervous while following the winding path down from the lodge to her inn.

Hers.

Impressive that she was taking it on. An educated guess

told me she was losing money just turning the lights on, particularly since there were no cars in the gravel guest parking lot on the west side of the property. Hopefully, I could get her to talk about that, see if I could help—hell, maybe she could help me get a handle on the mountain.

Or, maybe she could help me get a life.

I shook out my arms as I approached the little gate that opened into the yard of the inn. Tilda Saint had opened the place in 1980 after visiting the lodge to ski and seeing the need. The town was then much as it is now—a hidden gem just waiting to be discovered. If we could ever get people to us faster, we'd explode.

I had this thought about ten times a day. Part wishful thinking—that someone would solve my problem for me—and part reality—our mountain really was insanely good, and could compete with any of the top Rocky Mountain resorts in terms of vertical, snow averages, trails cut, etc.

The problems were numerous too, though—access to the mountain, and then access up it, since we only had one gondola, three lifts, a T-bar, and a rope tow for the bunny hill. We sorely needed an injection of capital to upgrade, but that would never happen if we couldn't get people to us.

I shook off that thought and took in the building: a white two-story house facing north with black shutters framing the windows and in desperate need of a paint job, certainly there only for the aesthetic appeal. It had a large brick chimney, and I remembered the living area with the big fireplace being a very welcoming, cozy space.

Second only to the lodge, of course.

The shingles on the roof were dark, somehow resisting the bleaching sun's effect, and the dark roof and shingles with the bright wood trim and red brick looked clean cut and charming.

The inside was filled with antiques kept in mint condition, all the furnishings real wood and high quality. It'd been a few years since I'd been inside and even longer since I'd been in a guestroom, but I'd heard good things from visitors and the town's visitors' bureau.

I hesitated on the front porch. I could walk in and it wouldn't be weird—not like it was her house, but it still felt like it might not be a welcome intrusion. Or at least, that it would be an intrusion. So I knocked on the side of the screen door, then stepped back to the edge of the porch and leaned against one of the posts that framed the doorway.

"Be out in a sec!"

I smiled to myself.

I liked this girl. Probably stupid how much without really knowing her at all, but I did.

"Hey, sorry for the hold up. I didn't mean to make us late," she said, pulling her long ponytail from the collar of her sweatshirt and zipping a thin jacket. The mornings had cooled off in the last week or so.

"No problem. We can't be late for something like this," I said easily.

Her shoulders slumped, evidently relieved, it startled me to realize. Had she really thought I'd be upset that she got out of the place a minute after eight?

"Let's go get some coffee," I suggested.

"Perfect." She let the screen door slam behind her. "Sorry, that door is so noisy."

"I think it always has been. I'm pretty sure Tilda could have gotten it fixed years ago but chose not to—I always thought of it as the replacement for a bell on the door."

The sun already hung high over Silver Ridge and its neighboring peaks, warming. When the snow started, I always felt like I couldn't love days without snow, but these quiet, late-summer mornings had something on me. Butter-flies flitted around the wildflowers lining the path between the inn and Main Street, and for a few moments, we walked one after another, me leading the way on the narrow path.

"We really need to put a sidewalk in here," I said to myself.

"Do you think? I kind of like it like this."

I looked back over my shoulder. "It's all right in summer, but winter, it gets tricky."

"I guess that's no surprise. Hard to shovel or plow."

"Yep." I stepped out onto the sidewalk that began with the official start of Main Street, then stopped facing the center of town.

"So this is Main Street." I made a grand gesture.

She snickered. "Oh really? Wow. Thanks so much for showing me—I never would have found it otherwise."

"At your service, ma'am." I grinned at her sarcasm, glad she was playing along, and we continued on to *Rise and Shine*.

The bell jingled overhead as we entered and joined the line. Bel and an assistant were rummaging around, pulling coffees, wrapping scones, slicing quiche, disappearing into the back to start a new tray of delights baking, no doubt.

"It smells so good in here."

The breathy quality to Wells' voice made me clench my fists to keep from touching her.

"It does. I have to stay away from here most days or I'd eat myself into oblivion."

She raised an eyebrow at that, but made no response.

"Wells, good to see you again so soon. And you—are you harassing this nice woman?" Bel eyed me behind the counter as she swirled a leaf in the foam of a latte and handed it to the woman in front of us.

"I am doing no such thing. I'm showing her around town," I said, annoyed that she'd started in on me so quickly.

Usually, Bel was fairly meek by herself. When she buddied up with Leo, that's when I worried. But she seemed feisty this morning, just looking for a fight.

"I'm sure she was desperate for a look around after only living here for *several months*."

That smart-alec look made me shake my head.

"I figured I should probably get the first-class tour from the town's golden boy," Wells said and shot me a dazzling smile.

I felt literally dazzled—kind of dumb and zippy in the wake of it.

"Golden boy?" I asked, trying to cover what she'd done to me.

"Don't try to deny it, Morrison. I may be a hermit, but I'm not an idiot."

She said this with a dead straight face, and I laughed.

That was one of many reasons I hadn't gotten up the guts to talk to her.

"I don't deny it. I'm just not sure I can live up to the name, but I guess you can let me know what you think."

"What'll you have?" Bel asked Wells as we stepped up to the counter.

"Black coffee."

"Anything to eat?" she asked, a smile on her lovely face.

"No, thank you."

"And you, golden boy?" Bel asked, clearly relishing Wells' comment.

"Black coffee for me, too, and I'll take a blueberry scone and whatever your slice of the day is." I pulled out my wallet to pay.

"Let me." Wells edged closer to the counter.

"I invited you on this tour—"

"So I'll buy the coffee."

She slapped a card onto the counter, and Bel glanced at me before running it through the machine's slide.

I nodded, not sure whether my offer to buy had made her uncomfortable or if I'd missed something. It wasn't a big deal, but something about her response struck me as strange. Guarded.

We settled at one of the front tables so we could look out at Main Street, currently as busy as it ever got midweek in late summer. Most area schools had started back last week so the locals who knew about the town and might visit were unfortunately now occupied.

I took a bite of the scone and held back a groan. "That is so good."

Wells eyed me, a small curve to her lips.

"Want a bite?" I held the little wedge out to her.

"No thanks." She smiled placidly, then her expression changed completely. "Actually yes. I really would like a bite."

She took the scone from my hand and broke off a corner, then closed her eyes and relished the flavor as she chewed.

"Wow. Bel is a genius," she said after a sip of her coffee.

"She is that, though she's not the baker. The woman who does the baking, Sadie, doesn't do much in the storefront—she's an introvert and basically lives to bake, but doesn't enjoy interacting with people. So you're unlikely to meet her any time soon. Bel's sort of the face of the place, and she also works for the family."

"What does she do for you all?" Wells asked, nodding when I held out the slice of bread slathered with thick, salted butter.

"She does our marketing. She got her degree at Miller State and did really well, but came back to town to care for her grandmother. She's been managing the bakery for about three years, and then does what we need on freelance. I wish we had more work for her, but we have no budget for marketing, and I refuse to abuse her relationship with the family by having her do it for free like she says she would if we'd let her."

"She's part of the family?" Wells asked, crossing a leg and leaning back in the wooden seat, her head tilting in interest.

"Not technically, but she's Leo's friend and has been for a few years, and my brothers are in love with her." I took a bite of the slice of the day—honey whole wheat, *man that's good*—and chuckled at her wide-eyed response.

"*Brothers* are in love with her? I didn't realize you had more than one, and also, how does that work out for them?" she asked, genuinely intrigued.

"Ah, yeah. Not that they'd appreciate me putting it that way. Dan is the youngest brother, and he's two years older than Leo. Then we have Jamie, but he's not in town very often. In fact, he'll be coming back home for the first time in quite a while in September for a family meeting."

A big crash behind the counter pulled our attention to Bel, who was standing, mouth agape, looking at me instead of at the mess that undoubtedly coated her feet from what sounded like a dropped mug of coffee.

"You okay, Bel?" I asked, noticing that Garrett, her teen-aged helper, was nowhere in sight.

She blinked, swallowed, and pushed through the swinging gate of the counter.

"He's coming back?" she asked, her voice shaky.

"Yeah, Bel. He'll be back for about a week. I think he comes in midmonth."

She swallowed again, nodding. "Okay. That's good. Good to know."

She spun on her heel and retreated to the kitchen.

"I gather that's a complicated situation..." Wells said quietly, and I just nodded. Not my story to tell.

She drained the rest of her coffee. "Ready?"

The day with Wells turned out... confusing. She was open and talkative about some things and completely closed off about others. I tended to be an open book, so finding places where she shut down had been unexpected.

And yet, I couldn't blame her. She hadn't known me even forty-eight hours yet. She hadn't grown up in this town, and she didn't know the kind of man I was. Based on a few of her comments, she'd escaped something she didn't want to discuss—a bad job, a messed up relationship, something.

It shed a little light on the way she'd kept to herself so strictly the first few months here rather than wandering around introducing herself and making connections that would help her business. Frankly, I'd expected a knock on my office door up at the lodge and had been surprised it hadn't come.

But today, we'd mostly talked town matters—the battle with the state to publicize access to us more readily, the challenge all the businesses faced if we didn't get more people in here for the upcoming ski seasons, and so on.

Just talking about it made my chest constrict. The lawyer and accountant had said they'd get the audit back to me before Labor Day, which was next weekend. It would come any day now, and then I'd have to face down the true reality of the place.

As we wandered back to the inn around nine-thirty, I found myself hoping I'd have an excuse to see Wells again. I hadn't learned much of anything about her personally, other than she came from Colorado before moving here and she wasn't close to her great-aunt, which I'd figured since I'd never seen her visit. I would have remembered.

"Thanks for showing me around, Liam." She tucked her hands into her pockets as we moved up the path toward the inn.

"Anytime. Not that you'll need to be shown around again anytime soon, but, you know, if you need anything. I know it's tough being new in such a small town, and I'd be glad to help you, any way I can."

"Thanks. I appreciate that."

She inched toward the door as I angled back to the path.

Then I remembered. "Like, maybe if you want me to lay on Jim about the liquor license?"

Her mouth dropped open a bit, then she shut it. "How do you know I applied for one?"

"I'm buddies with Jim, the guy who does the permits."

She crossed her arms. "Ah. The small-town effect, I guess."

"Yeah," I said, chuckling like an idiot because if I'd realized she was upset, I wouldn't have.

"Well, thanks. I think I'm good. See you around."

And before I knew what happened, the clack of that screen door sounded and she was gone.

CHAPTER THREE

Wells

I pulled on the sundress, a sweater, then sandals. I'd combed my hair out but refused to curl it—it looked like an imperfectly wavy mess of straight-ish hair, and if anyone cared, they could dive face first into a trash can.

Even that thought rang like a triumph.

The morning with Liam Morrison had thrown me off balance just as I was starting to feel like I'd found my footing and didn't need to hold onto the railing to stay upright.

It wasn't his fault. Actually, yes, but he hadn't meant for it to be. He'd been kind, charming, charismatic in a way that, had I allowed it, might have made me a little fluttery. He asked good questions, only some of which I answered directly, and he knew everything there was to know about Silverton.

Being around him made me want to smile and laugh,

and frankly, twirl around like an idiot—unsettling. He was fun and so handsome and so likeable. And that's exactly what had me running for cover. I didn't need to be getting involved with anyone right now. I'd let Preston determine almost everything about my life for almost two years—and if not him, then his tyrannical mother—and it'd happened faster than I ever would have thought possible.

When Liam mentioned the alcohol license, something in me had chilled. I'd been ready to say goodbye, to be by myself and try to shed this light, trotting feeling in me, but then he'd asked if he could help me and mentioned that specifically. Something he wouldn't have known unless he'd *asked* about it, or the inn, or me.

I'd been managed to within an inch of my life, and the idea that this hometown hero was trying to *look after* me or *help* me sounded all too disturbingly familiar. Preston would phrase his suggestions just that way.

"I don't mean to hurt your feelings, Serene. I'm just trying to help you. Your face looks fat when you pull your hair back, and I'd hate for you to look anything less than your best."

"I want to help you feel confident, and I know you're self-conscious about your chest. Why don't you try laying off the running and lifting, and stick with Pilates and yoga instead?"

"Your pants look a little tight. I just want to be honest with you. Do you want to meet with Mother's nutritionist?"

And if all of that wasn't enough, then he served up *"let me invest your money, and you'll quadruple it. You'll have a huge leg up on whatever business you might want to run someday."*

What kind of fool would fall for *that* when the person saying it was the same man who'd suggested I quit my job at the resort so we could spend more time together, so I could plan our engagement party, so I could plan our wedding... all resulting in my not having worked in the eighteen months before I finally woke up and got out.

I took a deep breath, filling every last millimeter of my lungs with this mountain air.

I'm fine. I'm free. I'm here. This is mine.

I had to remind myself sometimes, especially when I woke up, that I wasn't still caught trying to please someone who could never be happy with me. That now, I only needed to work on pleasing *myself.*

I grabbed my keys, though I never locked my door when I walked to town, and my sunglasses. Leo, Bel, and I were meeting at the *Elk Street Grill* at six, so the sun in the sky still fairly bright.

"Glad you came," Leo said with a wide smile and an upraised arm.

I leaned in to give her a light side-hug like the women I used to spend time with did, but she reached around with her other hand and actually hugged me.

Like full-on, chest to chest, heads side to side, squeeze and pat my back, hug.

Who is this girl?

She looked me up and down and shook her head, then said, "No wonder."

"No wonder what?" Bel asked as she sauntered up to the two of us standing outside the *Elk Street Grill.*

Leo smirked at me, then turned to her friend. "No wonder Liam has a crush on her."

My face reddened immediately. "I don't think—"

"Oh he does. For sure," Bel confirmed.

"I'm not looking for anything..."

Leo patted my shoulder and urged me to the door.

"Don't worry. It's just that it's quite rare to have someone new in town, especially who sticks around. Your novelty will wear off and he'll leave you alone soon enough."

Once we sat, after Leo and Bel had smiled, waved, or greeted practically everyone in the place, our waiter brought waters and menus.

"So tell us about you," Leo said, folding her menu, then her hands on top of it.

Her blond hair had been braided from a deep part on one side down to the other, highlighting her lovely, natural face. If they didn't share the same brilliant blue eyes and fair skin, I would never have guessed she and Liam were siblings, she being all light hair to his dark.

"Uh, what do you want to know?" I said, tucking my napkin in my lap.

"Everything. But none of the fake stuff. Who are you? Why are you here? Why haven't we seen you even though you've been here for months?" Leo asked.

Bel reached out a hand and set it on the table. "Forgive her. She's the baby of her family and my theory is that she can't boss around her brothers, so she has to take that out on everyone else."

Leo shot her a nasty look, but I chuckled and the tension in me eased. Maybe these two were as genuine as they seemed. I'd been surrounded by women, none of whom knew me, but maybe that had been because *I* didn't know me. I'd been slipping away from myself, trying to meet every one of Preston's passive-aggressive demands and the paragon image his mother wanted anyone coming into their family to have, and maybe they had been doing the same for their partners and families.

"Long story short, I came here because I had nowhere else to go."

The truth of that hit like a tennis ball to the chest at full speed.

Leo blinked. Squinted. Ducked her head and eyed me. "Explain."

I smiled and glanced at Bel, who leaned forward on the table just like Leo.

I ran a hand through my hair, took a sip of water, and let out a breath. Fine. *Here goes.*

"I was supposed to get married this past April. A few weeks after my great-aunt died and left this place to me, I was confronted by just how miserable I was in the relationship, and I used coming out here as a way to get out of the engagement." I took another drink of my water and waited.

Leo looked at Bel, then back at me.

"Well, I can see why you're not on the market," she said with a wry smile.

Relief washed through me. Of course I hadn't delineated the emotional abuse, or just how pathetic I'd been, but even running away from a wedding is ridiculous, and I'd had no idea how they'd take it. "Yeah, not so much."

"I guess you've had enough drama for a while, huh?" Bel asked, fiddling with her napkin.

I touched her arm. "Not so much that I wouldn't be able to listen if someone were to need to talk."

"What does that mean? Are you being cryptic, Bel?"

I would have laughed at Leo's blatancy if I hadn't seen how Bel blushed deeply and her brow lined.

Bel pressed her lips together for a moment, then sighed. "I overheard Liam say Jamie's coming back next month. Did you know?"

Leo's eyebrows shot up. "No. I guess I wasn't in the loop on his schedule. I know he was off tour as of mid-month, but it's been so long since he came back, I wouldn't have expected him until Christmas."

"Well, apparently he's coming back mid-September."

As before, Bel did not sound at all happy about this.

"I wonder if Danny knows," Leo mumbled to herself.

At that, Bel's whole face reddened. "I have no idea."

Leo seemed surprised by that, her head rearing back. "Why not?"

I watched as Bel struggled inwardly—maybe with whether or not to tell Leo, but maybe because I was there, this new person she didn't know if she could trust.

"Listen, I'm sorry—maybe I should go?" I offered.

Leo put her hand on my arm, just as Bel grabbed my wrist.

"No—"

"Please stay," Bel said, then frowned. "So Jamie and I have a history. And... so do Danny and I..."

"You were involved with both of them?" I asked quietly.

"No," she said, then let out a reluctant chuckle. "That's what's so stupid. I was never really with either one of them —not really."

I looked at Leo, trying to understand what that could mean.

Leo took a breath. "Danny has been in love with Bel since we were kids. Jamie's older than her and Danny by about two years. Bel had a crush on Jamie. He refused to acknowledge her—supposedly because he knew Danny had a crush on her and he said she was too young for him. But before he left, he and Bel had an—" she looked at Bel, then back at me, "—*encounter*. After that, he wouldn't be near her, wouldn't see her, just shut her out, then left for LA. And things have been strained with all of them since then— even her and Danny, who used to be really good friends."

Bel forced a laugh. "See? Drama."

"It sounds complicated. And hard, especially in such a small community, seeing each other all the time."

It sounded absolutely miserable, and all of Bel's body language reinforced that.

"Yeah. It helps that Jamie's not around much," she said, her eyes on her hands now in her lap.

"I'm sorry. I don't totally understand the dynamic, but I am sorry. I can see it makes you unhappy." Seeing the pain and sadness in every line of Bel's body across from me made that clear.

Her green eyes met mine, and she gave me a sad smile. "I'm sorry for whatever happened with you and your fiancé."

"Thanks," I said, and thankfully, the waiter arrived to take our orders.

We all ordered a cocktail, because it'd become clear we all wanted to relax and enjoy the time—almost like we had to wade through that hard stuff to get to the time when we could just relax. Once our orders were in, the waiter left us alone.

"So what's your plan for the inn?" Leo asked as she swirled her drink.

"Get it filled up with people, ideally. I'd love to get a small restaurant going like Tilda had wanted, but I think that's a few years out *if* I can manage to build out our bookings well enough."

I sipped my margarita, wishing I'd just ordered a beer or wine. But I'd always just ordered wine, if anything, with Preston. I hadn't had a margarita in years, and it seemed like something I should do if I felt like it, so I did.

"Bel, you got a secret marketing strategy to put this

town on the map and save everyone, by any chance?" Leo asked.

Bel smiled. "I wish. What we need is the state to change the signage—right now as you head into Weber Canyon, it says Silverton is 100 miles. No one's going to want to drive that! We can advertise until we're blue in the face, but until people know that we've shaved a solid forty miles off that commute by opening the dam road, no one is going to come."

Leo nodded. "Yep. And on top of that, we need more to offer—my family's place is awesome, and the mountain is just... it's insane. I've skied all over the world and I can say that honestly. But we don't have the infrastructure—we have one mid-mountain hut, one top lodge that's ridiculously minimal, and far too few chairs to get people on the mountain."

"So what do you do? I obviously haven't been thinking about these issues nearly as long as you have," I said, feeling the pang of disappointment at the thought of this uphill battle.

"We need cash. We get money from grants and build things up, and we start writing our reps and contacting the county and putting as much pressure on them to change the signage and their own ads to potentially include us. And we pray." Leo slugged back the last of her drink.

The food arrived and we dug in. Leo had demanded I order a steak, and because I hadn't had steak in just as many years as I hadn't enjoyed much of anything other than vegetables and chicken, I agreed.

"This is so insanely good," I said, swallowing another piece of steak.

"It is. Your cousin raises the best beef in the state," Bel said, smiling at me.

"My cousin? Wyatt?" I asked.

"Yes. Did you not know that?" Leo asked, then took a bite.

"He came to see me the day after I arrived. Other than that, we've only e-mailed. He said he's not in town much. I knew he ranched, but I thought he worked for someone else as a farm hand or something like that." I was ashamed I'd thought so little of him.

He'd been nice, if not friendly, though I couldn't blame him since I hadn't done much of anything to stay in touch. We'd barely seen each other over the years. I was relieved that he didn't seem upset about my inheriting the inn, though part of me still wondered if that was an act. It made a bit more sense knowing he was busy with his own business.

"Definitely not. About six years ago, he bought his own place and has developed an incredible stock and a great reputation. Most of the best places in the state use his beef, as do all of the places up here, of course. One good thing about isolation is that even the cheaper stuff gets more expensive once it's delivered," Leo explained.

"That's amazing. Good for him," I said, genuinely happy for him.

"And good for us."

~

The evening with Leo and Bel had been dreamlike. From the brusque way Leo had demanded honesty and personal details, to Bel's vulnerability, to the excellent food, it had been a night like I hadn't had since college. And even then, I hadn't felt as at ease as I had tonight.

I stomped up the stairs to the inn, wishing I had a reason to be quiet.

"Wells, wait," came the voice I'd already learned to recognize.

I spun around.

"Should I be concerned you keep showing up?" I asked, far too relaxed by the drinks and the night to censor my rudeness.

Liam held his hands up. "No, definitely not. I happened to be walking behind you on the path, going home from a night at the pub, and instead of calling out to you there, when you were all by yourself, I thought it'd be better here. I'm sorry."

He sounded genuine, so I let the door drop shut and tromped back down the stairs to meet him on the path. The sky was pitch black with only a few little diamonds twinkling, no moon in sight. The inn had lights strung around the eaves of the porch that came on at dusk every evening, and now, they provided the only real lighting.

"Why are you here, Liam?" I asked, coming to stand a foot from him.

He took a moment, his eyes sweeping over me, before responding. "You are..."

"I am...?"

"I just hadn't seen you without a hat. Hadn't really seen your face, I guess," he said, sounding off.

I shifted, something in me warming at his tone even as annoyance rode on its coattails. "Okay."

"Sorry. I just—I wanted to come apologize for the thing with the liquor license. I didn't realize it'd made you uncomfortable until... after."

After I essentially slammed the door in his face.

"Yeah, it did." I wrapped my cardigan tighter around my waist.

"I'm sorry. I wanted to clarify that I didn't ask about the inn, or *you*, specifically. Jim mentioned that there was an application in from the Silver Ridge Inn and that he thought it was interesting since there was no restaurant—that's it. And you're right, he shouldn't have said a thing to me. I guess he thought I might want to know since I'm dealing with all of this junk with my family's businesses and—"

"What junk?" I asked, suddenly no longer interested in listening to his apology. Hearing the truth—that he hadn't been checking up on me—had immediately eased my mind.

"Uh..." He shifted from one foot to the other, clearly caught off guard by the shift in discussion. "Well, I just got a financial audit back and it's not looking great. It's not sustainable. In the past, we've at least been able to cover our bases, even with a slim profit margin, but that was fine with everyone. It's not happening that way anymore."

He ran his hands through his hair and glanced up at the darkness veiling us.

"I'm sorry."

"Yeah. I basically have two seasons to turn this thing around, or we're done."

There hung a pull of desperation in his voice, a weight, that surprised me. He'd seemed concerned, but knowledgeable and capable, earlier. Any hint of worry over the town's business or the slow influx of tourists hadn't seemed as dire as it did now that I could hear how it influenced him so directly.

"No pressure, right?"

He forced a chuckle.

"Right. I'm sure you can relate," he said, then shoved his hands in his pockets.

"A little. Tilda was smart with the inn, and the operating costs are far less than a ski resort, but I can imagine the stress."

"I wouldn't quite say *resort* but it has its charms," he said, his smile self-deprecating and sweet.

"So you're the manager, or director, of the mountain?"

"Yep. It was supposed to be an interim position because it's not my end game, but I've been in the job since I got out of the Army five years ago. Well, I was assistant manager, then my dad had a heart attack and retired, and then I became interim manager. And because it's a failing prospect, no one with any amount of capability or quality wants to come in to deal with it."

"That's a lot. Especially as a member of the family," I said, trying not to sound as pitying as I felt.

"I mean, I love it in some ways. I love the mountain, I love the town, I love the lodge and I want it to grow. I want to see it succeed. But it's not my passion. Even saying that makes me feel so crappy, I can't even tell you," he said, kicking a rock from the path.

"What *is* your passion?" I asked.

"Beer," he said, then chuckled. "That sounds dumb, but I want to build a brewery. I want a pub and to have my beer be on tap in every decent restaurant in the state, the region. I want it to be *great.*"

The goal, the drive in his voice rang clear, and it only made me like him more. He seemed to feel about that the way I now felt about the inn. I wanted to make it amazing.

"At least you've gotten a start. I haven't tried any yet, but I will."

"Yeah, it's a start. A much slower one than anticipated, but you're right—it's not nothing," he admitted.

"Are your parents hoping you'll change your mind and want to stay?"

"No. They're understanding, and though I know they were a little disappointed, they understand my desire to have my own life. But there's no one else to do it, and so it falls to me. I don't want to be responsible for sinking this place just before its sixtieth anniversary. Talk about letting the family down and the world's most depressing anniversary celebration." He ran his hands through his hair again.

I suppressed a smile, enjoying how expressive he was. He didn't hide, didn't couch things in vagueness, and I wondered if that made him and Leo get along, or if it resulted in lots of butting heads.

"I worked in Aspen for a while, and they had consulting firms pitching them all the time. Why don't you reach out and see if you can get a few to come visit and see what we have here. If someone with resources could help find investors, or help with development—whatever—that could make a huge difference."

"That's... yeah. I've wondered about that. I actually contacted a few over the last few years, but they were all booked out or uninterested or had things we'd need to do before they ever came to visit. Maybe I should try again."

"It's worth a shot," I said, smiling at him.

He smiled back at me, and even though I could hardly see his eyes—it was so dark—my pulse picked up. He stood there for a moment, just... looking. Not in a heavy nor insinuating manner, but it felt like we were... connected in some way, relating silently. Like all the stars had held steady, the crickets and night sounds slowing, the air thickening with uncharacteristic warmth.

Just as quickly, it was gone.

He nodded, shoved his hands into his pockets, and stepped back. "Thanks for the pep talk, Wells. And sorry again for the license thing—it won't happen again."

"Don't worry about it." I waved back at him as he headed east to the lodge.

I stopped on the porch and looked out in the direction he'd gone. It was dark enough out there and bright enough above me now that I was standing underneath the porch lights to make him disappear.

As I stood there, staring out, a rush of gratitude filled me. I never would have guessed that opening myself up would feel good again. To Leo and Bel, and even Liam to a degree, who I'd decided earlier I should just avoid.

Maybe not.

Maybe I didn't have to punish myself by being a recluse up here in the mountains.

Maybe I could really *live*.

CHAPTER FOUR

Liam

I let my head fall onto the stack of folders in front of me and stay there. Jamie was coming home in four days. I'd spent every waking moment researching consulting firms that worked with businesses like ours, ones that seemed open to our level of risk. I'd sent inquiries to all of them and had already heard back from three—two had said no, and one had requested more information.

Better than nothing. The tension built in my chest, like a bee hive had been bashed with that damned audit, and now every minute that ticked by, another little swarm of bees flew out to fill the open spaces of my body.

The beehive in my chest image wasn't a perfect representation of the pressure I felt, but that's how my mind was working these days.

It felt like I'd done nothing else this calendar year but review every document that had ever come through the lodge manager's office. That included a wall of file cabinets buried in a supply closet—the office itself was actually pretty organized and welcoming.

The whole lodge was made of huge beams and granite stone, but they'd used pine sincc it was hearty and plentiful. They'd modeled the look after Austrian ski lodges with natural colors and clean lines, and I loved it. I preferred it to most places.

But it was aged. And if I didn't get my act together and find a way to save this place, it'd be gone. The report's clearest indication pointed out that if we didn't have two *big* seasons—at least big for Silver Ridge—then we'd be done.

I was glad Jamie would be here. He really had no idea about the lodge anymore—totally disconnected from life here, and sometimes that made me crazy, but mostly, I needed my brother. I needed someone to talk this through with.

If he could keep his head on straight with Bel in a one-mile radius, I'd be lucky. It never went well, but I was hoping enough time had gone by since the last time he'd blown through town. *Maybe* he'd be able to give me his fancy little face and help me out for the time of his visit without being totally mentally sidelined.

"Dude, you look pathetic," Danny, the third Morrison boy, said from the doorway.

I looked up to see my youngest brother, who'd inherited the only light hair of the men in the family and who perpetually had a distinctive goggle tan despite his light skin—well, goggles in winter, sunglasses in summer. He wore a filthy Sego Lily LTD hat—one he never took off this time of year. His sunglasses were perched on his head atop the hat, and he wore a ratty, fading T-shirt, cargo shorts, and hiking boots.

"Thanks so much, Dan." I leaned back in the chair and let out a sigh.

"Why do you look like you've aged a hundred years since I saw you running this morning?" he asked, and flopped down into a chair facing the desk.

"Because unlike some, I don't get to spend my days outside. I'm stuck in here and today, like the last few months, it's killing me."

That was partly true. I didn't mind office work, but the stress of this whole situation? Couldn't stand it.

"Poor big brother. You could always quit and come cut trails with me."

Like that was an option.

"Right," I grumped, and stood.

"Seriously though, why are you so stressed?"

"Because we're in deep trouble, brother. But I'll figure it out." I didn't want to bother him with a problem he certainly wouldn't attempt to solve.

He patted my shoulder as I rounded the desk, and we walked out the office. "You will. You always do."

He'd come to corral me for lunch, and I was glad for it. I'd lost track of time, and my brain had shut down, so no use trying to plow through.

"I've never tasted a better burger," I said as I bit into the one he'd pulled from the grill.

He smiled at me and flared his brows. "I am a master. I accept all such praise."

I shook my head, though thanked him after another bite. Lunch was one thing Danny stayed faithful about in the off-season, and it proved a big help. My parents and grandfather fended for themselves, as did Leo, but I'd found that if I wasn't careful, I'd miss the meal and end up nearly incapacitated with hunger by the end of the day.

Danny didn't do much that required commitment or responsibility—he had what we often jokingly termed *Peter Pan Syndrome*, because he stuck with jobs you might have in college or just after, but not really as you're rounding into your mid-to-late twenties and should be thinking about more serious things.

But as long as Danny and I didn't try to talk about those things, we were fine. We got along well, and he took good care of me in the off-season. During the season, I hit the cafeteria for lunch, so I had year-round lunch coverage thanks to his generosity.

"So why is Jamie coming to town?" He eyed me, crunching a few chips as he did.

I swallowed my last bite of the burger and inwardly grimaced at how I'd inhaled it. Good thing I remained unwavering about morning exercise because no way was my metabolism not slowing down.

"I have no idea. My guess is Ma and Da guilted him enough about it that he felt like he had to, but I thought he was taking a break this winter and coming back before he starts another tour in January, so I don't know."

Danny took a sip of water. "You know, I went to the library the other day?"

To anyone else, it might have seemed like an abrupt change of subject, but it was simply him avoiding *the thing we don't talk about*, a.k.a whatever was going on or not going on with him and Bel, and then who the hell knew how Jamie fit into it.

"Yeah? You finally reading, fella?"

"Ha ha. Hilarious. You know I'm an avid reader. I usually get eBooks from them, but I got desperate and for once, the place actually had a hard copy of what I wanted." He crunched another chip.

"I know you read. I didn't realize you read that much. So... how was the library?" I asked, at this point totally unsure of where we were going. Likely toward a punchline that would make me cringe or roll my eyes.

"I saw someone new." He raised his blue eyes to meet mine, and instead of laugh lines or something funny behind them, I saw a look that sent a little ache through me.

"Yeah? Did you talk to her?" I asked, gently.

He paused, frowned, looked out from the deck to the rise of the incredible mountain behind us and the bright yellow, white, and red gondola cars that dotted the main ascent. "Nah. But I saw her, at least."

I caught his eye. "That's good, Dan. I'm glad."

~

"I haven't seen you in a while," Wells said, an easy smile gracing that lovely, lovely face.

In truth, I'd been thinking way too much about that face. The only minutes my mind wasn't thinking about the lodge and mountain were spent trying not to feel pissed off that the brewery had basically ground to a halt, and anything left over circled Wells.

How are things going at the inn for her?

Does she have a boyfriend?

Would it be weird if I asked her out?

I hadn't been this interested in someone in a while. Part of it had to be because I didn't know anything about her. In a small town, especially after being here for the last five years without much more than an extended vacation here or there, I knew everything about everyone. It was just the way of it, especially when I had Grandpa and Danny to spread every lick of gossip out there.

But no one knew anything about Wells. Leo and Bel had been spending time with her—in fact, they seemed to see each other several times a week, if the word around town was to be believed, but when I'd asked Leo what she knew about her, she'd shot me a crusty look and told me to mind my business.

"It's been too long," I said, and stepped up to the entrance of the inn which now had a little arch over the pathway. "I like this."

I gestured to the arch.

"I'm late getting it in, but Aidan said hopefully next spring I can train some things up it, and it should be nice for lights at Christmas." She was kneeling down at the base of the wrought-iron archway.

"That sounds nice. Aidan knows his stuff, so you can probably count on that." I ignored the little pulse of jealousy flicking in me at knowing she'd spent time with Aidan.

Aidan Wallace owned the nursery and tree farm up here and was somewhere in his early thirties. An odd but extremely nice guy, I could see him charming Wells.

"I can tell. He can talk about vines for an hour. But super helpful." She looked up, flashing a half-smile.

"How's it going?" I asked, ignoring the presence of her very short shorts.

She'd been wearing them the first time I'd seen her, and as though she didn't already have long enough legs, these little things made them seem endless. I felt like saying a special thanks to Global Warming for sending unusually hot September mornings.

"Pretty well, I think. We had some people in over Labor Day, and we have some for the harvest fest weekend in October." She tamped down the soil with a trowel and stood.

I swallowed hard, taking in the aforementioned shorts and a top that must have been a shirt at one point but had been sawed off at the middle. It was—I was—

She pulled her gloves off and wiped her forehead with a wrist. "Sorry. I'm a mess—"

I turned bodily away from her and glanced at my watch.

"No, you're—don't apologize to *me*. I didn't mean to, uh, you know, uh, look..." I struggled, glancing back to find her squinting at me.

She raised one brow in question.

I cleared my throat. "Sorry."

She smiled, her cheeks a little pink, though they might have been already and I was just now noticing.

"How's it going for you? Any luck with consultants?"

I looked at the details of the archway, the daylilies still blooming, over her shoulder at the pile of weeds she must have spent hours pulling—really anything to keep my eyes from taking a leisurely stroll over her like they desperately wanted to do.

"A little. Maybe. Mostly no word, and two no's, but one requested more information, so I'm following up with that." I met her eyes to find her grinning at me from under her hat.

"That sounds like progress." She tilted her head to the side.

Something about the way she did that made my stomach flip—just this tiny thing, but she'd done it before, and it hit me just the right way every time.

"It is. And Jamie gets here next week, so that should help."

"Is he involved with the business side of things?" she asked, pulling off her gloves and sticking them into a pocket.

I laughed. "Definitely not. But we were always close. Still are in some ways."

"Just some?"

"Well, he's not here all that often, and though we message each other, we don't do a lot of heart-to-hearts over the phone or anything. But when he comes home, we pick up where we left off."

It was something I loved about him, even though I hated that we didn't do a better job of keeping in touch. Every time I saw him, I vowed I would– be a better brother, a better friend, a better support to him for both our sakes.

"It's hard long distance."

I nodded.

"It is. It's just life. It was the same with almost everyone here while I was in college and then in the Army." I could feel the conversation winding down, but now that I was here, I didn't want it to. "Do you have siblings?"

Her eyes flickered up to the bright blue sky. "Nope. It's just me."

And after that, atypical of me, but entirely typical of me with this woman, I couldn't think of anything to say. I nodded again, and smiled, and scrubbed a hand through my hair before saying goodbye. "Good luck with the gardening, Wells. The place is looking great."

"Thanks Liam. See you soon."

I spent the rest of the afternoon wandering around town aimlessly, alternately worrying about all the things I couldn't control and wondering why I got such mixed signals from Wells. Then I'd feel a justified flash of annoyance for that train of thought because she wasn't giving me signals.

She was just being a person communicating with

another person. And it had apparently been so long since I'd interacted with a beautiful woman I might be interested in that I could hardly handle myself at this point so early on, let alone when there existed absolutely nothing between us.

Okay, not *nothing*. I'd seen her eyes skim over me when she thought I wouldn't notice, but what she found there? Not sure. I took care of myself, was generally thought to be good-looking, and occasionally I drove into Salt Lake or Ogden and went out with people, but that was rare, and even more seldom in the last three years since my friend John Wallace (of the John and Nancy Wallaces, not the Orin and Janet Wallaces, Aidan's parents) and I finally got the brewery going.

We'd started with bottling and meant to get kegs into restaurants all over the state, but we'd halted progress at bottling. He'd been patient with me, and he didn't have any more capital than I did. But the time had come for him to leave his job at his father's law firm, *the* law firm in town, just as soon as I gave the word *go* and we could really push.

After finding my replacement for the lodge, I'd go for it. But first, I'd find the future full-time, non-interim manager that would still listen to my family and cooperate with us and be perfect. So... easy, right?

Shockingly, that person didn't exist, and the small handful of people we'd interviewed over the years had butted heads with at least two of the family, and more than that, seemed somewhere in the range of scared to terrified by the potential of moving to such a small, isolated town.

I nursed a beer out front of *Craic* until Leo sauntered by, all long hair and confidence, and sat down in the chair across from me. I could appreciate that she looked beautiful, and I knew that if she did someday date someone, which part of me thought impossible since I didn't remember her ever showing interest in anybody, I wouldn't handle it well. As baby of the family, she'd always be my little sister— whether she wanted that or not.

"You cut a sad sight," she said, taking in my longer than usual beard, the hair way past time to be trimmed, and no doubt my sad sack face.

"Yeah, yeah. You try attempting to save the family business despite the ridiculous odds, and then come talk to me about it," I grumbled.

"Danny told me you've been whining about that all day. When are you going to *do* something about it?" She crossed her arms.

God, help me not yell at her. Leo always pushed me— always. Maybe we were too alike.

"You know, I'm working on it. But it's not that simple, not that you have any idea." A low blow.

She sat forward in her chair. "All you have to do is ask and I'll help. Until then, I'll leave you to your beer and your hero complex."

She popped up, already across the street to *Rise and Shine* before I could respond.

Not that I would have. Leo baited me every chance she got. I tried not to rise to it, but days like today made it hard. She seemed to think that if *she* had control, or at least more of a say, then she'd make a difference.

To her credit, she knew every inch of the resort, but most of us did. She'd stayed as local as possible in college, going to Miller State a little over an hour away and coming home on weekends. She'd worked as a ski instructor, in KinderCare, as ski patrol, in ticketing, on lifts before she was really old enough—she'd done it all.

Except the back end. She'd never dealt with the financial end, never seen the slim margins we operated with, and certainly hadn't seen the doomsday audit I'd gotten a few weeks ago. Nor had anyone, because I couldn't bear to show them.

They all knew things were bad, so it wouldn't be too much of a shock, but the report showed we had about half as much time as we'd all assumed. Two seasons instead of four to get this place on the map and *moving*.

A swath of bright white caught my eye, and I looked across the street in time to see Wells skip across the front door of *Rise and Shine*. Her hair had been wavy down her back, her shoulders covered with a white sweater, and she'd shifted her sunglasses to the top of her head as she stepped in the door.

I shook my head at myself. "All right, Morrison. That's enough for today."

Enough wallowing, even if parts of my Irish roots demanded it from time to time. For now, a good meal, some rest, and I'd follow up with a few of the firms I hadn't heard back from.

And then, I'd skim the list of jobs one more time and see who we could trim from the staff.

CHAPTER FIVE

Wells

"Jamie should be in town soon," Leo said, quietly sipping her coffee next to me.

We were sitting at one of the small tables in the front of *Rise and Shine*. Bel was covering a few hours for the girl who did weekends, so we'd decided to meet here.

"Will she be okay?" I watched Bel talking with her current customer.

Bel was a beautiful woman, but when she smiled, she looked positively stunning. After spending time with her, getting accustomed to her genuine sweetness and thoughtfulness, it surprised me everyone in town wasn't half in love with her.

"I hope. It's been long enough since he was here last, and long enough since they've had to interact... maybe they can avoid each other."

I shook my head. "I still don't understand it."

They'd told me a bit more, and I didn't get the dynamic.

"If they happen to be in a room together and you witness it, you might understand a bit more then," Leo said quietly.

I knew Leo didn't want Bel to know she was concerned for her, nor did she want to draw any more attention to her brother's imminent arrival.

A jingle sounded at the door, and we turned and both smiled at Danny, who sauntered in like a cool summer breeze.

Danny was the true charmer of the family, from what I could tell—he took after their grandfather, for sure. He looked more boyish than Liam, but he was also five or so years younger. He had Liam's lighter coloring, but with a slight reddish tinge to his hair.

"Good morning," he greeted, an easy smile on his face. "What are you two doing here?"

"We're waiting for Bel."

Something in Leo's voice made me turn to look at her, but her face betrayed nothing.

Danny coughed. "Oh."

By the time I looked over at Bel, her smile didn't seem to come so easy.

"I'll go say hi," he said quietly.

Leo and I tucked our faces into our steaming mugs, but I knew Leo's eyes, just like mine, were on Danny. He stepped up to the counter, and a gamut of emotions crossed Bel's face.

Even though we sat less than fifteen feet from them, I couldn't hear a word. Danny was mumbling quietly, Bel nodding, and I had to bite my tongue to keep from yelling out *speak up!* From the looks of it, Leo did too.

The bell jingled again, but we made no move to check who'd come in—just kept watching whatever scene this was unfolding.

"Eavesdropping, huh?" a warm, deep voice said.

I tore my eyes away to smile over at Liam who was looking particularly good this morning—he'd trimmed up his beard, and even his hair, but he still had a delightfully disheveled look to him that wasn't usual.

"Did you roll out of bed and come directly here? How are you so rumpled?" Leo pursed her lips in disapproval.

"Your brother, Daniel, attacked me, if you must know," he said, donning an imperious expression and cutting her a look from the corner of his eye. "Wells, I wanted to mention I'd love to bring Jamie by while he's here and introduce you."

"I'd like to meet him," I said, wondering what the mysterious Jamie Morrison would be like.

There always hung a sense of awe when people talked about him, but also something forbidden—almost like he'd left the town on bad terms, but the people still loved him. Not even quite that, but there existed a dynamic there with Jamie Morrison and his family, Bel, and this town that made me curious.

"Great. Then I'll see you sometime this week. For now, I'm going to go break up whatever train wreck this is." He nodded toward the counter where I was happy to see Danny and Bel were smiling at each other.

"You'll have to tell me what you think of Jamie," Leo said, a little light of mischief in her eyes.

"Do you two get along?" I heard myself asking as we watched Liam pat Danny's back and say something that made Bel's smile widen.

Leo snorted into her coffee mug. "Jamie and I are almost nothing alike, so we get along great."

I took a bite of the daily slice, a pleasure I'd discovered when Liam had brought me here—so I did learn a thing or two, after all—and I'd enjoyed tremendously since. I'd gotten used to eschewing all forms of bread and anything one might consider a *treat*. But as we sat at this same table that day, I'd realized that the only reason I'd said no to his scone was because I was used to saying no to things like that.

So, I'd said yes. And it was amazing. And I'd gained a few pounds that first week because, and I was woman enough to admit this, I'd eaten every one of the best kinds of carbs—bread, cake, cupcake, pasta, fries. Things I hadn't eaten in years.

And do you know what happened when I did? *Nothing.*

Other than the pounds that had ended up coming off when I started running a bit farther and clearing out the cottage behind the inn for myself.

The world didn't come to an end.

Whether Preston would still find me beautiful, I could fairly say no. I was definitely too wild for him now, even in just these four months since I'd left Aspen. Even thinking that grated against my determination to avoid thinking of him, but satisfaction filled a part of me at the thought, along with the accompanying realization that I didn't care. No sadness in sight about that at all.

"Well, we're off to the airport," Liam said, now with Danny trailing behind him, both carrying to-go cups and small sacks, no doubt filled with something wondrous Sadie had made.

"Drive safe," I offered.

Liam caught my eye, flashed me a smile that, if I had to title it, would be called *the heartbreaker*, and off they went.

Leo and I swung our attention to Bel, who held up a finger to us because she was now pouring coffee and had her phone tucked to her ear.

Moments later, she sent the customer off with a latte, hung up the phone, and nearly skipped over to the table. She slipped into the third chair, beaming.

"So how was that?" Leo asked, clearly amused by her friend.

"So good. So, so good. I'm so..." she trailed off, covering her smile with a delicate hand.

"Good?" Leo supplied wryly.

Bel flicked her ear. "No. Relieved. Happy. He's fine. I'm fine. We're going to be... friends again."

Before we could talk more, the door swung open and a small group shuffled in, so Bel jumped up to go help them.

"That sounds good," I said hopefully.

"It does. I hope it's true."

I was nervous to look, but when I glanced up, a smile broke out over my face.

"I think it looks *so* fabulous, I can't even tell you. It was gorgeous before, but this just... I don't know. I think it suits you—looks fresh and lighter, you know?"

Lisa, the owner and lead stylist of the one and only salon in Silverton, leaned back and pursed her lips as she tugged and smoothed at my now considerably shorter locks.

I'd gotten the idea on Saturday. Something about Bel's relief at making up with Danny had triggered the thought. I couldn't pin down what it was about that, but as soon as I left the bakery, I'd rounded the corner to Lisa's and made an appointment.

The soonest she could fit me in was Tuesday. I'd had the momentum to sit right down and *do it*, but surprise of all surprises, Lisa's had been slammed, as was apparently always the case. She'd only fit me in on Tuesday because of a cancellation.

I'd talked about trimming my hair short for summer when Preston and I had been dating for about six months. He'd made clear that he preferred long hair, so I'd stuck it out. Then the next year, when I had an appointment a few months before summer, he'd mentioned again that he loved my long hair, and he'd be so disappointed with it shorter. My hair hung to my mid-back at that point, so I'd gotten about three inches off thinking he'd hardly notice and it'd be lighter for me.

He *did* notice, and he didn't speak to me for three days. *Three days*. And at that point, eighteen months in and a few weeks after our engagement, I didn't see how messed up it was. I just felt sad and guilty and knew I'd never cut my hair again if he didn't want me to.

Yeah. That's how fast it'd happened.

So looking back at my reflection, my hair brushing the tops of my shoulders and styled in loose, messy waves, I let the blazing smile crawl over my face.

"I love it." I swallowed down the emotion that cropped up at the surprising sense of freedom in this moment.

Lisa smiled at me, and she had tears in her eyes. She didn't know my story, but she was perceptive. "You are radiant. Go out and love your life."

I hugged her before leaving, feeling overwhelming gratitude for her skill, and her kindness, and her empathy. She didn't know what I'd come from, or what the hair cut meant, but she must have known a bit. Beauty was a personal business, and maybe she could tell I'd stopped letting myself decide about it too long ago.

I practically tap-danced my way back to the inn. I had dirty, messy work to do on the cottage to get it ready to move into before winter. Tilda had lived in it for years, but as the 2002 Olympic after-glow faded with each passing year and fewer people visited, she'd found it easiest to stay in a first-floor room in the inn itself.

It needed new weather proofing, a new roof, though the guy who'd looked at it said he thought I could make it through this winter, maybe, so I was counting on that. It needed to be cleaned and the floor resealed and stained and new windows... it needed almost everything, it felt like. I'd already cleared out the old rotting rugs and cleaned up the double bed and dresser. I'd paint or stain them at some point.

I'd never thought of myself as crafty or a do-it-yourself-type, but I liked it. I liked being busy with my hands. I liked doing things all day with my hands and body and mind and feeling exhausted when I crawled into bed at night. It provided a sharp counterpoint to the perpetual sense of dissatisfaction, the need for sleeping pills nine days out of ten, the sense of unease that had plagued me, even early on, with Preston.

I'd been a pretty little bauble for him, set on display, always shiny, perfect, presentable, and certainly never interacting with the things of life. Absolutely never ruining a manicure or tying my hair back to get something done.

I pushed out a long, hard breath and stood on the porch looking out at the inn's yard. Soon, I'd get some mums and other cold-hardy plants to liven it up.

I hated thinking of the woman I'd been because so

much of me couldn't make peace with how I'd stayed with him.

How could I have stayed? How could I let myself be turned into a trinket—a little figurine in a glass case? And of course, once he'd invested and lost all the money I had, of course I didn't have a chance at escaping.

God bless great-aunt Tilda.

My therapist, a former irregular feature of my life but who I started meeting with via Skype every week since the beginning of July when I didn't have anyone else to talk to and also couldn't figure out how to function without so much self-loathing I couldn't breathe—she'd say the gratitude was good practice. And when I'd told her yesterday that I was cutting my hair, she had been typically stoic, but ultimately thought it a good sign.

She'd suggested that hiding behind hats wasn't starting a new, open-living life. And that was true. But I wore hats partly because the sun shone bright, and partly because Preston hated them. He said I looked *odd* in them. Because of course he had an opinion about them as well. He also hated my hair in ponytails, so the ponytail-hat combo had been a lethal rebellion in the beginning. Now, I'd moved on to the haircut.

"Everything okay over there, Wells?" Liam yelled from the street.

I looked up and noticed I'd been standing there, gazing up at Silver Ridge and not moving for who knows how long.

"Just fine," I said, and trotted down the steps to meet him at the steps.

And then, I saw who was standing next to him and sucked in a breath.

Jamie Morris.

"This is my brother, Jamie," Liam said, clearly noting the moment recognition hit me.

I coughed, squinted.

"Hi. Wells Bryant," I managed, then pressed my lips together to contain whatever dippy expression might over-take my face.

Because standing in front of me was none other than People's Sexiest Man two years running. He was Grammy award-winning, world-renowned recording artist and rock god Jamie Morris.

Not Morrison.

But now that I saw them together, *of course.*

Jamie had those blazing blue eyes, just like Liam's. He had the dark hair, though he wore his like I'd seen it most often in photos—in a man-bun style that should have been trying too hard but hit just the right notes on the *I didn't even notice I* had *hair* scale of disheveled rocker without looking grungy.

He wasn't quite as tall as Liam—maybe an inch or two shorter, though they weren't standing on even ground. They both had facial hair. They both had beautiful straight teeth and killer smiles. And that was Jamie's flashing at me now as he held out a hand.

"Nice to meet you, Wells. I've heard a lot about you."

And the voice.

"I—, *oh.*" I stuttered, and then noticed Liam glaring at Jamie.

This was too much beauty. Too much. These two men, standing there like we were about to be friends. Liam was overwhelming—he made me uncomfortable in a way I wasn't sure I disliked, but then *this?*

Liam cleared his throat pointedly. "We're off to grab a

bite, but then Jamie's meeting someone. Can I swing back by and catch up with you?"

"'Course. Yeah. I'll be here. If I don't answer, just come on through. I'm working on some stuff out back on and off."

Relief at having rediscovered the power of speech flowed through me.

He smiled. "Okay. See you later."

Jamie held up a hand in a static wave. "Nice to meet you."

I forced my feet to turn and walk back to the porch, then to keep walking after I opened the door until past the Reception desk, past the lounge area, through the sliding door and onto the covered patio, then out into the field beyond and tromping down the path to the cottage set back from the main building.

"How is this real life?" I asked myself aloud, because once you get used to being alone and surrounded by nature, you do a whole lot of talking to yourself.

I shook my head. No wonder Bel was tied up in knots at the thought of seeing him again. I didn't understand what had come before, but if she'd been messed over by *Jamie Morris*, no wonder she tended to look seasick at the very mention of his name.

I wasn't really even a fan. I mean, his stuff was good, but I wasn't big into his style. But seeing him just standing there, acting like a normal guy out on a walk in his itty bitty hometown with his big brother...

Talk about unexpected.

As I pulled open the rickety door to the cottage, I found myself smiling. Not because I'd seen Jamie Morris in real life, which would have merited phone calls to all my best girlfriends if I had any who weren't either heartbroken by him or related to him. No.

Because of what he'd said.

"I've heard a lot about you."

Despite myself, I couldn't help but feel pleased to know I'd made the initial report from Liam. Fair enough—if I had anyone to report to, he'd definitely be in mine as well.

CHAPTER SIX

Liam

"This is going to be fun," Jamie said, and rubbed his hands together like he used to when he was ten.

"You think?" I took a drink of my beer and glared at him.

"I know." He gave me that rock star, famous guy, shit-eating grin of his.

"Did you have to say you'd heard *so much* about her? I already told you she's a little... skittish."

I would have smacked him in the head if it wouldn't have drawn even more attention to the awkwardness of the statement, let alone my traitorous blush.

"I did. Because I have. Because you're mildly obsessed with this woman." He leaned back with an arm over the back of the chair next to him.

"I am not," I grumbled.

His gaze wandered over the little pub. It wasn't technically allowed to even be called a pub according to state liquor laws, but we got away with things up here well enough. They did serve food—technically a partial menu from the Mexican place next door.

Ger had delivered a basket of tortilla chips and salsa when we sat down, thereby making our drinks legal. The place hadn't changed in the years we'd been coming. I was bracing against turning thirty-one in a few months and the horrible realization that it'd been nearly a decade since my first time there.

Jamie's eyes found mine again, and they looked typically twinkly.

"But you are, Li. And that's good. She may not be into you yet, but she's almost there, and she was definitely fighting a smile when I said you'd told me about her."

I heaved a sigh. "I think she was working on not falling all over herself in the sights of *the Jamie Morris.*"

"She did well, actually. I was impressed." He took a drink, set it down, glanced around again.

Good grief, he sounded like a jerk, but he'd had some terrible encounters with people over the years, so I knew he meant it as a compliment to her.

"I'm just saying it's a dangerous thing for me to introduce you to a woman I might be interested—"

"Let's not pretend it's *might.* You haven't acted like this since college. Own up to it. You like Wells Bryant, and you want to date her," he said boldly, flinging an arm wide like he was telling the world.

A few regulars at the bar snickered.

"*Fine.* My point is maybe I should keep you my dirty little secret," I said, and felt pretty smug about it, until I saw his face. "Aw, Jam, I didn't mean it like that."

He inspected the label of his beer—one of *my* beers. "I know."

I was always surprised by how much this place still influenced him. He kept up the front, stayed engaged with the family, but small moments like this let me know he was still hurting. Was still *hurt*. We'd always been good, but some parts of him were rough edges yet.

He took the last swig, tipping the bottle high, then set it down.

"Thanks for the beer—this one's still my favorite. I'm going to go find Leo and get the grilling over with. I'll see you at home?"

I wandered down the path toward the inn and wondered what I could do about Jamie. What I could do about the lodge, the town, the brewery, the family, Wells. I felt like I'd been underwater and climbing up, swimming with everything I had to get my head above water, but every time I turned around, I found some other problem that needed to be solved.

Not that Wells was a problem, per se. But she was in that she didn't respond to me the way I expected, and she wasn't overtly interested in me. And I wouldn't be able to make progress there unless I spent time with her, which neither of us seemed to have in great supply.

I knocked on the frame of the inn's screen door, behind it the way wide open, as usual. When no one answered, I stepped through and looked around.

Tilda had redone the place about a decade ago, updating the older wallpaper to light paint, stripping old carpet in favor of rugs over hardwood, and generally spiffed things up. The Reception area had a high wooden desk that Tilda's boyfriend Rex Woodruff, appropriately named since he was a carpenter, had made. Tilda's husband had died in his forties, and she'd sworn she'd never marry again. But she and Rex had found each other here, and they'd essentially been common-law married except that they never lived together.

The woodwork on the Reception desk was artful, clean. It elevated the whole space, which was saying something. It was an exceptionally nice place. From the outside, you might expect something more kitschy or eccentric, especially if you knew Tilda, but she was savvy and knew what would make people feel welcome.

Each room had its quirks, with oddities around, but overall, the place inspired confidence rather than a sinking sensation that the ghost of a Victorian-era child might haunt your room or the china dolls with vacant eyes might come alive at night.

"Wells?" I said loudly, hoping she'd appear and I wouldn't have to search for her, or startle her. I felt like I was always sneaking up on her, even though I tried not to.

"*Out here,*" she said from the back.

I followed the carpet to where I'd heard her voice—through an opulent lounge area and around the corner to the first room. I kept my hands on the doorway and leaned into the space, peeking my head in.

"You in here?" I said, taking in the room.

It was small—one of the smallest from what I remembered—with just a dresser and mirror, door leading to a bathroom, and a double bed. All of the furniture looked beautiful and matched, the linens on the bed pristine white, though in a jumble.

"How was your time with your brother?" she asked, still not actually appearing.

It sounded like she was on the floor on the far side of the bed. I stayed put.

"It was good. He's off to find Leo, but I'll have to pin him down and get his perspective on the lodge soon enough." Hopefully tomorrow.

Just then, she popped up, her face a little red, her hair disheveled and different-looking. She ran a hand through her locks, and an odd look crossed her face. "Strange."

"What is?" I asked.

"I got a haircut today and cut off about ten inches of hair. I keep forgetting until I touch it again and remember. I'm sure when I shower tomorrow, I'll be momentarily stunned by how little shampoo I need." She stepped around the bed and folded her arms across her chest.

"It looks good." It did.

Shoulder-length, or slightly shorter, it had a tousled look that suited her. I'd seen her with it pulled back in a ponytail, or on occasion down, and it'd been lovely. But she looked refreshed and clearly happy with it.

"It has been a long time since I've had an actual haircut. It was great," she said, then moved toward the door. "Want to sit outside and talk?"

"Sounds good to me."

We made our way to the kitchen area farther down the hall where she grabbed glasses of water and offered me a beer.

"Is that one of mine?" I asked with a wide smile, something about seeing her pull a beer my brewery had made out of the inn's fridge making me feel fuzzy.

She gave me a shamed look. "Well, yes, but it's one of the original six from the pack you gave me. I haven't been drinking much beer, I'll admit. But what better time to try it out than with the brew master himself?"

She led the way back down the hallway and out onto the back porch.

"Ah, well sorry to disappoint, but I'm not actually the brew master. My buddy John is. But I did help come up with the recipe, so I'm not as useless as a lot of guys on the business side of things."

We settled in Adirondack chairs set on the back lawn facing Silver Ridge.

What a view.

I'd never get sick of the sight of those mountains. They were in my blood. I felt a soul-deep connection with these peaks in particular, but I experienced a lightness, a different way of breathing, when in the presence of any mountains. It always struck me as a relief to come home and see them.

"You have an intense look on your face. What are you thinking?" she asked quietly next to me.

"I'm thinking how much I love these mountains." My head fell back against the wood of the chair behind me.

I snuck a glance at her and saw her smile, which made that fuzzy feeling grow. Jamie would be wagging his eyebrows at me if he knew.

"I can see why. If this inn had been almost anywhere else, I don't think I would have considered staying. I didn't really plan to until I got here—at least not indefinitely. But waking up every day at the foot of these giants... it's magic."

I looked over at her to see her eyes closed, her head tilted back so her chin jutted out, highlighting the perfect curve of her jaw, her chin, her neck.

"It is," I agreed.

We sat in silence for a while, until she spoke. "So, your brother is Jamie Morris."

I chuckled at the too-casual sound of her voice. "Yep."

"Yep?" She sat up and leaned on the armrest of the chair nearest mine. "That's all I get?"

I sat up and set my elbows on my knees, rested my beer between my feet. "What do you want to know?"

"I—I don't know. I guess... what's that like?"

I laughed. "I don't know. It just... is. It means we don't see him very often, but I think that's less about his schedule and fame and more about—" I cut myself off.

"More about...?"

"Family stuff, maybe. And other stuff you may have heard about," I said, hoping she would so I wouldn't have to spell it out and feel like I'd betrayed Jamie. Or Bel.

"Bel?"

I nodded. "He manages to convince me he's over it while he's gone, and if you see anything in the tabloids, you'd think he was living it up, though not as much as some musicians. But whenever he's back here, it's clear he's still... affected by being here."

She folded her arms across her chest, and I realized she wore only jeans and a short-sleeved T-shirt. Though September, the evening had gotten chilly now that the sun was almost gone.

"Here." I shrugged out of my jacket—it was nothing much, more like a sweatshirt, but perfect for these early fall days.

"Thanks." She took it and pulled it on, then zipped it up.

A small thrill snaked through me at her accepting it, and then at the sight of it on her.

"But she doesn't seem like... I don't know. I don't understand the dynamic." She shifted and looked at me, evidently hoping I could shed some light on it.

"All I can say is they're both idiots," I said, trying to lighten the subject.

"Well. I hope they can avoid each other, or have a peace-making conversation while he's here. Maybe it'll help them both."

"Maybe."

I doubted it, because we'd all been hoping that for years, and it'd never happened. This tense, heightened, painful awareness always hummed around town when Jamie was here, and not because of his star power, but because everyone was watching to see what would happen between Jamie, Bel, and Danny. Probably why Jamie avoided coming home.

"Enough about that. Tell me the latest on the inn. Did your liquor license end up coming through?" I asked.

She gave me a rueful smile. "It did. Thank you for asking. It's conditional on our food service, so it's really limited to breakfast and tea-time right now. Hopefully once I have the restaurant open, I'll be able to offer drinks all the time, even at happy hour whether I have a full meal displayed or not."

Wow. She had plans on top of plans. "A restaurant?"

She beamed at that. "Yes. Have you seen the space on the east side of the property? I want to set something up there, because there's just a field, and the property line extends quite a ways until the hill curves up. I'm assuming that's where Morrison property begins."

"Probably. I haven't looked at it with that eye, but the idea is appealing. What's your timeline?"

A curious mix flooded me—relief that she wasn't leaving, and disappointment that I now had no way of asking her if she'd sell when she was making long-term plans.

"Oh, *years*. First, we've got to have people staying here

regularly. But I think for an inn, it should have a restaurant. If we get more people in, we'll need more tables, just like we'll need more beds, you know? I'd love for us to have the problem of sell-outs and running out of lift tickets because we've met the max."

Her voice energized the air around us, just like her gestures.

"That sounds ideal to me. Do you happen to have a secret marketing strategy that's going to solve all my problems and bring in the people so you can build?"

She laughed softly. "I wish."

"It sounds great though. I hope it can happen sooner than later."

And I wanted to ask her—*will you stay after that? Would you want to sell this place? Will you want to start over every couple years?* But I didn't. Of course I didn't.

"Me too. Speaking of, what's the word on your challenge?"

"*Challenge.* That's a very positive way of framing it."

"My therapist is encouraging me to reframe the way I think of things..." she trailed off, stopped for a moment, then sat on the edge of the chair and squared herself to me.

Something about that made me sit up straighter too.

"Therapist?" I asked, feeling like I should based on the way she was waiting.

"I came here in a pretty desperate state. I'm still working through that, and I can't do it all on my own. So I do a video chat with someone online every week, and it has helped me work through some of my... issues."

"You mean your *challenges?*"

She flashed a smile. "Exactly."

"Are you okay though? I mean, you seem okay, of course, but—"

She set a hand on my arm to stop me, and other than our handshake, I was fairly sure that was the only time we'd ever touched.

"I am. I'm okay," she said, a hint of a smile on her face.

I knew my face looked serious. I was overwhelmed—by her hand on my arm, by this news that whatever she'd been going through was so intense, by everything.

"Do you want to… talk about it?"

I felt like an idiot, being so tentative, and sounding so unsure. I truly didn't have experience with this—with talking about hard things with a woman I barely knew.

She smiled fully now. "You're trying so hard to figure out what's right here, aren't you? I can practically hear your golden boy gears turning."

"You think I don't actually care? That I'm just trying to say the right thing for the sake of it?"

More offended than I should have been, sure, but it irked me she would think I was being anything other than genuine.

"I'm sorry, no." She looked down at her hands, both now resting in her lap, the large sleeves of my jacket swallowing her arms. "I don't really know how to handle you."

"Handle me?"

I watched as she looked out at the mountains, now masses of shadowed purple as the sun slipped past the horizon and the sky lit up in a blaze of pinks and oranges.

She stood up and turned, her arms crossed. "Will you walk with me out to the cottage? I'll show you what I've been working on."

I hoisted myself up and followed as she stepped out of the more manicured lawn area and onto a dirt path that cut through a small field before a pine forest began. Just at the edge, I could see Tilda's old, decrepit cottage.

Before I could ask her about it, she stopped. The grass was high on either side of us, crickets and other bugs chirping like they hadn't gotten the memo it wasn't summer anymore. We hadn't had a hard freeze yet so they were hanging on while they could.

I tucked my hands into my pockets, ever mindful of my impulse to reach out to her, but her body language made it clear that's not what she wanted.

"I was in a toxic relationship. I broke it off in April, but that was after years with a man who tried to control every-thing about me." She took a deep breath through her nose and let it out her mouth in a slow exhale. "I haven't been *me* in well over two years, and coming here was an act of desperation. But now that I'm here, I feel more whole than I could have hoped for. *Already*."

I studied her eyes, heart racing in my chest at the thought of someone mistreating her.

"I'm sorry." The futility of those words stood out in bold, but they had to be said.

"Thank you. I am too. A lot of what I'm working on is how to forgive myself." Her voice came out gentle—whether for my sake or hers, I wasn't sure.

"What would you need to forgive?"

She turned back to the path, and we walked side by side. "For letting it go on so long. For not realizing it was happening until I was too far into the relationship to feel like I could leave. For so many other things."

I grabbed her hand and tugged her to a stop. "I realize that my insight is exactly none on this matter, but I am positive that whatever happened wasn't your fault. And I'm also certain that you *did* get out, and you're doing what you can now to rebuild. That's impressive, if not miraculous."

Her eyes flickered between mine, and she gave my hand a gentle squeeze before releasing it. "Thank you."

We continued in silence, the only sounds those persistent bugs and the brush of our bodies against the tall grasses bordering the path. We stopped in front of a tiny cabin that faced east and looked straight up at the mountain.

"I'm hoping to move in before the season starts." She led me up the stairs and through the door.

I catalogued the features—weathered porch, collapsing front stair, flimsy door, single-paned windows. But inside looked far better than I would have thought.

"How much time are you putting in out here?" I slowly circled the small room.

"Any spare minute I have, which has been a decent amount since I haven't had many guests recently and I'm almost through sorting out Tilda's stuff. I cleared everything out, stripped the floors and refinished those. I've ordered new windows and a new door. And if you peek in there—" she nodded with her chin toward a door at the back of the room, "—you can see the shiny new bathroom. I hired a guy to deal with that though, and if the roof can last like he thought it would, I'll hire him to redo it next year when the snow's done."

"That's great. So you're really going to be here? I know you said you hadn't planned to stay but it sounds like you are."

I kept circling, admiring, wondering what it would look like when she filled it up with her own things.

She came to stand by me where I looked out one of the filmy windows.

"I wouldn't have thought I'd like such a small town, or living so far away from a big one, but I think it was exactly what I needed to rebuild my life, and now that I'm here, I can't imagine what else I'd want." She nudged me with an elbow and shot me a conspiratorial smile. "Except maybe a total tourist revolution in town."

After that, we walked back along the path, back through the inn, and we found ourselves yet again in the front yard.

"Thanks for showing me the cottage. You're doing an amazing job here, Wells, and the town's lucky to have you." I hunched, feeling the light chill on my arms.

"I'm lucky to have the town," she said, then turned to the door. "'Night, Liam."

CHAPTER SEVEN

Wells

I walked directly out to the back porch and took up the seat where I'd been earlier.

This man spelled trouble.

He was just so *nice*. And friendly. And even though he had the Captain America reputation and the golden boy persona in town, it seemed genuine. *He* seemed genuine.

Sometimes when he looked at me, it made my mind slow down, like it wanted to stop and enjoy those bright blue eyes on me. He made me feel muddled and messy, a little out of control in a strangely thrilling way.

Preston had never made me feel that way. Even in the beginning, I'd always been mindful of wanting to impress him. I'd spent an entire session on this with my therapist recently because I knew it was messed up. Why had I thought that was a good way to begin—having to seem as close to a perfect version of myself as I could just to attract a guy I barely knew?

But that's what we all did, to some degree. We created the image we thought someone wanted, or sometimes the images of ourselves we wanted to be but weren't quite.

This was one reason I'd told Liam about where I am. He needed to know I wasn't in a place to be something I'm not, and what I am is someone who is figuring out who I am. Who is trying to forgive myself, to make peace with the last few years, and to wade through this new life that is far different than the one I'd thought I was headed for—one in high society with a wealthy husband, one my parents approved of, and one I'd thought I wanted. I'd had no idea something different could even approach the satisfaction I already felt with this new version of life.

But Liam hadn't been fazed—well, not too much. He'd been thoughtful, and he was so transparent, I could have hugged him for it. I could see his mind racing to figure out what was okay to say in response—how to be gentle with me, but engaged. Utterly adorable.

He was fast becoming a valuable friend to me. I genuinely liked him and looked forward to seeing him.

And if I was honest, the thought of seeing him again sent little flutters through me. I smiled up at the mountain and snuggled into his sweatshirt, breathing in the scent that had lingered in the cotton—pine, clean soap, a hint of beer, and a twinge of wood smoke, like he'd stood next to a fire for a minute before walking over here.

Yes, if I was honest, Liam Morrison was too good to be true.

～

By Thursday of that week, I'd painted the walls of the cottage, fixed a few small issues in rooms in the inn, and we'd happily had a few bookings come through the website for November. I'd been working on finding some places to run ads, setting up deals with discount hotel websites and other vendors, all trying to get our name out there so we'd be full as often as possible this winter.

Not that I had any idea how to handle an inn full of people, but the thought of it made me giddy. After being here for months and months, I couldn't wait for the season to start.

But before that, we'd have a beautiful fall, and I'd keep getting things cleaned up and ready around the inn and especially in my little cottage.

Today, I'd decided to walk to *Rise and Shine* and grab a cappuccino. I was toast at only two in the afternoon. With this being a quiet time at the shop, hopefully Bel could sit and chat with me and I could hear how her week had been —had she run into Jamie?

The answer to my question came as soon as I stepped through the door, the bell jingling overhead.

In front of me stood Liam, who glanced at me immediately, a worried, almost pained expression on his face. As he stepped to me, I saw Jamie standing rigidly at the counter, his voice an unintelligible rumble from where I lingered.

And Bel. Sweet Bel stood with her jaw clamped shut, her eyes bright with unshed tears, her hands gripping the counter as though to keep her upright.

"What's—"

Liam put a hand on my arm and leaned in. "I told him this was a terrible idea. He insisted on coming."

His worried eyes found mine, then bounced to the two at the counter.

"Maybe they just need to get it over with—"

"Don't you *dare* talk to me like this is on *me*. Don't do that. *Don't*." Bel's harsh whisper cut across the room.

Her eyes snapped up to meet mine as though she'd just noticed she and Jamie weren't the only ones in the room.

"Wells. You're late," she said, an edge of desperation in her voice.

I cleared my throat. "Sorry. Just running a bit behind, and now I really don't have any extra time. Sorry to interrupt, but I really need to meet with Bel."

Jamie, who'd turned to look at me, his face blank of all emotion, stepped aside.

"Of course," he said quietly, then nodded to Liam.

Liam looked at me—we shared a thin, false smile, and the men left. Mercifully, there was no one else in the place. Bel came over, walking almost robotically, and sat in a chair, her posture perfect, her eyes on the bright yellow wall next to her.

"Are you..."

"I just need a minute." She sat there, no expression crossing her face except one of determination. After a minute, truly, she looked up, blinking me back into focus, and took a deep breath. "Thanks for being my excuse to get him out of here."

"Of course."

She stood. "Let me get you something—cappuccino?"

I opened my mouth, about to protest and tell her no; of course we should sit here and talk and she should cry, though nothing came out but, "Sure."

This was her workplace and also not the time or place to break down, though part of me wondered if Bel would let herself. Or, if she needed to. Was she sad? Angry?

That strained, loud whisper had sounded furious, sad,

hurt, longing... everything. Just thinking of it proved painful. But she'd locked whatever lurked in her down tight, and I knew it wouldn't resurface, just as clearly I sensed I shouldn't bother asking.

She brought me a delicious cappuccino with insanely detailed mountains designed in the foam. I'd hoped she'd sit down and we could chat about something—anything—but a few other customers trickled in and she was busy for the ten minutes I sat sipping my drink and scrolling my phone where I kept my to-do lists.

I left with a smile and a wave, the jingle of the bell at odds with the mood cast over the place, at least for me and Bel. The other patrons seemed oblivious. *Good.* No one needed to know that the long-awaited confrontation had come so publicly.

I stepped out into the street, the September day a gorgeous, sunny, mild pleasure. I wandered slowly back to the inn just in time to see my cousin Wyatt jogging down the front steps.

"Hey cousin," he said, his voice always surprisingly deep.

He was a true rancher by trade and dressed the part—wranglers, plaid snap-up shirt, cowboy hat, the works. The whole chiseled features, strapping chest, and muddy boots thing completed the picture, and I was amazed he hadn't been snatched up by some local girl ready to breed him his own little crew.

"Hi Wyatt. What're you doing all the way down here?"

He rarely came to town. His ranch was another thousand feet or so up on a kind of plateau area back behind one of the peaks. It took another forty-five-minute drive to reach, and I gathered the cattle game was incredibly demanding.

"I'm getting ready for the Almabtrieb—we bring the

cows down and dress 'em up, just like they do in Germany and Austria. The Meiers, the people who founded the town, kept the tradition with their small herd a century ago, and it actually makes a lot of sense. I bring the stock down to lower elevation in October. There's a festival that second weekend."

"Of course. No wonder I have like five rooms booked for that weekend. I thought maybe it was a long weekend for schools, but that makes sense. How fun."

I loved that about this small town—the founding family had brought with it some amazing traditions that had lasted. Between their German heritage and the Morrison family's Irish roots, unique practices happened all the time. I'd been sad to hear they'd decided to cancel this year's Oktoberfest, which usually took place in September, due to funding issues. I supposed money didn't determine whether the cows needed to come down or not, and for that I was glad.

"Glad to hear it. While I'm getting things ready, I thought I'd stop in. The place looks great. I saw Anthony in there at the desk and he said you're doing *swell*." He shook his head as if that were a shame.

I chuckled. "Anthony does love to use throwback language. He told me I was *tops* the other day. But I'll take it —if he's happy, that's fine by me."

Wyatt and I had rarely seen each other growing up, and when we did, it had been stunted, forced, and uncomfortable. Completely the fault of my family—they didn't want me to get my dresses dirty or tumble around with Wy and his brothers. That was all I wanted to do, and it had made for a tense time for my extremely stoic, almost antiseptically clean parents.

"Has anyone made offers on the place?" he asked, nodding to the building.

My brows shot up. "No. Were you expecting someone to?"

He frowned, shook his head. "I thought you might get a few—there were always rumors about people wanting to buy it from Grandma, but we all knew she wouldn't let it leave the family."

A stone settled in my belly. "Wyatt, did you want the inn? Why did she leave it to me instead of one of her grandsons?"

I'd been so wrapped up in my life, in this being the escape hatch I hadn't realized I'd need, I hadn't let myself fully realize the strangeness of the inheritance. Tilda had had one daughter who'd had three boys—Wyatt, Warrick, and Wilder. *I know.* The repeating first letter thing was very Utah, I'd been told.

"Don't think twice about it. We all had our own things going. She gave us plenty, and when she told us why she wanted to give it to you, we agreed it made sense. We had a family meeting about two years ago and she changed the will so you'd inherit the inn, the land, and the small sum to get you going."

Wyatt was so calm, so sturdy, talking about these things like it wasn't technically all *his* if he'd wanted it.

What kind of people just give away part of their inheritance?

"I—I don't understand. Why would she do that?"

I searched his face. His eyes were shaded by the brim of his hat but I could feel them piercing me.

"She said she thought you might need the mountains someday. She wanted you to have a place to come and get messy," he said, a half-smile on his face.

I clenched my teeth against the tide of sadness, shame,

and joy that brought. *Thank God.* Somehow, even though I'd never let her know me, she'd known.

"Well," I started, cleared my throat, then added, "Thank you. She was right."

He nodded slowly, then patted my shoulder. "You're good, Wells. You're doing just fine."

"I know." And I meant it. I was doing well, and I was getting better every day.

"I gotta get to a meeting, but I'll see you in a few weeks for the drive. Get the place nice and full so my heifers have a good audience, yeah?"

He tapped my chin with a finger and sauntered off, *all* cowboy now in a way that fit perfectly up here in the mountainous West.

A few weeks later, Leo found me in the cottage.

Or, she came tromping down the path, yelling at top volume, until I raced out the door and met her on the porch just as she hit the bottom, failing stair. Her foot nearly fell through right as I said, "Don't step there!"

"You're trying to kill me, I guess."

Her voice rang like a challenge—always pushing, even in jest.

"Oh, of course. My secret plan was to lure you out here when I had no idea you were stopping by and get you to step there and die from it."

She cracked a smile at me, her irritation faltering. "Fine. I forgive you."

"Okay. I suppose I'll accept, even if I'm not sure what for." I wiped the hair back from my face. "Now tell me what's got you shouting at me from across the field like there's an emergency?"

She scoffed.

"I was *not* shouting. I was hollering. Very different." She folded her slim arms across her chest, flipped her blond braid over her shoulder.

"Ah. Good to know." I leaned against the railing of the cabin's porch and stretched my calves, which had started cramping up a lot after the runs I'd been doing.

"I came to tell you that my brother has a crush on you, and I think you should consider going out with him." She quirked an eyebrow and let a smug grin curve her lips.

My body froze. I stood there, my mouth shaping letters in slow motion but no sound coming from my vocal cords.

I did love Leo's up-front approach. I did. *I know I do.* Somewhere, deep deep down...

"So?" she pushed, as though I should have planned a date with her brother in the ten seconds since she'd spoken.

"Uh, so, *wow*," I managed.

She narrowed her eyes at me.

"You like him," she said, more like an accusation than anything.

"We're friends, yes."

I'd had a few short conversations with him, but mostly, we'd seen each other in passing. Between the renovations to the cottage and the search for a new housekeeper, plus the guests I'd had for Wyatt's cattle drive and the utter insanity of that weekend, I'd barely had time to stop in to see Bel. I only saw Leo because we'd been trail running on Saturdays, and even then, we'd canceled last week's because of the cow festival.

"Yeah, but you like him. You're attracted to him. You think—"

"*Leo*. Please. Give me a minute to absorb this information, and then give me a minute to respond in my own words." I covered my eyes with the palms of my hands, then abruptly pulled them back when I realized they were coated in dust and paint.

"Fine, two minutes." She glanced at her watch.

She timed me while my mind raced.

Did I like Liam? *Yes.* Not hard to nail down. But wasn't it too soon for me to like someone, or date someone, or even think about that? Didn't I need a self-imposed penalty period, during which I was forced to be single and rely on myself and not fall into another situation where I lost myself before I even knew which way was up?

But Liam Morrison was nothing like Preston. If he had been, he would have elbowed his way into my life with backhanded compliments, gaining my trust in insignificant ways until he could force trust by, say, asking for investment money.

Anger washed over me. *Good grief,* I hated that I'd ever gotten into that relationship. I'd known he was manipulative, but at first it'd been with other people, and on my behalf. I'd been twenty-three and straight out of college and totally wowed that an older, cultured man like him would be interested in me. Pair that with the fact that somehow my parents found out I was dating *Preston Umbridge* and suggested *this was my chance* to nail down a respectable husband before my looks faded.

At twenty-three.

Right.

"Are you in there?" Leo asked, now standing in front of me.

I must have been deep inside my own thoughts. "Sorry. Yeah, I'm here."

"So, what do you think? Are you going to date my brother?"

I could see excitement where before she'd only been pushy.

"It's not that simple. Why do you say that he has a crush on me anyway?" I asked, mostly interested in delaying my own response, but absolutely willing to hear her reasoning because I wasn't entirely convinced Liam was interested.

I knew he found me attractive, but I also knew he was a genuinely nice guy. He was also, to a lesser degree than Leo of course, very straight-forward.

"I say that because he does. If you're around, he's looking at you or for you. If he hears you'll be somewhere, he accidentally shows up."

"This is a small town. That means nothing," I insisted.

"How many of our girls' nights has he happened upon in the last month?" she asked, arms crossed again.

"I don't know, I didn't keep count."

I must have grimaced because she smiled triumphantly.

"Yes you did. You do know because you totally kept track."

I pursed my lips together, then reluctantly agreed. "Fine. I did. He showed up to every one."

"Exactly."

"We're friends though. And I'm... kind of a wreck. There's no way he's interested in my baggage when he could have anyone in town."

Because as much as he'd been watching me, I'd been watching him.

He charmed old ladies he helped crossing streets. He chatted up the veterans' group, joked with the younger kids, and caught the eye of every woman he walked by, married or not. And women sidled up to him at restaurants, in the coffee shop, even on the sidewalk. I didn't blame them. If I wasn't trying to make peace with my own dating history, I probably would have been more overtly flirtatious myself.

But that wasn't me—certainly not anymore.

"That's true. He absolutely could. But I've never seen him act like this about any of the women in this town. He only acts like that with you."

"You should probably let him talk to me about this. This isn't really any of you—"

"Stop right there. *Obviously* this isn't any of my business, but I'm in it anyway. He's my stubborn, perfect, idiot brother and you are my stubborn, brilliant, idiot friend. You're not likely to decide you can date without a little push. He'll be too busy being polite and chivalrous and you'll be too busy self-flagellating. I'm circumventing that and years of angst with this one small method of interference."

She'd shocked me speechless again with her willingness to peg us both so neatly and yet fairly accurately—at least for me. I didn't know if he'd avoided being more open about his interest for my sake, but I'd certainly been punishing myself by not allowing myself to even consider dating someone like him.

"If I see him again sometime soon, I'll... try to make it clear I'm open to dating. Or something. Maybe."

She smiled, satisfied.

"And don't you *dare* tell him I'm interested in him. Let him figure that out on his own." I gave her a hard look, but rolled my eyes when I could see she'd probably already had this same conversation with him.

Someday, when it was her turn, I'd make sure I was knee-deep in her business.

CHAPTER EIGHT

Liam

I hadn't talked to Wells in two weeks. It was now the second week of November, and I couldn't believe how close we were to the consultants arriving, and more than that, to the season opening. We'd had a decent number of season pass sales, but they'd been typical—not a big uptick, which I'd known would be the case, but still a disappointment.

We hadn't spent any time together—no time for it. I'd been scrambling from one thing to the next, coaxing the consultants—The Bauer Group—to come before the season. They'd wanted to see the mountain open, but I'd urged them to come before then when I could give them my full attention.

Beyond that, I'd been reassuring John that I was serious about the brewery and that I wasn't satisfied with the way things were. He wasn't either, but his job was strictly nine to five and not quite as unwieldy as the lodge, so he generally had more time to dedicate to it. *Thank God*, because without him, we wouldn't have any beer to sell or submit to contests, and that was essential to ever getting to a place where we were brewing more, selling more, making more, and so on.

Leo had come to visit a few weeks ago. She'd asked what I thought of Wells. Immediately, a red flag had planted itself firmly in my mind.

If Leo wasn't provoking me into a fight, she was actively arguing with a decision I'd made, or making a suggestion that was bound to make me want to shake her. So this *had* to be provoking me.

"Why do you ask?" I leaned back from my desk to stretch a bit.

She sat in the seat opposite mine. "Because I'm curious. You seem interested in her, and she's my friend, so I thought I'd ask."

I eyed her. No sign of the usual mischief—no troublesome little twinkle like Jamie got, no smile being bitten back by a literal bite of her inner cheek. Maybe she was being genuine.

"I like her a lot. I'm glad I've gotten to know her a bit, and I'm looking forward to... doing that more, if the opportunity should arise." I inwardly rolled my eyes, but didn't let her see it. Leo picked up on any sign of weakness immediately.

"Hmm. Good."

That's all she said.

"Why *good*?"

She studied me, arms crossed, face serious, which surprised me. "I think it's a good idea for you to spend more time with her if you want. That's all. For once in my life, I'm not saying anything else."

She popped up out of her seat, twirled around, and bounded out the door before I could respond.

I'd sat there for probably twenty minutes, wondering what she'd really meant. But the thing about Leo? She usually said what she meant. At the same time, it seemed far too simple for her to be saying I should spend more time with Wells.

Maybe she could tell I liked Wells. Maybe she wanted me to be happy and so thought it'd be nice if we dated.

Though that was not really a Leo frame of mind, at least not for my case.

Maybe she knew Wells liked me. Maybe she wanted *Wells* to be happy, and thought by some miracle I could be someone to help her with that.

My pulse ticking up a bit, the thought made me smile to myself, which I quickly wiped away for fear Leo would pop back in and catch me and tease me mercilessly.

What the exchange had done was leave me certain I wanted what Leo had suggested—I wanted to spend more time with Wells, get to know her, and more than that. It'd been a long time since I'd been this attracted to someone physically, but the beauty of Wells was that the more I'd gotten to know about her, the more I liked her.

So today, before I made the hour-and-a-half drive to Salt Lake, I thought I'd stop by the inn and offer to pick something up for her—see if I could bust out a tiny version of the old knight in shining armor gig. And, if she had anything she needed, then I would have another excuse to see her when I delivered it later today.

Win-win.

"Hi Anthony."

"Hi Liam Morrison," Anthony, who was twirling a pencil in his fingers and leaning on an elbow at the inn's high-top Reception desk, responded. "She's out back with some coffee. I'm sure she'd be happy to have you join her."

He winked, then returned to his pencil-twirling as I thanked him.

I pulled open the door to the back and smiled seeing Wells hunched under a blanket, a knit cap on her head, her hands cupping a mug, her body tilted toward a fire built in a metal pit in the middle of the patio area.

"This looks cozy," I said as I approached.

"Care to join me?"

Her broad smile made my stomach flip.

She'd gotten more generous with the smiles—an insanely gratifying thing.

"I'd love to, but I'm on my way to the city." I sat next to her on the bench she'd scooted close to the fire.

She took a sip of coffee and huddled down into her blanket further. The morning was cold—it felt like snow was coming. A gray snow sky hung over us, the forecast calling for it to start later. Once it started up here, we were likely to have it on and off for the next few months. I'd be doing my best snow dance every morning after Thanksgiving weekend to ensure it was more *on* than *off*.

"What're you up to in the city?" she asked, then shivered.

I smiled at her, because being near her like this did that to me. She was all bundled up but clearly still freezing, and it proved a difficult thing to keep from wrapping an arm around her and pulling her to me.

"Running a few errands, but mostly meeting with our bank. The consultants get here tomorrow, so they'll be contending with the storm if it does hit." One of my concerns, but in the end, having a decent early snow was only a good thing.

They'd insisted on their own transportation and doing whatever they had to in order to mimic what a regular family might experience when making their way to the town and then the lodge. It was a good plan and would help them understand some of the barriers to access people had, as well as some of the unique challenges our resort had that others just didn't.

But I was nervous. Understandably. And I had arranged this last-minute meeting with our bank to see if we could secure a loan to install another lift or two at spring thaw. Or at least, to be able to say it was under advisement. It was one of the many projects I'd been working on—proposals and requests to the loan officer at the bank to help give us the infrastructure to support more people. I'd bumped up my proposed timeline by two months and was praying I could effectively communicate with the guy. He'd been easy to work with in the past, but after our audit this summer, I didn't have a lot of hope.

"Do you like visiting Salt Lake? You went to school there, right?" she asked, resting her mug against one cheek.

In that simple movement, she'd made me feel a startlingly visceral need to touch her cheek, to cup her face in my hands and chase away the cold, kiss her chilled lips, and warm her in other ways.

I took a breath then blew it out.

"I did. I went to the U and then left for three years in the Army. I like going there every once in a while. After being away from here for almost seven full years, I've been back five years, but I'm still always glad and relieved when I'm back and don't have to leave again any time soon."

She smiled again, and my blood pumped faster. I laughed at myself then.

"I guess it makes me feel pretty small-town, but I'm a small-town boy at heart." I flashed her a chagrined smile.

I'd grown up here, and instead of coming to hate it as Jamie evidently had, I'd nestled into it and loved it. Danny and Leo had even more than me, the two of them leaving only when absolutely necessary.

"If I'd never been here, I might think you were crazy. But it's kind of wonderland."

She looked up at the mountains with the same expression I knew I had—longing, nostalgia, awe.

Something about her accepting this place so fully when not everyone did made my heart thump gleefully in my chest.

"I've got to head out soon, but I thought I'd see if you needed anything from anywhere in the valley. I'm happy to get whatever you want, and I can drop it by this evening when I'm back."

Her surprise was clear, but not uncomfortable. She looked in my eyes and bit her lip as if trying to solve a puzzle. Then her mouth tugged up into a grin.

"Actually, I do have a few things, if you don't mind."

I assured her I didn't, and she asked if I'd go to a favorite grocery store there, and another home décor store. She had a few other small items, but most of it would be from the grocery store.

"You really love this place, huh?" I asked, marveling at the very specific items on her list for Trader Joe's.

She nodded. "I do. It's one of the only things I actively miss while I'm up here. Hector's is fantastic, which was a pleasant surprise, but I do miss Trader Joe's. This is so awesome of you. I have a cooler I can give you—probably not totally necessary considering the weather, but just in case."

I followed her to a large storage room in a part of the inn I didn't know was there, stuffed with organized bins of decorations and who knew what else. Each clear plastic bin was itemized with a list on the top and side, from what I could see. On a shelf near the door sat a small collection of camping and outdoor gear, as well as a cooler.

"Is this all Tilda's stuff?"

"This stuff is mine, but yeah, the rest is her seasonal décor and some kitchen items that don't get used right now, things like that. I went through and organized and took a detailed inventory. She had good records, but this room had gotten out of control, and if there was a method to the madness here, I couldn't figure it out."

That's when I realized Wells was a neat freak.

"This is... intense. Maybe scary intense. Are you this organized in every part of your life?" I asked, feeling the delight at this discovery tiptoe over my mind.

I was surprised to see she blushed, just slightly.

"Uh, yes. Probably?"

"You're probably this organized in the rest of your life?"

She made a face. "Yeah. I'm not big on clutter or disorder. Maybe it's my desperate grasp at control, but I feel better when things go in their place. And in a business, it's so important. If taking the inn has taught me anything, it's that."

She gestured for me to exit in front of her, and then she followed me out after turning out the light.

"I agree. Completely. It's something I've tried to explain to Danny about a thousand times."

I thought of the absolute disaster zone that was Danny's side of the room when we were kids. Most likely, not much had changed since he was still functioning as a teen taking a gap year before college despite the fact he was twenty-five. I shuddered to think what the inside of his apartment looked like.

"I can see him being kind of a slob. It's always the real charismatic ones who just don't have time to stop and pick up the socks on the floor," she joked.

"And me? Am I a slob, do you think?" I asked as we stepped onto the front porch.

She eyed me, taking in my hair—actually cut and styled today thanks to Lisa—my close-trimmed beard, and my long wool jacket over a suit. I looked particularly corporate today, and though it didn't make me uncomfortable, I was less confident now that her eyes skimmed over me head to toe.

"Never," she said with a short shake of her head. "I think you like to be in control of everything."

"Not everything," I protested, a flash of embarrassment shooting through me.

"I mean you like to make sure things are taken care of. You're a doer, and you're a problem-solver, and leaving a mess grates against those things. If you ever did leave behind a mess, I'd guess it'd be for the same reason you sometimes go too long between haircuts or your beard gets shaggy."

I kept my breathing even, but honestly, in that moment, my heart soared at a gallop. It was a mustang racing through the salt flats, just blasting through the distance. That comment told me a lot, and my body knew it—she'd watched me enough to notice my hair, and whether it was or wasn't cut.

Call me pathetic, but that was all the encouragement I needed.

I stepped closer—not too close. I wasn't crowding her,

but I wouldn't deny it if someone accused me of standing closer than I had before.

"And why do I let my hair get too long?" I asked, my voice low.

She blinked, but didn't look away from me.

"You're too busy. You're too wrapped up in taking care of everyone else to take care of yourself," she said, somehow close enough that I could feel her breath on my lips.

"Boss-lady, you've got a call in here."

Anthony's voice shot through the door, through the moment, and we both backed up.

She nodded to the door as she backed up. "I better get in there. Thanks for coming by and asking—that was thoughtful."

"I'll be back around six—I'll come straight to you."

The words felt miraculous considering the pace of my pulse, the pump of my blood through my body, the furious wanting that had arisen from being so close to her for the first time *ever*.

"I'll look forward to it," she said, and disappeared behind the door.

I thought about the interaction with Wells the rest of the day. That had been flirty. That *had* to have been flirting, right?

I knew it was. I wasn't so out of practice that I couldn't recognize it. But it was also... genuine. I flirted sometimes, but that had been... real—a walk sign where there had only been the red hand flashing as cars blazed past.

That had been her giving me the green light.

For what exactly, I wasn't sure, but I would certainly be

a fool if I didn't put myself out there a bit now that she'd given me something to go on.

One of the best surprises of the day was when I made it to the home décor store, my first stop—I found that she'd sent me a message.

"I got your number from Leo. We should have exchanged a while ago anyway. Was hoping you'd grab another one of those frozen pizzas on the list, and a bag of their arugula, and then join me for dinner?"

If I hadn't been walking into a store, I would have high-fived myself.

I responded immediately. *"Sorry, just got this. Sounds good. I'll let you know when I leave here."*

How completely idiotic that my body had reacted so violently to reading a text message from her. My heart was racing again, adrenaline coursing through me like it was ready for a challenge, a thrill, something.

After the store, I had to shove those thoughts far from my mind as I prepared for the meeting at the bank. That was doable since I'd been preparing for this meeting for months, and I had insane amounts of adrenaline accompanying me now, my body channeling that natural reserve, demanding I succeed.

I strictly avoided the sense of impending doom circling my mind—the sense that if I failed at this, and if the consultants didn't like the lodge, or the family, or the town, there was little chance we'd make it to our sixty-year celebration.

That's right. *No pressure at all.*

CHAPTER NINE

Wells

I was unprepared for the horror that seeing my mother's name flashing on the caller ID of my phone would summon in me.

That's exactly what it was—horror.

"Hello?" The bewilderment sounded loud in my own ears.

"*Serene*," came my mother's crisp voice.

"Dana."

Don't think me cold—I'd called her by her first name since I'd turned sixteen. She'd asked me to.

A pause. Typical of any conversation with either one of my parents, but this one infuriated me.

"Please tell me you didn't call me to then sit in punishing silence. Call me back if you're not—"

"*Where have you been?*" she asked, her voice hard, edged.

What a large emotional display, and it only served to raise the tiny hairs on my arms and the back of my neck.

"I've been in Silverton. You knew this."

I'd called them the day I left, in the cab on the way to the Denver airport, to tell them I was leaving Preston and leaving Colorado, that I was severing ties with him and moving to Utah to take the inn.

"Don't jest, Serene. Where are you?"

"Dana, I'm in Silverton. I told you this is where I was going, and I'm here. Managing Tilda's inn and creating a new life in which I'm not controlled by a man who doesn't love me and his dictatorial mother."

Silence again.

"Well, thanks for calling—"

"You've embarrassed the family."

There it was.

"I can't apologize for that. I understand that my breaking the engagement with Preston was inconvenient for your image, but it was outright *damaging* to me. I can't imagine what would have happened if we'd gotten married."

I'd thought of that too often in the early weeks, simultaneously crushed by the reality that the person I'd fabricated in my head from the very beginning of our relationship had never existed, and by the knowledge, somewhere firmly rooted in me, that if I'd stayed with him, he wouldn't have stopped at emotional abuse.

"Don't be a child, Serene. You've never been particularly smart, but I had no idea you were this insistently stupid."

I gritted my teeth, forcing the rising swirl of smallness and shame back, hating myself for caring what this person said to me. "If you refuse to believe that he was emotionally abusing me, that's your problem. I'm not ashamed for leaving—I'm only ashamed it took me so long. If there was social fall-out for you, that's also your problem."

"Whatever you think you're doing there in that pathetic little town, clinging to that god-awful extended family and lapping up the leavings of an eccentric, self—"

"So nice to chat, Dana, but must go. *Cheers.*"

I ended the call and fell back on the bed, squeezing my eyes shut and breathing in the scent of fabric softener where my face was buried in the comforter.

I'd touched on this with my therapist. I'd told her about their hands-off way of raising me, their repeated insistence that the only thing I had to offer was my beauty. I still didn't understand it, but I wondered if it was because that's what my mother thought of herself.

She hadn't gone to college, but had married well. She'd been a trophy wife, eventually volunteering and organizing luncheons and charity auctions in all the right circles, and she had keys to any kingdom she wanted, except maybe the elite circles of women who'd gone to school right alongside their husbands and knew everyone in an even smaller inner circle.

Or maybe it was because my father had cheated on her ceaselessly throughout their marriage.

Who knew?

I was working toward apathy on the subject, or more realistically, simple peace about it. I'd been working on that for years, even before Preston sauntered his way into my life, but now, therapy forced me to confront that their way of speaking to me might have made me more susceptible to someone like him.

Wow, did that hurt.

As I've been reminded, something hurting isn't always

bad. It's part of the process. Refusing to let ourselves feel or address feelings? That's where we could get into major trouble.

So I let myself lie there, face pressed into the fluffy white comforter, heart aching rabidly, and refused to feel ashamed of that ache. I let myself cry, let myself wish, for a moment, I'd been born to the daughter of Tilda Saint and not Elsa Wellington.

Elsa Serene Wellington had been my mother's mother and Tilda's sister. I never knew Elsa—she passed before I was born. I'd never been able to reconcile how different great-aunt Tilda was—grounded in these mountains, genuine, loving—with the way my mother was. Tilda's only daughter Jane had settled close by for love of her mother, and her kids had mostly stayed close to home now that they were grown. From what I understood, my mother hadn't spoken to her mother in over two years before the latter died.

My phone buzzed next to me. That's when I saw Liam must have sent the message he was leaving Salt Lake hours ago. The clock said it was after seven, and he hadn't showed up yet.

When I went outside, I saw why. The snow was already six inches deep and falling fast—if it'd started in the south, he might have hit bad traffic all along.

I paced around the inn, straightening a mirror here, dusting off a shelf there. Tala watched me pace back and forth past the Reception desk. She'd arrived at five for the evening shift since we had a few couples staying the weekend.

"You're driving me insane." She spoke without lifting her head, her face still focused on the book in front of her.

I read a lot—a book a week, probably, but Tala read

voraciously. She read literally hundreds of books a year, in all genres.

I smiled placidly, enjoying the swirl of dark braids tucked into a neat bun on top of her head. She shook her head as though she could feel me watching her even as her eyes skated across the page in front of her.

"Sorry. I'm expecting someone. Are all the guests back from dinner?"

It wasn't my job to keep tabs on people, but when we had only two couples, I did it anyway. I was nosey and wanted to make sure people had the best time possible, so me knowing a bit about what they were up to helped me prepare accordingly.

"I believe so, yes. One came through about ten minutes ago when you started milling around the upper hallways, and the others ordered in, and I haven't seen them since they came in this afternoon and asked for another bottle of champagne to be stocked to their room," she said, a small smile on her face.

Though she read all genres, Tala was a romantic at heart and I noticed she spent quite a lot of time with romance novels.

"Good for them."

Liam came stomping up the front steps just as I began pacing back toward the front. He was completely covered in snow.

"How far did you walk?" I asked, pulling open the door and pushing the screen out for him.

He slid by me, his long black coat completely white.

"From your parking lot to the door," he said, his voice muffled by the scarf he'd wrapped around his head. "This is insane for November, but we'll take it."

He pulled the scarf down and revealed a wolfish smile that had my insides fluttering.

"Come in. Let me take a bag." My hand brushed his as I reached for one of the four brimming Trader Joe's sacks he carried.

"Hi Tala," he said with a nod, then followed me as I walked to the kitchen.

"Hey Liam," she said as we moved down the hall, only slightly delayed.

She seemed to sense when someone was a customer and when it was me or someone on unofficial business—she was charming and helpful to guests, but reluctant to pull her eyes from her book for even a moment unless for business.

As we made our way down the hall to the kitchen, nerves started creeping up. "How did your meeting go?"

"I have no idea."

I heard the doubt in his voice.

"But you don't think it went well?" I set the bag down and shoved things into the fridge and freezer.

He sighed, then reached into one of the bags he'd carried and started emptying the contents onto the counter where I could put them away.

"I don't know. The loan officer seemed generally posi-tive, but I'm not sure why they'd take a chance on us. When I look at it with a lack of familial attachment, I don't know that I'd invest in us."

I pulled out a bottle of red wine, opened it, and filled two stemless glasses, then handed him one.

"To you. For making the drive, for doing your best in that meeting, and for bringing me groceries." I was inca-pable of dampening the bright smile on my face, because being here in the kitchen with him was the best part of my day, no question.

"And to you, for carving your own path here and reinventing yourself. Cheers," he said, his blue eyes light as he smiled while we sipped the wine.

"Let's get the pizza in. I'm so hungry, and you've got to be starving." The stretch of driving after a day full of meetings would have been a killer.

"I am. Yes. I have been dreaming about this pizza since you described it this afternoon. I hope it's going to live up to my imagination." He opened the box, then sliced through the plastic with a knife from the block.

I washed my hands, pulled the pizza onto a stone, and set it into the pre-heated oven. "Okay, fifteen minutes and we're done."

Twenty minutes later, we sat in the lounge, where the only indoor tables during bad weather were kept, each sipping wine and crunching salad and destroying our pizza.

"I can see why you like this." He took another huge bite.

"I'm glad. Thank you for offering to go—I have only made the trip once a few weeks after I got here, and it was so exhausting I swore I wouldn't go again for a year. I'm sure I won't last that long, but it's nice to have some variety."

"How was your day?" he asked before diving into his salad.

I had to stop myself from staring at the delicious way his jaw flexed when he chewed. An entirely mechanical feature of someone's body—the hinge of a jaw at the point of biting something—and yet I could hardly look away. The stubbled jaw was apparently catnip to my feline soul because I could think about nothing else but the fact that I wanted to rub my cheek against his.

"Sorry?" I asked, breaking the trance.

He narrowed his eyes at me. "I was wondering how your day was."

"Oh. Good, then great, then terrible, then fantastic." I smiled at him.

I'd been doing that a lot—smiling, and feeling a bit untethered to reality, because sitting there with him, and feeling really happy about it, was unexpected and a sensation I wanted to strap to me and never let go of.

"Do tell," he prompted, then waited patiently as I finished chewing, took a drink, prayed no arugula had stuck in my teeth.

"Morning was good, reasonably productive. You came around and offered to buy me groceries, which was great. The rest was okay until my mother called, which was terrible. And then you came back, bearing all kinds of goodies and your snow-blown self, which has thus far been edging further and further into the land of fantastic," I said, surprising myself with how forthcoming I was.

I eyed my wine glass, realizing I'd had a glass and a half on a very empty stomach, so I was possibly going to remain a bit more forthcoming until I'd eaten all of my food.

"I'm glad to hear about that last part." He paused to give me a real, full smile, which served, as it always did, to make me feel giddy and warm. "But I'm sorry about the call with your mom—do you want to talk about that?"

"Uh, no. I don't want to ruin this perfectly lovely evening by dragging the Bryant family drama in. The short version is, we don't get along, and this is the first we've spoken since I left Preston, and Colorado, in April."

"Preston? That's his name?" Liam said, clearly disapproving.

"Yes, that's my ex. And my mother is none too happy about my *embarrassing* them by leaving the abusive jerk."

His eyebrows rose high. "Wow. You'd think they'd be happy for you that you got out of a bad situation. You'd think she'd be asking what she can do to help you, or support you."

His whole body emphasized his words with the energy that always seemed to fill the air around him.

"That just shows you had a nice family growing up. You'd only think those things if Wayne and Dana Bryant aren't your parents."

"I had an idyllic childhood. I can admit that. But I'm sorry yours was so different," he said in that low, gruff voice I'd only heard a few times.

Oh, I liked it.

"Thanks. If I ever have kids, I hope I can give them idyllic. Growing up here seems like a nice place to start."

I turned my attention to my glass of wine as I realized that might have been a strong implication. Most guys would be scared away by the suggestion that I wanted kids and that I wanted to stay *here* when I had them. Somehow, I doubted Liam Morrison would be.

"It's a good start," he said.

And there it was again. Our eyes met, and all the heat from the room swirled around us as we shared the moment. I was the first to blink away and ask him if he knew how long the storm was supposed to last.

We ate and chatted, laughed together, and it was all completely wonderful. By the time we'd finished our food, I felt relaxed and sated in a way I hadn't in quite a while.

"This is so good, thank you," Liam said as he took the final bite of pizza.

"You can't thank me when you brought it all the way here. Which reminds me, how much do I owe you?" I asked, enjoying the way he sat back in his chair and let out a long breath that I would swear was one of contentment.

"If I said nothing, would you believe me?" he asked, his eyes challenging with an upraised brow.

"No. No way are you buying my food." A frown threatened, as did a twinge of something familiar and dreadful.

"Are you sure? What if I insist?" he asked, a playful smile on his mouth now.

But my face fell, I knew. I could feel it and see the change in him as he saw me fold in on myself. It was too familiar—manipulation tucked into a nicety that ended up leaving me in debt.

He sat up straight in his seat. "Wells, I'm joking. I'm just flirting, being stupid."

I swallowed, but still felt the dry, raw feeling in my throat.

He reached out a hand to me, but stopped short of touching me from where he sat. "Truly. I'm sorry. I didn't mean to make you feel uncomfortable."

I took a drink of wine and watched him. Let my mind review his words. All of them genuine, and none of them ones Preston would have used to coerce me into getting his way. Certainly, he wouldn't have said *sorry*.

"It's okay. That's just... that's the kind of thing my ex would do when he was trying to manipulate me. He'd start out making it sound sweet, like something fun that he was doing because he cared about me, but there were always strings, and I always felt I had no choice but to go along with whatever he wanted because I owed him for this or that."

Liam's face moved quickly from stricken to determined. "Then I demand payment immediately."

I chuckled. "I don't actually have my wallet on me, but I—"

"No excuses, Wells. I won't have you indebted to me. Go grab your wallet and pay me—I'll wait here."

I waited for him to crack a smile, but he was committed to this. I took another large gulp of wine and hauled myself out of the seat. When I got back with the cash, Liam had turned his attention to the fireplace next to him and stared at the flames.

"Everything okay?" I asked, wondering if my reaction to his joke had ruined the evening.

He turned and shook his head once. "You got that money you owe me?"

I laughed and wagged the money in front of his face, impressed with myself that I had cash for once. "Now we're even."

Something in his eyes shifted—maybe the flame of the fire reflected there, but I felt heat radiating from him in a new way. He stood to meet me where I'd stopped, pulled the bills from my hand, and tossed them on the table.

"That's right, we're even," he said, his blue eyes crackling with intent.

I opened my mouth to say... something. But before I could, a warm hand reached out and cupped the back of my neck. His touch on my bare neck felt shocking, enticing, and as he inched toward me and pulled gently on me to meet him halfway, I was riddled with nervous excitement.

Our mouths met softly, lips brushing gently, then more pressure, and a bit more, until he deepened the kiss with a tilt of his head and mine.

It'd been months and months—possibly even a full year, since I'd been kissed, and never like this. *Never.* Preston had kissed as an obligatory first step to whatever came next— whatever he was after. The two boyfriends I'd had in college had been largely the same—hurried, a bit sloppy, uninterested in lingering there when they thought there was more to be had.

Liam Morrison kissed like he had nothing else to do. He kissed like he'd been waiting to do it, and now that he was doing it, he didn't intend to stop. But it wasn't rushed, frantic, pushing for more. It was savoring and mesmerizing.

As I kissed him back, relishing the slide of tongue and teeth, I thought—I actually thought this—I *could do this forever*.

And that thought broke me out of the moment, had me pushing gently against his chest where my hands had been clutching at his shirt only moments ago.

That thought had me stumbling back a bit, then steadying myself on the table.

I couldn't be thinking like that. *I couldn't.*

I brought a hand to my mouth, as if to verify that it had in fact detached from his, because part of my mind was still back there, reveling in the texture of his lips, the occasional scrape of his chin against mine, my heart pounding out of my chest and my hands staying put only because I'd ordered them to.

"I'm sorry. I shouldn't have—"

"It's fine," I said, not ready for him to apologize even though he must have thought I was upset. "I just… thought I better clean this up in case anyone wanted to come have a drink out here, and you should probably be getting home before you can't move your car. You have a big day tomorrow."

He stood there a moment, eyes a little frantic as they assessed me, and then he let out a breath.

"Okay, Wells. Can I help you clean up?" he asked as he pulled on the suit jacket he'd draped over the chair.

"No. Please just… get home safe, okay?" I stacked our

plates, praying my hands wouldn't shake so much the china rattled.

"Sure. Yeah. Thanks for tonight," he said, his face painted with complete dejection.

And I couldn't blame him. I'd pushed him away, hadn't explained a thing. I'd kissed him back like my life depended on it and then pushed him away.

CHAPTER TEN

Liam

I pulled my front door shut and brushed the snow from my sleeves, then shrugged out of my wool coat, which had been completely useless in the storm, and hung it on the coat rack.

I'd left my car at the inn since I'd had a few glasses of wine, and I didn't feel like digging it out even if I hadn't had a drop. More than anything, I wanted to get out of there and examine every minute of the evening in privacy.

I shut my eyes and took a deep breath.

What a wonderful, terrible night. It wouldn't ever be simple with Wells, but the confusing part? It *was* easy with her most of the time.

When she forgot to be worried. When we moved around in the kitchen as naturally as a couple who'd been together for years. When we talked about our days. When we joked over dinner. When she melted against me, into the kiss I'd been wanting to give her all night, all day, for months.

But I'd messed up—I knew that. I was glad she'd told me what I'd done wrong, and now I knew—don't push. Not a simple thing because I was pushy by nature, used to being in charge and telling people what I wanted, how we'd get it, and then making the task happen. But with Wells, she'd been hurt, and deeply. I didn't want to be constantly dredging up bad memories of when she was in such a terrible place.

Preston. Yeah, the name sounded preppy and high-handed, just like the man himself. I doubted he'd ever show his face here, but if he did, I'd hear about it and make sure I had a chance to speak with him.

That kiss.

I could have stood there and kissed her for hours. My hand threaded in her hair, the other eventually having landed on her back, her hands fisted in my shirt and pulling me close—my breathing came fast just thinking about it.

But the break away, the shaken, undone look she'd given me... I would have smiled, relished it, if I'd thought it had come from being overwhelmed with pleasure, or... almost anything else than what I thought it had been.

Because it had looked like Wells deciding kissing me back had been a mistake.

I dragged myself down the hall, surprised to see the oven clock blinking 12:17—must have been a power outage.

I lived in a small outbuilding of the lodge, the dedicated lodging for the mountain manager. It'd always been meant for that, anyway. And one of the perks Da had lured me into the interim job with had been the simplicity of living there, not worrying about rent, while I got the brewery up and running.

He and Ma hadn't lived there at the lodge, of course—our family home was a few miles away, accessible by snowmobiles and skis in the winter, another element of the idyllic in my childhood. But about fifteen years ago, he and Ma had spent the money to fix up this building, which used to house a snowcat and any broken ski patrol mobiles, but which had really always been superfluous.

He'd known he couldn't do the job forever. Grandpa Will had done it until he was sixty, then promptly turned it over to my da, who'd been working alongside him for decades already. And Da had always planned to turn it over to me when I was ready.

And here I was, about to let a third-generation business die out.

In the end, I'd stayed in the job far too long. I'd had no choice, but it was true. That thought weighed heavily on me as I went through the motions. I took a shower and eventually felt my core temperature rise enough not to feel that internal chill that had taken over since the moment I'd seen Wells' face.

Add to that my useless wool coat, my frustrating meeting with the loan officer that would likely yield nothing, and the time had clearly come to put this day to bed.

~

Jonas Bauer was not what I'd expected, and neither was his partner Karla Ritter.

The family had gathered to greet him. Leo, Danny, and I were waiting at the lodge, dressed in our usual snowy day attire. I'd been tempted to wear a suit, but in the end, the idea of the trip was to see how things worked here, and if they wanted a real picture, then here we were.

Danny was in snow pants, boots, a waffle-knit shirt with a T-shirt over it, his face somehow already looking like he'd spent hours on the mountain despite just having walked the trails in the snow from the day before.

Leo was her usual deceptively sweet-looking self. She had long blond braids that hung down to her ribs. She wore tight jeans tucked into heavy snow boots and a fleece jacket that fitted close to her body. This was practically her uniform on lodge days, and it turned heads even as simple as it was. I could admit she looked stunning, even if it made me want to punch anyone who took a second glance.

And me. I wore jeans, heavy snow boots, a long-sleeved T-shirt with a lightweight jacket. I'd pull on the heavier stuff if they wanted to go out in it.

For their part, Bauer and Ritter were surprisingly casual too. Part of me had expected a sort of steely New York feel. Their communication was direct, brief, and extremely professional—no casual chit chat or friendly exchanges.

"Welcome to Silver Ridge Lodge." I extended a hand to Ritter, then Bauer. "I'm Liam."

"Pleased to be here, Mr. Morrison. I see the season is setting up well for you," Bauer said, his face surprisingly stern despite the compliment.

He was tall—taller than me, which was rare, frankly. He must have been six-three at least. He was built, but not in an imposing way—no, the imposing element came from his demeanor. He had blond hair silvering at the temples, a slim nose, sharp jaw.

And since this was the first time we'd spoken, all other interactions having come via e-mail or his administrative person, I detected a slight accent. *Interesting.* I'd been given to understand the company was an American one, and it was, based on the research I'd done.

"It looks like it," I said, smiling at both of them. Ms. Ritter smiled back, and Bauer nodded. "Let me introduce my brother Danny—" I gestured to Danny who'd stepped up to shake hands, "—and my sister Leonie, though we call her Leo."

"Nice to meet—"

Just as her hand met Bauer's, her voice broke off and she sucked in a breath. I looked over sharply, but couldn't detect anything amiss. The two dropped hands, a normal thing after a handshake, and neither one looked any different.

Huh.

Bauer spoke to me next, not acknowledging anything. Usually, Leo jumped in and started up conversation, peppering questions and bald statements that might make me cringe just as likely as they'd make me beam with pride. But no, she stayed quiet.

I shook myself out of the distracting train of thought and responded.

"Have you had lunch? I'm happy to take you to one of our local restaurants. We'll have dinner here at the lodge this evening, if that's acceptable."

"We'd like to see the lodge, maybe a quick pass on the gondola if you have it running, and then we'll go to the inn," Ms. Ritter said, her accent far more pronounced than Bauer's. She had a narrow face, yellow-blond hair cut into a short crop and styled simply, and blue eyes.

"Certainly."

We wandered through the halls of the lodge. It really was beautiful.

The front room faced the foot of the mountain only several hundred feet away, the whole side of the lodge built out in huge panes of glass only occasionally interrupted by wooden beams.

The wood was light, the accents gray, cream, neutral. Ma and Da had visited ski areas across Europe a decade or so ago and Ma had fallen in love with the aesthetic she'd found in Austrian lodges—clean wood, lighter colors, plush materials layered on top of natural ones.

The old look wasn't far off from this, and I thanked Grandpa Will for that. He'd fought in World War Two with the 10th Mountain Division, and like so many of his peers, he'd brought his love of skiing and the mountains back with him. He and his friends are credited with bringing Alpine skiing to the US, at least as a more accessible sport.

At some point, he'd seen the natural look of the wood, and so rather than staining it or use darker wood, he'd stuck with the raw pine aesthetic. It had worn and aged well, and still looked surprisingly fresh and bright for a building nearly sixty years old.

A huge stone fireplace sat at the far end of the main cafeteria room where people could sit and read and relax while their kids took lessons or until their legs recharged and they could attack the mountain again.

The cafeteria was small, but could serve people quickly and efficiently, and it filled me with pride to say the food was excellent.

The tables and chairs were carved and finished wood, some of which had been done by the one and only Rex Woodruff. The aesthetic was different from the darker, polished look of the inn, but the craftsmanship was equally sturdy and appealing.

I love this place.

Showing Bauer and Ritter around only confirmed it for me. It deserved to flourish and grow. People needed to see the lodge, and even more so, the mountain.

We loaded the gondola that Jiff, one of our perpetual lifties, ran for us. He was sixty-something, and I knew nothing about him other than that he'd worked for the family for more than twenty years, had never wanted a raise, never wanted a promotion, and seemed perfectly content to operate lifts when he was scheduled and ski when he wasn't, or cut trails and hike them if there wasn't snow.

He and Danny were kindred spirits, but any time I had that thought, I banished it.

"The mountain is extraordinary," Bauer said, squinting out at the peaks of Silver Ridge.

It was bright, though still snowing. Fortunately, the visibility wasn't bad, so we could still see many of the front-facing runs and one of the other lifts that started mid-mountain.

"It is. If we have one asset, it's the mountain. We need more lifts, another aid station or two if we can open the back lines with a lift..." I didn't want to list all of the deficits I was tracking. He could probably already see them, if his resume was fact and he'd evaluated more than ten other small American resorts.

"I love it, Jonas." Ritter spoke in a quiet, low voice to him, a hand on his wrist.

Leo and Danny were minding their own business, sitting on the other end of the benches on either side of the gondola car. Sturdy and well-maintained, the cars were six-seaters and got people to the top in about fifteen minutes.

I watched out of the corner of my eye and thought I saw a nod—*maybe*. Hard to tell as we bumped along the lines up to the top station, but I thought I saw it. Maybe that meant he'd heard her opinion, or maybe it meant he loved it too.

Please, God, let him love it too.

That's what we needed. For these people to see the place and love it and advocate and fight for it with *their* resources and connections.

The top of the mountain was one of my favorite places.

I was repeating myself, but I couldn't help it. I loved the view, loved the air that was just a bit thinner at the top, loved that I could see miles and miles around, and yet still couldn't see to the end of the back runs.

Only expert skiers skied the back now, partly because it had no lift so only the most dedicated did that, and partly because that's where our avalanche risks were highest due to the grade of the mountain face there. Our ski patrol blasted regularly—one of Danny's favorite things in life— and that helped, but until we managed it like the main mountain, which we had no reason to do until more people skied it, it would stay essentially out of bounds.

After walking around the small lodge at the top—only about ten tables, a minimal service area for warm drinks and food the lodge team packed up in the early morning, plus restrooms and a deck with glorious views on a clear day—we headed back down.

We bid farewell to Bauer and Ritter, who were going to check in at the inn and relax a bit before dinner, and Danny, Leo, and I conferred in my office.

My siblings sat in the chairs next to each other across my desk.

"So?" I asked.

"They love it. I can tell. She's definitely MF, and I think he is too, but he holds any expression or interest close to the vest," Danny said, ever exuberant.

MF was *mountainfolk*, a term we'd all used for years to refer to people who had mountains in their blood, their soul. The Morrisons were all mountainfolk, even Jamie, which was why he couldn't avoid the siren call of Silver Ridge when it came for him.

"Leo?" I asked, very curious to hear her perspective.

"I don't know yet," her response clipped out.

Danny and I looked at each other with wide eyes.

That was as typical as finding a flamingo on the front lawn in the middle of January. Leo *always* had an opinion, always wanted her say, and never withheld judgement.

Instead of ribbing her for it like I might normally do, I nodded. I'd been happy with her reserved approach to the meeting, and I didn't want to provoke her into a fight that would bleed over into her being more aggressive or use her more typically demanding strategy at dinner that night.

"Okay. Then go enjoy a few hours to yourselves, and I'll see you both back for dinner. I'll call Jamie and let him know how it's going."

Dinner went well. The chef, who'd arrived just this week for the season, had done a great job with a simple Italian dinner. The conversation flowed despite Leo's eerie quiet, though she had spoken a few times, and Danny did a fantastic job charming Ms. Ritter despite her likely more than ten years of seniority.

Bauer seemed pensive, reserved. I wasn't surprised he wasn't babbling about how much he loved the place—I doubted I'd ever see him like that, though that might be judging him too quickly.

We kept the meeting short, knowing they'd come from the east coast and were working off eastern time. When I checked my phone after dinner and saying goodnight to my family, I saw I had a message from Wells.

"Could we talk sometime soon?"

I responded immediately. *"Of course. You say when."*

Her response took only moments. *"Are you free tonight?"*

I hadn't let myself think of her, though my mind had begged to go there more than once. Every time Bauer or Ritter said something about their lovely room, the staff at the inn, how much they liked the place, I'd wanted to ask if they'd met Wells, what they thought of her, how did she seem.

Of course, entirely inappropriate, so I'd locked that up tight.

Now she wanted to see me. *Tonight.*

I told her I'd be down in a few minutes. I was exhausted from the day—first anticipating the arrival of the Bauer Group, then meeting them and showing them around, waiting for the dinner, and then slogging through it since I had realized, though it'd all gone well, we probably should have called it a day and let them do their own thing rather than forcing dinner on them.

They were meeting Danny early tomorrow to walk some trails, see more of the mountain. Then we'd meet after lunch to go over the detailed financial reports. They already had much of the information, but we'd talk through it together, in person, again.

That evening, we'd all go our separate ways. They could confer, and I could breathe. And pray.

I stomped down the sidewalk, which had been shoveled and salted, though the snow had slowed and I'd bet it'd be mostly melted down here by middle of the week. We'd need several more big dumps before we could open a whole run, or even consistently make snow for the main mountain.

I stomped my feet on the large mat on the porch to

knock off some snow and water, then stepped through and did the same inside the door.

Tala was at Reception, as usual this time of night, her nose in a book. She didn't look up when she said, "She's in the lounge."

"Have a good evening, Tala," I said, though I was sure she hadn't heard me.

My pulse picked up as I approached the lounge, the same room where we'd had dinner and then kissed, and I would have nearly skipped right in there despite how things had ended except the sight of Ms. Ritter, Bauer, and Wells all laughing heartily, beers in hand, caught me up short.

Wells saw me first and rose while I heard Bauer say something to Ritter. *Ah, German.* It made sense now, of course, with the last names, and even their features, but I wondered if they were an international company.

"Hi," she said, a shy smile on her face as she approached.

"Hi." Nerves cut through the joy of seeing her.

She reached out to me, pulled me close, and hugged me. It took no more than a second to respond, for my arms to wrap around her and pull her close.

Okay then. This is good.

"I was just talking with your guests." She took my hand as she walked the handful of steps back to the table where Bauer and Ritter sat observing us.

"*Herr Bauer, Frau Ritter, si kennen* Liam Morrison," Wells said in what I assumed was deft German since Bauer's stoic face lightened slightly and Ms. Ritter's smile shone bright.

"Good to see you again, Mr. Morrison." Bauer stood and offered his hand.

I'd seen the guy not an hour ago, but we were still on

formal terms. Fine by me—when they decided to take the job, then we'd get to first names.

"I don't mean to interrupt," I said, feeling foolish for barging in on their time together, and aggravatingly, also fairly jealous that someone else had gotten to laugh with Wells.

"Not at all. We're just retiring to bed now." Ms. Ritter nodded to Wells as she and Bauer stood.

"*Schönen Abend Noch*," Wells said, a lovely smile on her face and flush to her cheeks.

"*Ihnen auch, Fraulein Bryant*," Bauer said with the sparest smile I'd ever seen.

They walked slowly around the corner to the Reception area. Their room must be on the east side of the inn where they'd see the mountain in full display at sunrise. A perfect choice for them.

"Do they have one room or two?" I asked, realizing it was nosey and possibly a breach of privacy.

Wells raised a brow.

"Not telling, sorry." Her eyes glittered at me.

She seemed so happy, directly at odds with how we're parted last night.

Evidently noticing my demeanor change, she took my hand and pulled me to the plush couch on the far side of the fireplace, the opposite to where our table had been last night.

"I'm sorry for how I... responded last night. I didn't anticipate... that, and I didn't know what to do," she said, leaving me fully in the dark.

What does that mean?

"I'm sorry for upsetting you. I would never want you to feel anything other than happy to be around me, so please don't apologize for how you felt. Now I know, and I won't kiss you again. I promise."

The words tasted like chalk in my mouth, but I ground them out, heat rising to my cheeks as I did.

Was there anything worse than apologizing for kissing a woman you'd wanted for months?

Answer—no. No, there wasn't.

She looked down at her hands, making me afraid she was going to cry. I heard a quick inhale of breath and saw her body jolt, and I *knew* she was crying.

What had I done now?

But then, she raised her head and her cheeks were bright, her eyes smashed shut, but her mouth was smiling. *Laughing*.

I opened my mouth to say something, but found no words. That, and watching her laugh, had me smiling, then chuckling along with her, despite my inner turmoil.

She finally came up for air and leveled me with a look that struck me straight in the chest. It was sweet, earnest, and with her face still glowing from the laughter, she looked gorgeous.

"I shouldn't have laughed. That apology was so sweet and honestly, so unexpected, it just... hit me right. I never would have expected you to apologize. We had a great evening, and I wanted you to kiss me, and you did. I kissed you back. But then I freaked out, and that's not your fault."

She smiled up at me, then lay a hand on my arm.

My ridiculous heart was beating double-time from my apology, her laughter, and then her saying *kiss* a small handful of times—definitely enough for me to be picturing myself kissing her again, which wasn't quite where we'd gotten yet.

"That's good to hear. I mean not the freaking out part, but... the rest of it is."

Wells tied me up in little Celtic knots. I didn't know what happened to my brain, my tongue, my lungs when I was around her, but I usually felt fourteen trying to talk to my first crush.

"Good. Then we're clear on that," she said, then took a breath. "But I need you to take back that promise."

"Promise?"

I searched my mind. What had I promised her? I'd thought of plenty of things I'd like to promise her, even if it made me roll my eyes at myself, but I'd been careful never to voice them, not to come on too strong.

"Just now, you promised never to kiss me again. I want you to take that back." Her eyes bore into mine, bright and blue and serious.

My pulse raced, and I swallowed. "I formally rescind my promise never to kiss you again."

"Good."

CHAPTER ELEVEN

Wells

Staring into Liam Morrison's eyes proved to be an experience—an intense one, and it lit a match in me, one I hadn't felt light before.

I'd gotten bold thanks to the twenty-four hours since our first kiss, the confidence I'd built up in myself, the quick meeting with my therapist this morning, the interaction with congenial acquaintances this evening, and now with this man sitting here, looking penitent and nervous and adorable as we sat alone together.

I shouldn't have laughed, but I'd felt the tension ratcheting tighter every hour of the day, and finally, I couldn't wait any longer. I'd messaged him, even though I'd known he'd be busy with work, but I didn't want to go another day without talking to him, clearing the air, and clarifying that I was interested.

Because I'd come to terms with the fact that I was, and

as my therapist had reminded me and I'd been reminding myself all along, there was no magic number. No number of appropriate months to be broken up with an ex before you date someone new. That's *my* choice, along with the guy I'm dating.

And the beautiful part was, Liam knew about my past. Not all of it, but enough to realize I had issues that I'd need to deal with as we went. But the reality? I was mid-twenties, he thirty—I wasn't sure if there *were* people without issues at our age.

In truth, I hadn't felt much of anything but a low-lying dread and fear of Preston for at least a year. He'd proposed about eight months into our relationship, and at that point I definitely cared for him. I hadn't woken up to his manipulations, and the ones I did notice, I chalked up to him just being *a man*. Being particular. Wanting what he wanted, and not feeling shame for being the woman who happened to give it to him.

Even if those things took too much away from me.

We hadn't been physically together most of the winter —he'd been working on whatever investment project he'd taken my money for, and he'd never given me many details. I cringed at the memory of him insisting I was being too pushy and suspicious by asking him where he was going.

"Why do you need to know that, Serene? Why would you question my faithfulness to you when we're getting married in six months?" His golden hair was perfectly styled with a combed part and just enough gel, his suit tailored and flattering, his shoes reflecting the overhead light of my bedroom.

"I didn't mean to question you. I just like to think of you, so when I know where you are, I can picture you there." I pulled the blankets up higher around my chest, holding them closed at the back.

He'd come to visit me that morning because he was leaving. As usual, he didn't undress but I did. I convinced myself I loved being with him, that we were making love and that was good because we'd be married soon enough, and then he'd be done and leave me before I'd gotten cleaned up or dressed.

"I know you miss me. I know it's hard for you to do much of anything when I'm gone, but this isn't something you need to worry about, Serene. Just relax, take care of yourself, maybe hit a Pilates class today."

I straightened, wondering if he could see the way my stomach, even as tight as it was, rolled a bit when I slouched.

"That's a great idea."

That was the last time we'd slept together. He'd be gone for weeks at a time, and when he got back, he'd be too tired. I started finding ways to be busy or unavailable, which he didn't like, but he'd usually only take a day or two between trips—to wherever he went—and so my method worked.

By January, four months before we were supposed to get married, I knew something was wrong. I didn't want to be with my fiancé, physically or otherwise. I started seeing my therapist, who helped me recognize the problematic dynamic of the relationship. It had only taken a few weeks for me to realize how messed up it all was, and how lost I was.

So when Preston came to me in March and explained that all of his travel, all of his efforts had been for *me* to save the money *I* invested so poorly and which he'd lost in the end, I saw through it. I'd known for over a month I couldn't stay with him and had been waiting until he'd gotten home to break things off.

I'd been slowly extricating myself from his family—not showing up to the mandatory family dinners on Sundays, even when he was gone. Taking a bit longer to respond to his mother when she checked in to see if I was going to fit into my wedding dress.

The problem was money. I had no visibility on the money he'd taken—essentially the entire trust from my parents that they'd been more than willing to hand over to him after he'd convinced them he was going to take care of the money *for* me.

So when he said the money was gone, I panicked. I had no idea how he'd respond to that loss—would he blame me, even though I'd had no hand in that failure? I wasn't sure how I'd do... anything. I hadn't worked. I had nothing saved. His anger drove him to storm out rather than stay and talk to me, like it was my fault he'd lost all my money and probably a big lump of his own, and I'd cried and prayed like I'd never done. I'd never wanted to be anywhere else more than I did that night.

Two weeks before our scheduled wedding day, a lawyer named John Wallace had called me to say that Tilda had left me the inn and a sum of money to help me transition—I just had to come to town to sign. I'd told him I didn't have available funds to make the trip, and he'd offered to advance me the money, like my guardian angel.

I scheduled a flight the next day. I hired a lawyer, to be paid upon completion of the project of severing all ties with the Umbridge family, and high-tailed it to Utah, straight to John Wallace, Sr.'s office where I signed all required documents, opened a new account at the local bank, and had all the inherited money transferred there, where Preston had never and would never have access.

After that, I couldn't tell you exactly. I walked around the small town, not seeing it. I felt relieved, but ghostly. I felt like I'd disappeared and had a dreadful feeling that I'd never rematerialize into myself again.

Six weeks passed before I was able to hold a full conversation with anyone at the inn. It'd been closed anyway, but I stayed there, ate little, lost weight for the first month. At some point in May, I woke up and realized I had nothing left to be sad about unless I kept lying there. I'd been on anti-depressants and had kept up with those, but only finally venturing out and taking a walk in the woods behind the inn had snapped me out of the haze. I'd smelled the air that day—it had been clean, fresh.

Don't get me wrong. I'd still cried every day. I'd sat numbly and stared at flames dance in the fire pit. But doing those things in the shadow of the mountain had given me a blanketing sense of peace even with the sadness, the grief.

It had almost never been grief over the loss of the relationship, but rather a grief for myself—who I'd been, why I'd ever gotten into the place of feeling trapped, accepting the abuse, and now of picking up the pieces of me that were left.

It was now mid-November. It'd been over six months since I'd had that awakening and well over a year since the relationship had effectively ended for me emotionally and physically. I'd done the hard work in therapy, with myself, on the inn, in my life at large.

And all of that came down to the one thing I'd realized over the last day. It was okay if I went out on a date with a nice guy like Liam Morrison.

I took a deep breath and let my eyes wander over his face. Every carefully shaped feature looked so *beautiful*. It felt overwhelming to sit next to him and resist touching him in some way other than my hand still on his wrist, but I'd been resisting that for weeks now.

I cleared my throat, pulling out of the tangled thoughts, the longing. "I hope you'll also consider going to dinner with me sometime?"

The intensity of his eyes quelled just a bit, and one side of his mouth slid up into a smile.

"I will absolutely consider it." He looked at the ceiling, his brow furrowed, chin bunched like he was thinking. "Okay. Yep. I'll go to dinner with you."

"I'm glad that didn't take too long."

"I've been hoping to take you to dinner for months now. So you asking me to dinner didn't take too much thought."

He smiled, that blazing charm opening the cage of butterflies in my chest.

"Months, huh? Well I guess it's a good thing I finally asked you."

He shook his head emphatically. "Yes, it is."

We smiled at each other, and I wished he'd just lean over and kiss me, but he seemed to be holding himself in check. *I wish he wouldn't.* But Liam was smart, and intuitive, and I hoped he wouldn't stay polite for too long.

"I didn't know you speak German," he said then, breaking our doofy little trance.

"Just casual conversational. Nothing business-level. Jonas and Karla have always been kind about my ability." I tucked my hands under my legs and let out a satisfied sigh at the chance to catch up with them.

Liam blanched at that. "You know them?"

"I can't believe we hadn't talked about it, but yes. I interacted with them several times when I worked in Aspen. They didn't end up accepting the job at the resort where I worked, but we'd gotten to know each other. I'd heard them speaking German and so I'd greeted them in their language, and they'd made a point to stop and talk with me. One day they took me out to lunch—they were great."

"I had no idea. What a coincidence," he said, his tone odd but not withdrawn.

"Isn't it? I'm glad for you though. They're the best, and if you get them, they'll make a difference. I'm rooting for that, no question."

He stood then and held his hand out. I took it, and he tugged me up, then pulled me close. My heart raced, but instead of dipping his head and kissing me like I'd been willing him to do, he wrapped his arms around me and engulfed me into a hug.

"You are a beautiful person, Wells. I'm so glad I know you."

He spoke softly into my hair, then released me from the hug, though I would have happily stayed nestled there in his arms for much longer.

I searched those blue eyes again—fast becoming my favorite pastime. "You are too, Liam."

I walked him to the door after we'd made plans for Thursday, the day the consultants left. He said he didn't want our first date to be him dropped in his chair with exhaustion and only half a brain.

We'd laughed, but it'd given me an important insight I'd never had—Liam Morrison was human and *did*, in fact, get tired of charming everyone and taking care of all the problems.

I'd spent nearly all week working on the new rooms. They were really coming together. I wished Rex could have done the furniture, but he'd retired, and his kids weren't in the business, though two still lived in the area. He'd been lovely on the phone when I'd asked him—he'd said he and Tilda had discussed it and decided ordering from a store in the valley was better at this point. I felt good knowing I was doing what Tilda had planned to do, even if she'd been pretty far from the point of actually doing it.

The floors were finished, the walls painted, the bathrooms fitted with all fixtures and only needed shower curtains, complimentary soaps, and those few touches we'd add for seasonal décor. The rooms just needed furniture and wall-hangings, and the light fixtures.

They looked great. Ten more rooms at the far end of the west building. At one time, they'd been staff rooms, storage, Tilda's room, offices, but over the years, things had shifted around. Ultimately, I guessed she'd always planned to build more rooms, but maybe had run out of money. I'd used some of the inn's budget that had been earmarked for upkeep and some of the money she'd left me to finish these up.

I knew, somewhere deep in me, that we would get this town on the map. That there'd be a day in the next few years when every one of the twenty-two rooms would be finished, and maybe we'd expand. I *loved* the thought of growing this place into a success, and with it, the town around it.

And with all this, Liam's family's business would grow, the whole community would flourish. He'd get to focus on his brewery and creating his own legacy.

Jonas Bauer and Karla Ritter had left early that morning. I had new guests arriving tomorrow for a quick overnight, and then a good group for the following Thanksgiving weekend. Tonight was really our best shot at a date before the season opened and things got insane.

We were keeping it casual with Mexican, but that was

fine with me since it was some of my favorite food, and I'd only been to *Guac* a small handful of times. It'd been great every time.

I cleaned up and pulled on a long-sleeved dress, thick leggings, snow boots, and my knee-length puff jacket. Far from sexy, but when you spend most of your time walking around a wintry town, it made no sense to try to be anything but warm.

I'd done my hair in loose curls down to the tops of my shoulders and put a little more makeup on. I felt confident, but comfortable, and it felt *so good.* I'd wear a knit cap to walk to dinner because the wind was whipping around and made the temperature so cold now that the sun was setting.

Liam wandered up right on time, also bundled in a down jacket, his head covered in a hat, and I ran out the door. We walked side by side down the path to town, and since *Guac* sat right next to *Craic*, the first building at this end of town, we had a mercifully short walk.

Snow flurries flitted around us, glittering on our jackets, melting as soon as we stepped inside of *Guac*'s sunny, bright, and blessedly warm interior.

"Bienvenidos amigos!" Luis hollered from the back.

He was owner, chef, and an active part of the community. He knew everyone and was well-loved. His kids were nearly all grown, only one left in high school. The others were spread out, one in the military, one in college, and one had just moved back, though I hadn't met him.

We were seated, placed our orders, and served in record time. Or maybe it wasn't all that record, but I was too immersed in being there with Liam, enjoying how free he was, enjoying how he nudged the basket of chips to me like I should eat them instead of having them taken away. We both got margaritas and toasted to deep snow and a long winter.

"What is the hardest part about living here?" he asked, crunching on a chip as he watched me.

"I guess it's not being able to run to Target or any of the familiar chain stores. But once you get over that, it becomes less important. I think that was hardest this summer, before I'd figured out my purpose and made a list of things to do around the inn, and also while I was still used to that retail therapy habit."

"Makes sense. I can't believe it's already been almost six months since you got here."

"More than, actually. I got here mid-April." I ate a chip, enjoying the salty crunch and the tang and bite of the salsa.

"That's impossible. I could swear you got here in June." He squinted his eyes like it would help him remember.

"I got here in April. And then I barely left the inn until end of May. So it's possible you didn't ever see me until June," I explained.

His brow dropped and furrowed. "What did you do all of that time?"

I took a drink of my margarita. "I stayed in bed, mostly. Cried a lot. Thought about how I'd gotten there, and how long it would take to get to where I could look at myself in the mirror and not cringe."

He stretched his hand across the table, grabbing mine. "I'm sorry, Wells. I hate that you went through any of this. I wish I could change it. I wish I could erase it for you."

His voice was pleading, his grip firm but not unwelcomed, and a pang of tenderness for him hit me.

"Thank you. Part of me wishes I could change it—I'd be lying if I said I didn't wish that sometimes. But I'm past the self-loathing, for the most part. And I've learned so much about myself. I'm glad it's behind me, and I'm looking forward."

I hoped he'd understand I wasn't *done* processing the feelings, the years of my life influenced by someone who had fundamentally been unkind to me. But I also hoped he could hear that I wanted to move forward, not just look.

"I'm happy for you. I hope you're proud of how hard you've worked to get through this stuff."

He pulled his large, warm hand back, and I wished he'd left it there, but then saw why he had as the waiter set down our food.

"What is the hardest part about living here for you?" I asked, reveling in the delicious chimichanga piled with guacamole.

He finished chewing, wiped his mouth with a napkin. "Everyone knowing everything about you, or thinking they do."

"You mean your golden boy status?"

"Exactly that. It's fine, but sometimes it's a little..." His eyes scanned the restaurant, which held three other couples and one family, all at decent distances from us despite the small size of the room. "It's confining. And it often makes me feel like a fraud."

"How so?" I scooped up another bite of the layered fried tortilla stuffed with savory shredded chicken.

"I already have enough of a complex. Sometimes I see it, other times I don't, but I get it. I want to be the good guy, the one people go to when they need something, the man who saves the day. That's in me. But I'm also selfish, and needy, and small." He paused, studying his plate. "I don't think I'm explaining it well."

"Leo doesn't let you get away with anything. At least she's here to keep you in check," I joked.

He rewarded me with a laugh. "That is correct—she won't let me color outside the lines, that's for sure. Jamie doesn't either, but it's easier between us. I think Leo and I are almost too much alike, and that's why we butt heads over stupid stuff right along with the stuff that matters."

I tilted my head to one side. "I suppose you are alike in some ways—you're both straightforward—you say what you mean, and you mean what you say. But you have more of a filter, a bit more tact than she does. You're a little more old-fashioned, and she's more of a romantic. But overall I'd say you are pretty similar."

"You think *Leo* is romantic?" His disbelief stitched into every syllable.

I nodded. "I do. She is so torn up for Bel and Jamie, and even Danny, it's crazy."

"Bel's her best friend these last few years, and Jam and Dan are her brothers. Of course she cares, but she's not a romantic," he countered.

"It's not just that she's concerned. She takes it personally, almost physically, when Bel is dealing with Jamie stuff. And beyond that, she gave me a talking to about giving you a chance," I said, dropping my neatly wrapped bomb on the table.

"What? When? What did she say?"

I couldn't help my smile. "She came over a while back and said you had a crush on me and I should get over myself and spend time with you."

I smashed my lips together to hide my smile as I watched his neck and cheeks redden. Then he scraped a hand down his face.

"That girl is going to be the death of me."

"Do you think? I think maybe you should thank her, if you really have been wanting to go out with me for months.

You would have continued being considerate of me by not asking me out while I was adjusting, and I wouldn't have believed you were interested in my mess if she hadn't said something."

His blush faded as he took a bite, chewed, swallowed, and pointed his fork at me. "Point taken."

"Good. Because Leo is my friend. I know you guys have your... dynamic, but I don't want to feel like I'm in the middle of you two if we keep... or, you know, if we go out again."

"I hope we will. I can tell you, Wells, that I am most certainly interested in your mess. I'd like to be in it any chance I get."

CHAPTER TWELVE

Liam

The date with Wells was coming to a close, and I'd already decided I was going to kiss her again. I hadn't the night we'd talked about the first kiss because I hadn't wanted to rush her, or me, or anything.

But tonight? Yep.

I was going for the classic doorstep scene approach, both because of the previous stated desire to eliminate the rushing, and because I had to be up at the crack of dawn to talk to Jamie, who was somewhere impossible and opposite our time zone but had requested a video chat.

I should have changed that.

I had to work, too. We had about six days until opening day, and our seasonal employees were all going to need in-processing.

We walked hand in hand back down the path to the inn, and I cursed the unusually cold November air for preventing me from feeling her palm against mine, even if holding her gloved hand was better than nothing.

And really, I couldn't curse the cold air. It was creating perfect snow-making weather, so the team was on that for the base layer, and we had another storm coming in Tuesday, supposed to be huge. The valley and airport would hardly see anything but flakes, but we were projecting eight to ten inches at base, and nearly fourteen inches at the top.

That's the stuff of dreams.

Stopping in front of the door, we faced each other. The bright light of the porch made it feel like we stood in a spotlight. But no one was around, and no one was staying at the inn, so no chance we'd be interrupted.

"I'm glad we did this," I said, tugging her hand so she'd step a bit closer.

"Me too." She tilted her face up to mine.

I happily took the invitation. I leaned down to her, met her lips with mine, and savored the warmth of her as the cold swirled around us. We stood in the spotlight, snow drifting past us in whirling waves, and pulled each other closer.

There was no hesitation in her response, as though she'd been waiting for me to kiss her. I smiled at the pleasure of our lips touching, our mouths meeting, our closeness, and the impenetrable little bubble we'd created.

I was surprised when I pulled back and the area around us wasn't melted, but coated in a dusting of snow.

"Will you come over tomorrow? I want to show you something."

Her breathlessness made me feel like I'd been pummeled in the ribs, my chest achy and sore, but looking at her made it worthwhile.

"Of course. I have a call in the morning, but I could

come after that." I already eagerly awaited seeing her again, though we hadn't parted.

"Good. I can make you lunch too. Just let me know when you're coming and I'll be ready."

The call with Jamie was short, and I'd wanted to complain about it and tell him he should have just e-mailed, but I could hear the exhaustion in his voice. I could tell he wasn't doing well, and he needed to be done filming whatever ad or modeling campaign he had on the books.

He was a musician, but as I often told him, he was also the prettiest of the Morrison men, and he frequently had jobs in Asia and Europe for modeling. The US companies weren't using musicians as often, and not his style either, but I also suspected he didn't like seeing ads of himself when he was here.

He'd be back for a few days at Christmas this year, and my parents had agreed to come in from Arizona for the holiday. They'd become fair weather winterers after Da's heart attack, and though it felt like a part of the mountain was missing when they were gone, it took a weight off my mind to know they weren't dealing with shoveling snow before I showed up first thing in the morning, or digging out a tractor to help plow a road the county hadn't gotten to yet.

They'd come for a week, and it'd do us all some good to see them. I looked forward to introducing them to Wells too. They'd love her, and I hoped she'd love them. They were certainly different than her own parents.

I hung up with Jamie at six, and despite my best efforts to fall back to sleep, I got out of bed at six-twenty when no amount of counting backward could stop my mind from jumping between the subjects that constantly occupied it—the lodge, Wells, the brewery, when the consultants would decide, what the bank would say, Wells.

I went for a long run on the treadmill after looking out the large window in the living room and seeing the coating of ice and snow on the trail I usually took for runs. It made me sad to see the time for trail running pass, but that meant ski season was almost here. I did my usual routine of squats, lunges, and other quad-building work followed by stretching that Leo constantly nagged about to make sure my legs were ready for that day, and then got cleaned up.

Still only nine-thirty in the morning. I sat in my office, nudged the pile of mail sitting in one corner that Danny or Leo must have grabbed yesterday, scrolled through my e-mail, and then messaged Wells.

She was all I wanted to think about today. I wanted to put aside work, the feeling that I was constantly failing someone—the brewery and John, or my family and the lodge—and just go be with a woman I liked too much for my own good.

Or, the hopeful part of me thought, maybe exactly the right amount for my own good. Maybe I could be good for her, and she for me.

She messaged back welcoming me anytime, which made me ridiculously happy. I thought about doing something to occupy myself for another twenty minutes before I hiked down the road to the inn, but I knew it was futile. I wanted to be there *now* and there was no benefit to playing coy. She knew I liked her, and she seemed to like me enough to keep agreeing to hang out, so I wasn't going to complain.

Though I absolutely would be complaining to Leo the

next time I cornered her. What was she thinking, telling Wells I had a *crush* on her like I was a preteen girl?

Granted, I absolutely *did* have a crush on Wells, but that was none of Leo's business.

Wells thought it was cute, said it was all Leo's fault we'd managed to go on a date. But I knew better. I couldn't have held off asking her to go out with me much longer. I couldn't have resisted seeing if she'd be open to a date.

And I wouldn't resist ribbing Leo about being a romantic, which I had no doubt she'd hate the sound of. I could see it, once Wells explained it. I knew she felt... *a lot* when it came to the Jamie and Bel thing. I knew she wanted them to make peace, and I knew she hated disagreements and strife even though it felt like she was always the one provoking it with her "brutal honesty."

She was young, and despite herself, she still had a naïveté that was a little charming, a little maddening. I was seven years older, and I wanted to shake her and ground her sometimes, but she was smart. Sometimes too smart, and maybe just one more reason why we disagreed on many things.

Leo had been mad when I said we were bringing in consultants—she wanted us to magically generate income, customers, and infrastructure. I had no other ideas about why she would be so against it.

Her reaction to Bauer had been borderline rude, and her contributions to the interactions with him and Ritter over the week they were here, when she even showed up for a meeting, had been stilted at best.

I'd have to pin her down on it soon. It was possible she had *real* objections, and I needed to hear those. It wouldn't necessarily change things, but she wasn't Danny, who had no desire to shape how things went. If anything, she wanted more of a say, but I couldn't give her one.

I knocked on the door of the inn and Wells threw it open almost immediately. She wore black leggings and a large sweater, one shoulder exposed with lovely, bare skin begging to be kissed.

Whoa, boy.

Yeah, I wanted to skim that shoulder with my lips, run them up her neck, and find my way to her lovely, curved mouth.

Her hair was pulled back into a ponytail but small wisps fell down here and there, not quite long enough to be contained.

She looked relaxed, comfortable, and utterly delectable.

"Were you waiting by the door for me?" I asked with a sly smile.

"Definitely not." She crossed her arms over her chest, then unfolded them just as quickly, reached out to me, and pulled me into a kiss.

"Okay, maybe I was," she said against my lips.

We melted together for a few minutes until a sharp *ahem* rang out from behind her and we jumped apart.

Leo stood behind us looking severely annoyed—a face she wore frequently around me, but right now, I couldn't be bothered to care. If Wells hadn't jumped back, I would have kept right along enjoying her greeting.

"Sorry," Wells said as she turned to glance at Leo.

Leo pursed her lips to hide her smile. "It's fine. I'm just claiming all the credit. And I'm definitely leaving now."

She grabbed her jacket from the coat rack to the right of the front door.

"You don't have to leave just because he's here—"

"I do," Leo said, just as I said, "She does."

Leo and I eyed each other, and I was glad to see she wasn't upset; rather mostly, she was trying to contain her laughter. It could have been worse.

We bid Leo farewell, Wells a bit more fondly than me, and then stood in the entryway of the inn for a moment. I would have been happy to pick up right where we'd left off, but Wells didn't seem so keen.

"What were you and Leo up to?" I asked as she turned and led me to the lounge where the fire roared.

I suspected this must be her favorite room in the inn, and I could see why. It was warm, inviting, and with the fire, looked like a perfect place to spend some quiet time with someone you wanted to talk to.

Or make out with.

Whatever. You choose.

"She stopped by to talk—nothing major." She was facing away from me, and something about her very casual tone sounded off, but I wasn't sure in what way.

"Yeah?" I asked, hoping she'd elaborate, or... say what she really wanted to say.

She dropped onto the small couch where we'd been before. "Listen. I can't talk to you about Leo stuff, okay? She said some things in confidence that have a little to do with you, but she's not ready to talk to you yet. I wish she'd confided in Bel instead, or maybe she did, but she needed a sounding board and showed up at seven this morning to pin me down and dub me *it*."

I took a seat by her, close, and tucked an errant strand of hair behind her ear. "I understand. I appreciate you telling me that you can't tell me."

She blinked once, twice. "Wait, really?"

"Yes?" It wasn't really a question, but I wasn't sure why she was so surprised by my response. I let my hand slide down behind her ear to rest gently at the back of her neck.

"You'll just... take my word and accept that I'm not going to tell you every little thing, even when it has to do with your sister?"

She looked truly perplexed by this—it had to be because Preston would never have taken something like that well. It must have been why her voice had shaken, just a bit, when she'd said it.

"I trust you, Wells. I get that I don't know you super well yet, but I like that we're working on that. And I know you have a friendship with Leo that exists independently of me. I don't expect you to tell me everything about your time with her any more than you expect me to catalogue every second I spent away from you. Does that make sense?" I searched her face, her eyes, willing her to believe me and let me believe her.

She nodded once slowly, in a kind of rapt slow motion. "I guess it does, in theory."

"I feel like there's a but coming."

She let out a big breath, her shoulders sinking, her whole body sliding back in her seat. I let my hand fall away, but set it on her hand nearest me. I didn't want there to be any chance she could forget who she was with, or who *I* was. I hoped I could continue showing her what kind of man I was, but I knew some of this would eke out over time, with no way to anticipate it. All we could do was handle it when it came.

"It's not a but. I guess I'm just waiting for the other shoe to drop," she said, an odd, thin smile on her lips.

I ducked my head to look her in the eye so she could see what I meant.

"I get that adjusting to what life is like with someone

different is going to take time. I'm not scared by that. You can wait for the other shoe to drop, but it's already on my foot, tied up tight. No shoe will be dropping. I also get that you won't trust that until we've had some interactions like this, where your ex might have leveraged a situation to get something out of it. I won't do that."

"So much of me knows that's true, but the other part of me is thinking *how do you know that?*"

She'd folded her arms, drawn into herself a bit. It wasn't hot and cold, all over the place—just a slow but systematic pulling back, almost like a reflex she'd formed over time.

"I won't be manipulating you because I really like you, and I like pretty much everything about you, and all I want to do is spend time with you. I don't want anything from you except to get to be around you. The only thing I'm going to leverage is the miraculous potential that you might like me too and want to spend time with me too, and then, if that's the case, I'd like to give you what you want."

She bolted up and threw her arms around me, pulling me close and hugging me fiercely. "Thank you," she said in my ear.

"Thanks for telling me what you're thinking and giving me a chance to understand what's going on in that gorgeous head of yours."

I kissed the side of her head. We stayed like that, hugging close, for a minute or two before she pulled back.

"I think you might be a unicorn." She bit her lower lip to tuck away her smile.

"Yeah? Being a golden boy *and* a unicorn might be a bit much, don't you think?"

"Good point. I take it back. I'm partial to the whole golden boy thing." She stood and grabbed my hand.

I trailed her down the hall that went west in the

building and quickly found I'd never been this direction. As far as I knew, all the rooms to rent were on the east end, some facing the ridge, some facing the field and the pine forest just past it.

She stopped in the hallway just before an opened room.

"I want to show you something." She clasped her hands in front of her.

She looked heartbreakingly lovely in that moment, appearing confident and excited, casual and open.

"Show me, please."

She stepped back and gestured for me to enter the room to her left. I peeked around the corner, then stepped inside.

The room smelled a bit like paint and sealant. The walls were a clean, warm blue color, the baseboards white. A large rug lay in the middle of the room and on it, centered between two windows, sat a large, dark-wooded bed with fluffy white linens that looked amazingly inviting.

For an idiotic half-second, I thought maybe she was inviting me into her room, and my stomach did a backflip, but I adjusted mental course when I saw the basket of small towels on the countertop of the sink through the doorway on the opposite wall.

The bathroom looked pristine, with marble counters, large mirrors, great lighting, a standing shower with a glass wall and a sparkling tub next to it.

"This looks fantastic," I said, not entirely sure what I was seeing other than a beautiful new room for the inn.

"It's one of ten new rooms that should be ready before Christmas."

I whirled to look at her. I could see she stood on her toes, practically bouncing with excitement.

"How? Or... I don't even know what to ask. I though the

inn had twelve rooms. Why would Tilda not open these years ago?"

One ugly part of my mind thought about how much more valuable the inn would be with these rooms finished. I should have tried to make the deal this time last year.

But good for Wells. It *was* good for her, and I was glad.

"They had different purposes over the years. Initially, she couldn't afford to outfit them like she had the other half, so she'd planned to finish them slowly over time. Other things took priority and in the end, they sat here, especially when there was no real demand for more space." She frowned, then twirled halfway around to take in the far side of the room.

She turned back to me. "When I got settled in and started functioning, these rooms were the perfect project. Everything else in the inn is fantastic, so it wasn't like I had to come in and revamp it. Tilda was smart—always hired good people, had a qualified accountant and lawyer who made sure things were organized... other than the storage room, there were really no changes to make except this western wing."

"This is huge. This will more than just double your capacity—it makes you significant enough to put you on the map. To host smaller conferences. All kinds of stuff."

Her smile widened at my excitement for her.

"I hope so. And eventually, if we can get things filled up and turn a profit, I want to add cabins out by the one I'm redoing for me. And I want to build on the acreage between here and the Morrison property line to create more rooms or maybe even a small conference area. I don't know. There are so many options. She actually has a ton of land, which I wasn't expecting."

"That's good," I said, a small strain in my voice.

Of course we had the mountain, but what we needed was space to build a hotel. We needed space for more buildings, to accommodate more people. The note we'd been given by Bauer stated that, and it'd stung.

I knew as far back as my grandfather, the family had tried to increase their holdings on either side of the property where the lodge itself sat. One problem was how it sat on a hill. Another was that much of the base area's space made up a parking lot. We couldn't eliminate that. So we needed *more*.

And here Wells sat, rolling in it. And I hated myself for even thinking it, because I *was* glad for her. I was so happy she was happy, that the inn was going to do well and get more business. That was good for everyone in the town.

But what if the space we *didn't* have was a showstopper for the consultants, or barring that, then for potential investors?

"What are you thinking?" she asked, clearly noting the change in my face, or energy, or whatever it was.

"I was just thinking you've done an amazing job with this, and you've kept it so quiet. I was wondering why." That was also true.

"A few people knew we were finishing the rooms, but the plan had been next spring. After about six weeks, I begged everyone involved to push their dates, to prioritize the project, and get them done before the season was in full swing. And they did." The fondness in her eyes at the thought of the people who'd helped her shone clear.

Some lame part of me felt bad I hadn't been one of them, even though I hadn't known her then.

"I'm glad they could pull it off. That'll let you get them selling, and get more people on the slopes," I joked, as though filling the mountain was my only concern.

She shook her head and smiled, then took a deep, satisfied breath.

"You're an impressive woman, Wells Bryant." I stepped to her.

"I'm not sure about that, but this feels good—like I was meant to do this. Does that sound hokey?" She reached out to take the hand I'd extended.

"No." I stepped closer, my feet bracketing hers. She was tall—probably five-nine, but I still had to tilt my head down to speak right to her. "You fit here."

I meant here—Silverton, the inn, yes—but a larger part of me felt she fit *right* here, with me, in my arms. She'd integrated into a small town that, while welcoming, wasn't an easy place to live. She'd embraced the distance, the isolation, and she'd done something significant in just over six months of living here.

Her eyes met mine. "I think so too."

She leaned up on her toes just enough so our lips met. But no sooner had we started kissing than her phone rang, jarringly loud, and we had to separate.

"Hello?" she asked, her cheeks flushed.

She mouthed *sorry* to me while I chuckled at the frustration and chagrin racing through me.

I wandered around, checking the view from the rooms, noting the tall bars above each of the two windows where she'd likely hang long drapes.

"Must've been a wrong number or a robo-call," she said, perplexed.

"I think the real question is, why is your volume set to eardrum-destroying level?"

She'd come to stand in front of me again, and my heart beat, beat, beat with the hope that she'd kiss me again.

"When I've got music on and I'm working here, or especially in the cabin, I've missed a few calls, so I turned the volume up. I silence it when I sleep though," she explained, reaching out and taking a handful of my shirt in her hand.

Her knuckles grazed my chest, and I wished it was her hand directly on my skin. I let one hand settle on her hip and used a finger to trace the line of her shoulder where the sweater hung off the side of her arm. I heard her breath hitch as the pads of my fingers ran over the perfect curve of the cap of her shoulder, then down and back across her clavicle to the dip at her throat.

She swallowed, her eyes on mine, all the energy in the room pushing us together.

We crashed into each other, the anticipation after that first sweet kiss having built an irresistible pull between us. I slid my hand along her bare shoulder and cupped the back of her neck, pulling her closer by the nape and hip.

Her hands threaded into my hair, her fingertips skimming my scalp and her whole body urging me closer, closer.

"I'm glad you got the *get a room* memo, but next time, close the door before you go at it."

Leo's voice somehow penetrated the fog of desire that raged in me, and I lifted my head to see her standing in the doorway, back turned to the room.

Sure enough, the door was propped wide open. Whose idea had that been? What a terrible error.

Wells drew back, released me with a grin, and pushed some errant strands of hair out of her eyes as she said, "Okay, Leo, the coast is clear."

Leo turned around, her face unreadable. "I forgot to tell you I spoke with Jonas Bauer earlier. He called as I was walking past your office, and I answered—the light was on so I thought maybe you were in there until I saw your chair empty. Anyway, you're supposed to call him back when you can."

More than a small part of her was absolutely delighted she'd had even the most ridiculous reason for coming back and interrupting us. Wasn't she the one who'd pushed us together?

"Will do. Thanks. See you later." I grabbed for Wells, who shuffled out of the way, biting her lower lip in a way that sent a burst of heat through me.

"I'll see you out," Wells told Leo, and gave me a look that said *don't go anywhere.*

As if I would.

CHAPTER THIRTEEN

Wells

I stood at the door and watched Leo descend the steps, then trot down the path and out to the sidewalk.

I couldn't decide whether I should kill her or kiss her.

She'd been all too pleased with herself for interrupting me and her oldest brother, and I certainly hadn't felt grateful at the time.

But as my heart rate slowed and my mind cleared away the fog that kissing Liam created *every time*, I saw the wisdom in slowing down a bit.

In the end, we were just getting to know each other. We knew we wanted each other, yes. In fact, it felt like every time we saw one another, a burst of cosmic chemistry poured out in the room where we both stood.

I thought about him constantly. I wanted to be near him

all the time. I wanted to be under him, on top of him, *with him.*

At some point in the last few weeks, he'd worked his way into my brain, and no way was he getting out. And that was fine... becoming increasingly, more and more, something I might even call good.

But what scared me most was waking up and finding myself in the same boat I'd been in this time last year and the year before that. Logically, I knew Liam was nothing like Preston. A strong personality, yes, but not a manipulative abuser with no conscience or sense of honor.

Also, I'd never been certain whether Preston was even capable of love. I'd thought he'd cared for me in his own way, and I'd tried to talk myself into loving him in the early months, but he'd never loved me.

I *knew* Liam loved. He loved his family. He loved friends. He loved the mountains and the town and so many things, I couldn't help but wonder what it might be like to have him love me.

I wandered back to the room, happier than usual that Tala wasn't due until our guests arrived later today.

Liam stood tall at the window, looking out over the street and up toward the peak you could just see if you looked due east. He was tall, broad-shouldered, fit, and I felt his pull like he'd tied a rope around my waist.

I approached, and he turned when he heard me.

"She manage to find her way to the door?" he asked, a sardonic brow raised at the silly question.

"Of course," I said, wanting to touch him, but knowing that would only lead to us trying out the linens on the new bed.

I'd left the door open just to check myself. His eyes flicked up to note the open door, then back to me.

"I should probably go." A small smile graced his perfect, delectable lips.

I nodded once. "You probably should."

"Walk me out?" he asked, waggling his fingers in my direction, then taking my hand when I held it out to him.

We walked silently, each of us holding our thoughts in. I was both glad and frustrated by this.

He stopped at the door, grabbed his jacket, and pulled it on, the look on his face a tick shy of devastating. The only reason I hadn't plastered myself to him was because I had employees showing up any time now, and guests not long after that, and whatever it was between us wasn't something that would die out in a matter of hours.

"Are you free again soon?"

His fingers traced my shoulder again, like his hand was drawn to my skin there. I'd never been so happy about a lazy, schlubby style as this one.

"Absolutely."

The next few weeks were an absolute blur. After the weekend, we had a one-day break, and then people started arriving for Thanksgiving weekend. The town put on a great mini-parade and apparently, it had a decent draw for tourists. I was even able to book the room I'd shown Liam, though I hadn't gotten the beds for the other nine new rooms, so that was killing me. I'd actually had to turn away a couple who'd wanted to book for the weekend last minute—a good problem to have, but one I wouldn't have had if I'd gotten my furniture shipment.

Thanksgiving went well. Because I was working, and the lodge officially opened on Thanksgiving Day, Liam and

I were at odds schedule-wise. Before I knew it, it'd been more than two weeks since I'd spent any time with him.

That wasn't *quite* true. It was a small town, and we did run into each other. And when we did, we stole moments together, mostly to make out.

No, really. We were like sixteen-year olds who'd been grounded and snuck out to see each other to steal kisses. It was ridiculous and exciting and only made me like him more, though I wished we could spend actual time together.

I knew it from the time I'd interned in Aspen, and even living there and observing—winter was the busy season for people in what was essentially a resort town. Yes, summer had its draw, and hopefully, Silverton could figure out how to make it a bigger draw so the whole year's income didn't depend so heavily on ski season, but ultimately, November to March, *maybe* April if it was a great snow year, was the time when everyone worked themselves into the ground.

It also turned out to be the most fun. Energy filled the air with the lifts running. The whole town felt alive now that tourists and adventuring locals from neighboring towns came to ski and shop and eat.

It had been so long since I'd been this happy. I could remember the feeling—right as I was about to graduate college. I'd thought the world lay ahead of me and my life was about to finally begin. I'd completed my degree in hospitality, I was only two years away from my parents' trust becoming available to me and giving me true separation from their influence, and I was ready to get to work.

My therapist and I had talked about whether I should have known something bad was coming—that my life had been too easy up to that point. I was destined to be knocked off my little pedestal.

But of course, I couldn't have known what would

happen, nor should I feel guilty or sad for not somehow predicting I'd end up on the tether of a manipulative jerk who was most likely a sociopath.

Now that life felt good—*so, so good*—and I was fully awake, tasting and feeling like I hadn't in years, that irritating, illogical, but ever-present voice, tapped at me. *What's coming for me? What's next?*

We'd talked through that feeling in therapy. I knew it wasn't founded in truth. I knew that being happy and feeling excited about life wasn't a sign that I was doomed for some new challenge or pain.

I shoved that away while waving to Anthony on my way out. This Friday in mid-December, I was sneaking in a lunch with Leo and Bel before the weekend guests arrived.

I'd made a habit of personally greeting every new guest, both as a way to make them feel welcome and to show my investment in their visit. I wanted their needs to be met, their time to be so wonderful, that they'd come back and bring all their family and friends.

We were meeting at *Guac*, which sounded divine. I'd had an early breakfast and forgotten to eat anything since. I saw Bel first and gave her a big hug. We'd only seen each other in passing at the coffee shop a handful of times because I hadn't been visiting as much now that the inn was occupied.

With Marcella back from maternity leave, just in time for the busy season, we put on a glorious breakfast every day, and a fairly elaborate brunch on weekends. We still got many of our baked goods from *Rise and Shine* because Sadie's bread was, in my carb-loving opinion, the best bread on the planet.

Bel looked as fantastic as she always did. She was easily one of the prettiest women I'd ever seen, and she had that effortless beauty that felt a little mean-spirited after all the years I'd spent dyeing and manicuring and plucking and coloring every inch of my body. Of course, I'd let that all go, and so far Liam hadn't seemed to mind, but at this point, I'd decided I was only doing that stuff if I felt like it.

So far, I hadn't but for some unibrow prevention measures and bikini line maintenance.

But Bel looked like one of those women who just rolled out of bed and little birds helped her dress in simple, classic clothing. She was slight, but strong. She hiked with Leo sometimes, and she was big into running. I wished our schedules would sync so we could go together, but lately, I'd been fitting it in right when her morning shift would start.

Her caramel-colored hair shone in the blaring winter sun, her golden skin fresh and somehow dewy despite how dried out everything about me felt, her minimal makeup basically perfect.

She's someone I bet mean girls hated. If there even were mean girls in Silverton, which part of me doubted.

"You look fantastic, as always," I said, hugging her tight.

"You should talk. You're practically glowing." She looked me over with clear approval.

"I'm happy. Maybe that's it?"

"Yes, it's the glow of happiness. And maybe also some beard burn from making out with my brother." Leo sauntered up to us and pulled us both into a hug with one arm hooked around each of our necks.

I immediately reached up to touch my chin and cheeks. Beard burn, for the record, was a real thing. But I hadn't gotten to see Liam... or be close enough for beard burn, in almost five days.

Leo caught me and pointed, then laughed. "I knew it!"

"You knew what? That she and your brother are kissing? You *already* knew that," Bel chided.

"I did, but for some reason, I get a sick amount of pleasure from teasing them both. I made him turn beet red the other day when I accused him of falling all over you whenever he sees you." She pursed her lips to hide a grin, a pleased look on her face.

We took our seats at a table and settled in. "I can't wait for the day when you're interested in someone. From what I've heard, there hasn't been much of anyone so far, so when there is, I'm going to be there, and I'm going to be merciless," I warned.

Leo's face shuddered. "I'm not worried, nor is that an even remotely scary threat. There's no one I'm interested in in this town."

She held her chin high and shoulders square as she pointedly reviewed her menu.

"Not *in this town*, sure," Bel teased, then hid behind her menu when Leo shot her a dirty look.

"Don't even ask what she's talking about. She's crazy and if she says a word—" she then gave Bel another murderous look, "—I'll have to kill her."

Bel pressed her lips between her teeth, and we all perused our menu in silence until the waiter came and took our orders.

"Are you done sulking?" Bel asked gently. She had a knack for handling Leo's moody moments that felt like magic.

"Yes, Mother." Leo leaned her elbows on the table and picked out a chip to dip into the huge bowl of guacamole that came with it.

We all crunched our chips and guac in delight, and after inhaling my fifth chip piled with the green goodness, I had to ask. "How on Earth does he get so many ripe avocados up here? This time of year?"

"He gets his food just like the grocery store does, but he also has a hothouse where he grows citrus and avocado. He has his own little indoor California out in his back yard," Leo explained.

"Genius." I'd forever be grateful for Luis' commitment to fine guacamole.

We chatted and ate, and eventually all stuffed ourselves so full of delicious food, we leaned back and breathed like our lungs had nearly run out of room.

"Bel, you know Jamie comes in next—"

"I know." Bel swallowed.

"He's only staying for a few days this time. He has a Christmas concert or something, but was trying to overlap with my parents to catch them before he leaves."

Bel nodded again.

Liam's parents, the famous Mr. and Mrs. Morrison, had been gone since I'd arrived. They'd been traveling, visiting her parents, who'd moved to Arizona last spring, and Liam's grandma had asked the Morrisons to stay and help them get settled. By the time it was getting cold here, they'd decided they'd stay the winter because Mr. Morrison had felt so much better there than here in the cold.

Liam and Leo had both mentioned how different it had been to start the season without their grandparents and parents, but they were both glad that each of the couples was doing the right thing for their health. Mr. Morrison had had a heart attack in the last few years and his health had been up and down since.

I smiled to myself, thinking about Liam's face when he'd said how much he worried about them coming out, even for a few days. *What if they slip on the ice?* He'd been so upset at the thought after getting off the phone with them, and I'd had to hug him and kiss him because his concern for them was so endearing.

"You'll be okay?" Leo pressed.

Sometimes, it seemed like Leo tried to get a rise out of Bel, but I knew that wasn't right. It wasn't quite that, but I couldn't figure it out.

"I'll be fine."

"That's what you said in September," Leo said, a frown pulling at her lips.

Bel wrapped her arms around herself. "I would have been, if he hadn't stormed into the shop. But he'll be busy, and I'll be busy, and it'll be over before I even see him."

Leo's bright blue eyes flashed. "So you're not coming to Christmas dinner this year?"

Bel pursed her lips and exhaled slowly. "I'll be with Gran. We'll be fine."

I could tell Leo wanted to say something more, so I cut in. "How is your Gran?"

Bel's face relaxed. "She's well. She's over that cough and the doctor said there's no need for concern. She's tough and ready for winter."

Her smile looked genuine as she thought of her grandmother.

Her grandfather had died before her teen years. Her parents had moved away when she left for college, and they'd always been "absentee," as Leo termed them. Bel wasn't quite so harsh, but it was clear that in many ways, Mr. and Mrs. Morrison were much more involved in Bel's upbringing than her own parents.

I'd met her gran, Ella, only once, but she was charming and spunky and sly. Clearly, she enjoyed having Bel here with her, though I wondered sometimes if she knew Bel was stuck.

I only saw it because I'd been there. Totally different circumstances, but I could see Bel slogging away at the coffee shop, barely using her marketing degree, and I wondered how much it ate at her.

"How's the marketing for the lodge going?" I asked, remembering Liam had mentioned there would be a new marketing plan in place.

Bel perked up even more at that. "I think I'm on to something really good. Liam wants me to pitch the Bauer Group my idea so they can see we already have something solid and ready to run with, that they wouldn't need to track down an agency. I know I'm a novice, and I don't bring a lot of experience to the table, but—"

"You're awesome. Liam was blown away by your idea, and the haughty jerks at the Bauer Group will be too. Trust me."

"I hope so." Bel folded her napkin neatly at the side of her plate.

"So you and Liam are..." Leo started, but trailed off.

I raised my brows but stayed silent.

"Hanging out? Dating? In love? A long afternoon by the fire away from engagement, what?"

My face reddened even though I willed it not to.

"You are obnoxious," I said, feeling both annoyance and delight at her teasing. "We're dating. I think."

"Haven't defined it?"

"Not exactly, but I'm not dating anyone else, nor do I plan to, and I think the same goes for him."

Just saying it aloud, I felt a drop at the thought that we hadn't actually defined it. Was I being naïve in assuming Liam wasn't dating—and kissing—anyone else?

Bel set her hand on top of mine and patted it. "You have nothing to worry about with Liam. He's not the kind of guy to date two women at a time in the first place, but I'm *positive* he only wants to date you."

"Positive, huh?" I asked, relishing their assurance, even if it made me a bit needy.

Leo, unimpressed as ever by the relationship, even though she was secretly our biggest cheerleader, agreed. "She's right. He's head over heels. It's just a matter of time before—"

"*Leo.* Let the man have something for himself." Bel shook her head, then looked at me with raised brows.

"Fine." Leo scooted her chair back. "I have to get back up there. I have an afternoon lesson."

We hugged goodbye and went our separate ways. I found myself smiling as I wandered the snowy path back to the inn.

Jamie would arrive later today, along with several new guests including the illustrious members of the Bauer Group. I was anxious to meet Mr. and Mrs. Morrison, who'd arrive in a few more days.

And most of all, I was counting the minutes until Liam would duck into my room and we could take a moment together.

I'd failed to get the cottage ready before the heavy snow came, mostly because after the first snow, it became clear that the roof wasn't as sound as we'd hoped. It'd have to wait until spring, so I kept my small room right off the lounge. But I'd managed to get the rest of the rooms ready, just in time, and had even aired them out enough to get the paint smell completely gone.

The knock on my door made my heart race, and I ran on my toes to answer it. I was in jeans and a sweater and thick socks, because once Liam left to get Jamie, I'd be back to reality with the inn.

But for now, I could enjoy this.

Just as I pulled the doorknob open, I felt it push toward me and Liam stepped smoothly around the door and closed it behind him. His eyes ran from the top of my head to the seam of my socks.

"You might get prettier between visits. It's that, or I'm suffering from withdrawals." His eyes darkened as they took another tour of me.

"Glad you could come." I stepped to him and leaned up on tip-toes to reach his mouth with mine. "I have coffee," I said, then kissed him. "And croissants..." and a kiss. "And other stuff..." one last kiss before he chased me and captured my lips again.

Before I'd caught my breath, we were lying on my bed, hands dipping under sweaters to find warm skin, legs entwined.

"I'm not hungry for any of that," he said, his voice as rough as his trimmed facial hair.

I stroked his cheeks, traced the sharp curve of his jaw, let my kiss be my answer.

Our hands searched each other, taking the rare opportunity to explore without ten layers of down parka between us. He trailed kisses down my neck, to my collar bone and bit lightly, then smoothed over the mild sting with his lips.

"I can't think about anything but you," he said, his breath chilling the trail of kisses.

"I know the feeling." I pulled at him just enough to get him to rise back up and kiss me again.

"It's stupid, how much I want you." He pulled at my sweater to kiss a line over the top of my shoulder.

I ran my fingers through his hair. "I've always had a thing for dumb guys."

His dark chuckle had my toes curling, my body rising to press against his.

"How long until you have to go?" I whispered, then nipped at his ear.

He froze, then dropped his head to my shoulder. "Ten minutes."

My hopes sank even as I smiled at the dejection in his voice.

"I'm sorry." I nudged his head with my shoulder so he'd look at me.

Those blue eyes leveled me with a smoldering look.

"It's not your fault." He dropped his head again for a moment, then rolled away and sat on the side of the bed. "Let's eat something."

He sounded so put out—ridiculous. Except I knew how he felt and wished we'd had more time, even though I'd known from the beginning we didn't.

We sipped coffee and talked about work—new guests, new runs opening, when his family was arriving. We managed to steer clear of any heavy business talk. I wanted to ask him if he'd heard good news from the Bauer Group, but I suspected he'd share more after their visit. They were coming in now, right before the holidays, and would fly out on Christmas Eve.

"I'm glad the storm isn't here until tomorrow." I hugged him and nuzzled my face into his neck.

He let out a big sigh, and we released each other. He

looked at me with a smile and shook his head slowly. "Why couldn't he just hire a limo or something? I mean, he's Jamie Morris. He has the money. He could easily save me the trip."

His words rang full of mock-complaint.

"My guess is you offered. Or maybe, he didn't want to hire someone to come all the way up here because it's a trek and they'd lose other business."

He shrugged. "No. Jam would pay them well enough to make it worth it. You're right. I told him I was getting him so we could catch up before he's inundated when we get back. Bauer will be here and I want Jamie's thoughts on him, and I just... need a minute before the madness hits."

I smoothed his hair down where I'd run my hands through it and placed a soft kiss on his lips. "Go. Enjoy Jamie. I'll see you Christmas Eve, right?"

CHAPTER FOURTEEN

Liam

Nothing in my life up to this point could have prepared me for the squall of problems coming at me left and right. And more than that, nothing could have prepared me for falling in love in the midst of it.

Fine. I said it.

I was tired of telling Wells I liked her.

I like you—it's too simple. It's too sweet. I suspected I was a man who loved ferociously. Not in a territorial, animalistic way, but in an encompassing and deep and lasting way. I'd never done it before—never fallen fully in love, so I wasn't sure when you hit bottom.

As I waited curbside for Jamie, I thought about how much I wanted Wells.

Physically, yes. But I wanted her—I wanted her commitment, her care. *Her.*

Knowing what she'd come out of not even a year ago, I knew it was too soon to say anything. Between the physical frustration, our schedules never matching up, and the total inadequacy to express myself, I felt electrified in her presence and almost struck dumb by her. It was getting ridiculous.

The back door was thrown open and a bag dumped on the seat, then Jamie jumped in and pulled the door closed. "Go."

I would have hassled him, but that must have meant he was getting looks, or there'd been an incident. He always traveled as incognito as he could, but he was at that insane level of fame where it didn't really matter. People knew him, and because they knew who he was, they wanted something from him.

"Was it bad this time?" I asked, knowing sometimes, the holidays offered an odd kind of anonymity for him because people were so harried.

"Not so bad, but I heard some people talking on the escalator after my security escort peeled off to deal with something else. Figured it'd be better to get out while I could than to start signing autographs or be accused of having no Christmas cheer." He looked out the window, eyeing the mountains as we drove, then settled back into the seat and shut his eyes.

"Well, I'm glad you made it in one piece," I said, and let the quiet of the drive settle over us.

After a while, I felt his eyes on me. "Yes?"

"You look good, brother," he said, and roughly patted my chest with a back-turned paw.

I knocked his arm away with my elbow. "Thanks. I feel both excellent and terrible, so I guess I'm glad the overriding look is good."

Jamie sat up more and stretched his neck side to side. "All right. Tell me all about it."

So I did. I told him about the bank denying our loan. I told him Bauer and Ritter were coming in, short notice, to meet with us tomorrow, and that I wanted his opinion. Needed it.

I told him the resort wouldn't last more than another two seasons, including this one if we didn't make some progress, and fast.

The silence felt heavy as he eyed me and I drove. "Just say it."

I could see the flash of his smile out the corner of my eye. "You realize, I can invest. I can—"

"Absolutely not."

"Absurd. Let me do this. It's the least—"

The burn in my chest felt like pure, white heat. There was no question here. "Under no circumstances are you riding in on your white rock star horse and saving this business. It's a bad idea. We need it to become viable on its own merit, or we need to accept the loss."

Even if the thought of losing the lodge and mountain would feel like death—truly, death of a legacy and so much of my life—no way would I let Jamie sink his own money, though I knew he had an insane amount of it, into this business. He'd offered once before and I'd told him the same— the more desperate circumstances hadn't changed the answer.

The miles ticked away before either of us spoke again.

"Bauer's that selective? It's been almost a month since his first visit, hasn't it?" Jamie asked as we wound our way up the Weber Canyon.

"They are. *He is.* He's the best. Wells even confirmed it —his reputation around Aspen and anywhere else I've inquired is stellar. And his record speaks for itself." I told him about a handful of resorts he'd rehabilitated, and one in Idaho he'd been to the year before.

"Well damn. I guess we need him."

"Simple as that. We do. And I think we almost have him —or I thought we did. But something about this trip has me nervous." I gripped the wheel a bit tighter, then released enough to let the blood back into my knuckles.

"What do Leo and Danny say?"

"Danny is all for 'em. He says they're *MF*s and that's all he needed to know. He took Bauer on the trails and said the guy is a beast—just a machine, eating vertical and on Dan's tail like no one he's met. And Ritter's in love—you can see it. She said as much on day one, but they both keep it close to the vest."

"And Leo?"

I let out a breath. "I don't know. I don't know what her deal is, but she's been... odd about this. Maybe you can get her to tell you what she thinks."

A pause lingered, and I glanced over to see why. Jamie was staring out the window, contemplating that, I guessed.

"What?" I asked.

"I'm just processing what you just said. You said 'maybe you can get her to tell you what she thinks,' like Leo isn't the most freely opinionated woman on the planet."

"I know. That's what I'm saying. She's acting crazy— quiet, thoughtful, just kind of brooding. She's channeling you circa 2010."

His head jerked, and I could feel the daggers in his eyes.

I shook my head, unable to wave him off thanks to the curving road and my inability to pull a hand from the wheel.

"You know you were a disaster then. And you know

what I'm saying—Leo's being weird, and I don't know what's up. I even asked her point blank about it and she wouldn't give me anything. Danny's always off doing God only knows, and so I'm left figuring it all out." I let out another deep breath.

"Poor put-upon Liam. Trying to save the family while the rest of us burn it down," he mocked.

"I'm not trying to be like that. I just want some input. I already feel enough pressure—it's already on me to save the family business, the legacy of our grandparents and their parents, and I don't have a—"

"*Listen.* Li, you're doing a great job. And I'm sorry for being so checked out—I'm a selfish jerk, and I'm sorry. I'll be around more after February, and we'll figure it out."

He was just trying to appease me, but I hoped with every breath that he'd do it. He wasn't one to make empty promises, not to me, and I needed him.

"Thanks. You're not all bad."

"No?"

"Nope. You pull off the man bun almost as well as Jared Leto did."

He punched my shoulder as I laughed, letting loose some of the tension that had been circling me constantly.

"What've Ma and Da said?" he asked once I'd quieted down.

I thought about how to say it best, without sounding like a martyr. "They've all but stepped completely out. Ma doesn't want to stress Da, nor do I, so I'm not pushing it. If Bauer takes the job and can get our numbers up, get us an investor, or talk to another bank, *something*, we'll see things turn around."

We sat with that, listening to the tires on the road, until he spoke again. "And Wells?"

Just the sound of her name made my pulse race. I pushed a breath out my nose and tilted my head in his direction, wishing I could look at him to see his response. "I like her."

Understatement.

"Yeah? Never would have guessed." The smile in his voice rang clear as he snuggled down in his seat.

I was impressed he'd managed to stay awake this long—he usually passed out the minute he found himself in a moving vehicle.

He roused a half-hour later as we rolled into town, his senses evidently alerting him to being home. He scooted up in his seat, his eyes out the window as we inched down Elk Street, curved around, and hit Main Street. I watched his gaze follow *Rise and Shine* from the moment he saw the door until he couldn't see it because it was too far behind.

"You going to talk to her again this time?" I asked quietly.

It took a few minutes before we reached the lodge and I pulled into my spot. I turned the key and shut off the engine.

"I have to try."

My parents arrived just before the storm hit, and then it started dumping.

Perfect timing—a Friday night, so by Saturday, the slopes were packed by ten and the traffic didn't let up. I messaged Wells to check in, and she said she'd turned away more than twenty callers asking for a room that weekend. The smart people had all booked in advance for the weekend before Christmas.

Bauer and Ritter shook hands with my parents, who'd run the lodge for thirty years. It was nothing more than courtesy, but Bauer seemed to see value in it and had asked more than once if he might have a word with them, just to say hello.

This was something about Jonas Bauer I respected, even if I hated my inability to read him. He understood we were a family business, and he wanted to buy in. I had yet to mention that Leo seemed, at the very least, perturbed by their presence, though since I didn't really understand what that meant for her, there was nothing to say.

Bel came to the lodge early on Saturday morning since she didn't work that day, and Bauer and Ritter were only there another night. She presented her ideas, all built around the vintage ski posters from the days when resorts were just starting, and Bauer and Ritter were pleased—enthusiastic, even, which was saying something for Bauer.

As we came out of the last formal meeting with the two enigmatic visitors who made up the Bauer Group, I felt hopeful. Between the storm, the packed mountain, and Bel's presentation, they had to be pleased. He had to want to take us on.

I was chanting it, willing it, begging it, praying it into happening.

I walked into town to see John and check in with him. He and his dad were knee deep into a big project, but he'd come out of his office long enough to say we needed a sit-down in the New Year.

"We're due for a talk. It's time to buckle down and make progress."

I knew what that meant. He wanted me to put up or shut up—he wanted to move out of bottles and expand. He wanted me to find investors like I'd said I would years ago.

He wanted my mind and energy in the game, and he wanted it so he could justify quitting his practice and move into something he loved doing full time.

I knew exactly how he felt. Our situations were eerily similar, except for the nuance that he was the youngest of three sons, not the oldest of four kids. One son already practiced law at their family business and wanted to keep doing the job, so John leaving wasn't a betrayal of the family, thank goodness.

I shook his hand, wished him Merry Christmas, and prayed that by the time I saw him next, I'd have information for him. If we could get the lodge on solid ground, we could draw someone in who cared about the place, and I could finally wash my hands of it without feeling like I was leaving it to die.

All the while, I'd been counting the minutes until I'd see Wells. She was coming Christmas Eve for our big dinner. She'd meet my parents, and I'd introduce her, but the night before, the snow started dumping. Downright raging. Jamie made it out on his flight, but Bauer and Ritter were stuck, as were four other guests who'd planned to depart on Christmas Eve.

I knew it was coming, but seeing her text say she felt she had to stay, make the night special, help Marcella who was pinch-hitting a fancy meal with no notice... a kick in the gut. All I wanted was my girlfriend, who I'd never even actually called *girlfriend*.

If I couldn't see her, I had to clear that up, at least.

Me: *So... you're my girlfriend, right?*

It took hours before she responded. Ma and Da insisted Bauer and Ritter attend our dinner, but in the end, they opted to stay at the inn since Wells had so many others in the same boat.

Wells: *Am I?*

I smiled to myself as I sat in bed, unable to concentrate on the book I was reading.

Me: *Yes, please.*

She sent a little smiling face back, which I took to mean she agreed. Then a few minutes later, my phone rang. I answered while still fumbling with the device.

"Hello?"

"Hey. Sorry it's so late." Her voice rang raw and tired, but still sounded so good.

I curled onto my side and held the phone to my ear. "It's okay. I'm glad to hear your voice."

"I think I've almost lost it. We served cocktails and wine and *wow*, Jonas and Karla can put it away. Plus there was another couple, the Rawlins. They're from Kentucky or Georgia or somewhere and these people... I'm telling you I don't know how they were still upright."

I savored her husky laugh, a pang of yearning so intense flooding me, I crushed my eyes closed. "It sounds like a great night."

She sighed into the phone and I thought I heard her breathing slowing.

"Yeah, it really was. I will never be able to thank Marcella enough, but it went off like we'd planned it instead of the ultimate shoot-from-the-hip. I guess now I have that under my belt, I won't be surprised when it happens again."

I could hear the smile in her voice, the satisfaction at a job well done.

"You're amazing." My heart thumped in agreement with my words.

"I just did what needed doing, but thanks. It sounds like things are going well for you too. Jonas seemed very pleased with everything. I'd almost call him jovial."

"*Jovial?*"

"Yes, no lie. And I don't think it was the booze either. I think he's had a great few days, and I honestly thinks he loves this place, Liam."

Her voice was warm and a little rough in my ear, and I wished I could fold myself around her and keep her with me.

"I hope so," I said softly.

Then we were there, both exhausted but unwilling to hang up.

"This is so stupid," she said, just above a whisper.

"What is?"

"That you're literally a quarter mile from me right now, but we're in separate beds, we haven't seen each other in days, we're likely not going to see each other for another few if I remember our schedules right."

Frustration tinged her voice, but I'd only heard one thing.

"Separate beds? That's a concern of yours?"

I heard her tsk before she responded.

"Is that all you heard?"

"You can't expect me to hear much after that, can you? We have yet to share a bed. I can think of nothing I'd rather be doing than sharing a bed with you right now."

She chuckled into the phone. "Well, you could always brave it and walk down here."

"Or you could walk up here. You haven't even been to my house," I said without thinking, only to realize it was true. She'd been to the lodge a time or two with Leo, but we'd almost always met at the inn or in town.

"That's true, I haven't."

"Maybe we should fix that. Sometime soon." I stifled a yawn.

"Let's do that. For now, let's say goodnight."

"Alright then. Good night, Wells."

"Goodnight, Liam."

The next day, after spending the day chatting up skiers, making the rounds to all the lifties and patrollers and every other employee on the mountain, I was ready to collapse into bed. But it was only five o'clock, and I had dinner with my parents. They were only here another few days, and they wanted as many family meals as we could muster. I had half an hour to get cleaned up and to their house, about a ten-minute drive in the blaring snow.

Someone rang the bell, and I assumed I'd open it to find Danny or Leo wanting a ride, but instead, I swung the door open and found a bundled Wells on my doorstep.

A better sight, I'd never seen.

She set down the small bag with her and jumped into my arms. Literally. I stumbled back a bit, but steadied and leaned into the embrace with all I had.

"You're so handsome. Did you get more handsome since the last time I saw you?" she asked, her face still bundled by a fleece neck gator and the collar of her coat.

"Are you even under there, or is this just a shovel with a bunch of clothes on?"

She swatted me and pulled her hat off, then shimmied down until I released her and her boots hit the floor.

She stood there, right in my entryway, and unzipped the two-foot-long zipper of her puffy coat. She pulled the neck gator over her head, unzipped the fleece sweater she was wearing and stripped it off, and finally stopped in only her tight snow pants, boots, and a crew turtle-neck base layer that clung to her like a second skin.

I blinked, and blinked again, because... what was I supposed to do with that? "So, not a shovel."

"Not so much," she said, a shy smile on her face.

She was still fully clothed, but something about the moment made it feel like she stood there in my entryway naked. I could not have been more attracted to her—though to be fair, if she wanted to keep going, I'd be happy to test the theory. Instead of letting any of those asinine comments escape, I grabbed her hands and pulled her into the living room.

"What are you doing here?"

"I told you last night, it was driving me crazy that we weren't going to see each other—that the storm we've been looking forward to would have the real-world consequence of keeping us apart on our first major holiday together." She ducked her head to look at a family photo on the mantle.

I came up behind her and embraced her from behind, my arms folding her up in a big backward bear hug. I closed my eyes and sighed at the feel of her, and wished it wouldn't be out of place to tell her how much I cared about her.

"What's wrong?" she asked, twisting in my arms to face me.

I scrambled, certain we shouldn't have the *feelings* conversation tonight. "Uh, I was just realizing I hadn't told you about the bank."

True enough—I hadn't. It wasn't something I'd wanted to tell her at all, but she'd want to know. And it might explain why I was feeling even more stress than I had been.

"Oh."

Her voice held a grave note, like she knew what was

coming. She probably did, since I would have told her immediately if it'd been good news.

"Yeah. They declined the loan."

She held my arms at my biceps and caught my eye, her jaw set. "You'll get through this. Bauer's going to get on board and they're going to make things better. They'll help you find the money and make the changes you need, and help people find Silver Ridge and realize how amazing it is."

I smiled at the determination in her voice. Taking her cheeks in my hands, I searched her face. *My goodness, she's beautiful.*

"Thank you." I touched my lips to hers. "Now, will you please come to dinner with my family tonight? Meet my parents and hang with us and then come back here and make out with me by the fireplace?"

She grinned broadly, and my heart leapt. "I wish I could."

I dropped my head dramatically and she picked it back up, slowly pushing my dead weight until I was upright again and she was giggling.

"I promise, if I could, I would. But Marcella is doing me a huge favor by cooking again tonight. It looks like the roads are done, and most everyone's flights are going out tomorrow. So maybe I can join you another night before they leave?"

"They're only here for a few more days, so tomorrow is really the last chance for this visit. I understand if you can't swing it, I really do."

"No, I want to. If everyone really does get out, I definitely can. I have new people checking in, but I don't need to babysit them and feed them dinner."

"And can I have you after the dinner too? Will you come back here with me?"

It was forward, if you wanted to call it that, but at this point, we'd been friends for months, dating for two... I wanted her alone, all to myself, for a few hours in the midst of this wintry madness. The pace wouldn't let up until after the New Year, and even then, weekends would be insane, and hopefully, many of the weeks would be too if people took their ski vacations with us. She'd be swamped, as I would be, especially if John had his way with things.

She swallowed and nodded.

"Yes," she said, then cleared her throat, her voice bolder when she said, "I'll stay with you."

The air around us must have crackled, because I would have sworn I heard the sound of the electricity pulsing into the room at just that thought. We smiled at each other, anticipation and nerves and excitement and those *feelings* I wasn't mentioning swirling around us.

She glanced at her watch. "I should get going."

"Yeah, me too. I've got to get cleaned up before I head up there."

"Can you message me tomorrow and tell me a little about what I should expect at your parents' house? What to wear, if they have any... quirks or things to mention or not mention..."

I smiled at her show of nerves. "Of course. But I'll warn you now—while they are spectacular people, they are ultimately very normal, unexciting, and quite reasonable. I think they're going to love you, so please don't worry."

I pulled her into another hug as we walked to the door.

I helped her layer back up—fleece, neck gator, hat, coat, gloves, which I hadn't actually ever seen her take off.

She put the small bag she'd had on the table where I left my keys. "Leave that until tomorrow, okay?"

"Okay..."

"It's just something small. Just a little present. Don't worry if you didn't—"

"I got you something."

That stopped her, and she pressed her lips together to hide her grin, which I wished she wouldn't do, because I wanted to collect every one of them.

"Alright then. I'll see you tomorrow. Have fun with your family."

"Good luck with the dinner. I can't wait to have you all to myself tomorrow night."

CHAPTER FIFTEEN

Wells

"I can't wait to have you all to myself tomorrow night."

His words had run through my head all night and all morning. Just thinking of him saying it, his voice low and his brow wrinkled and serious—*hi*. Hard to think of much else.

I'd said farewell to Jonas and Karla, and my other guests, right on time. They'd checked out, and the housekeeping team had swept in to overhaul the rooms in time for the new crush of guests we had. Mercifully, we only had six full turnovers for the day, so they could manage without my help.

It'd been busy, and after I'd greeted the afternoon's new arrivals and left Anthony to get them settled, I went to get ready. Before I stepped into the shower, the phone rang, and without looking, I answered.

"Merry Christmas, Serene."

Preston. My skin crawled at the sound of his voice.

"How did you get this number?"

"Your parents, of course. They're eager for us to reconcile, so they were shocked when they discovered I'd misplaced your new number, and were more than happy to provide it to me."

Ugh, he was slimy. I wanted to hang up and not deal with this. But in some ways, I'd known it was coming, and I wanted it done with.

"What do you want?" If he'd expected anything other than a glacially cold reception from me, he was an idiot.

He sighed dramatically into the phone, and I cringed. I could picture him now, loosening his tie like he was coming down to my level.

"Serene, I'm done with this. You've had your fun, sown your oats, *whatever*, but now it's time to come back home and publicly reconcile."

There it was.

Publicly. He didn't like that he'd been embarrassed, and must have thought he could leave it up to me to fix it.

Not happening.

I rolled my neck and tried to find the words, even as his use of my first name, my given name, pinged around my head like a fly. I'd never liked it, probably because of the way my mom used to say it when I was in trouble, but also because when I had been with the Saint boys, they'd nicknamed me Wells. I'd loved it. I fit right in with them—Wyatt, Warrick, Wilder, and Wells, the tacked on little girl cousin, but they'd loved me anyway.

When I'd introduced myself as Wells, Preston had smiled like he knew a secret. Turned out he did—he knew my father from golf, and he knew my name was Serene Wellington Bryant. He'd never once called me Wells, never once introduced me as Wells, and I think to him, the name was a kind of rebellion.

I took a deep breath, praying we were nearly done.

"I would have thought being contacted by my lawyer and severing all legal ties, returning the engagement ring, and removing all my belongings from the state of Colorado would have clued you in, but apparently not. So, I'll say this for you plainly."

I waited a moment to create dramatic effect. I wanted there to be no potential for misunderstanding. No room for his sociopathic brain to even consider the possibility that I'd return to him.

I spoke slowly when I continued. "I will never come back to you. I will never marry you. I will never reconcile with you. I will never be with you in any way ever again. You will never contact me again. You will not speak to my parents again. You will not say my *name* again."

I was shaking with adrenaline by the time I'd finished.

He was quiet for so long, I started to think he'd hung up.

"You worthless idiot. What makes you think you can do anything but sit around looking pretty? What makes you think you can run a business? Your unused degree and your internship of less than a *year*. You were lucky I ever took a second look at you. You know your father *asked* me to?" He chuckled into the phone. "He told me you worked in accounting at the resort, told me you'd just *love* to meet a man like me with a firm hand and a good head on my shoulders."

My chest caved in.

My father had told him to date me. The little piece of our relationship I'd thought had come naturally—even that was false, manipulated. I couldn't find words to respond, my mind whirling.

He spoke again.

"Everything you've got, you've been given." He made some sort of disgusted sound, then, "I'll be fine without you, *Serene*. I shudder to think what you'll do without me."

~

I knocked on Liam's door at ten after the time I'd said I'd be there. I was still in a daze, still felt like I was watching myself move around the room.

And so much self-hatred swirled in me for that. For letting Preston determine anything about my day other than being a small annoyance. For letting his words affect me at all.

Liam opened the door, all handsome, bearded, charming smiles, and strong arms for a warm hug.

I leaned in and breathed his pine and spice scent, wondering at how safe I felt with him in a way I never had with Preston at any point.

"Is it okay if we go?" he asked, peeking at me under my hat.

Though only a quarter mile separated the inn from his house, it was cold and windy, and I just hadn't been up to making the trek by myself in the dark, much less the journey home.

"Of course. I'm sorry I'm late."

I wanted to apologize for the shell version of myself I was too, but I didn't want to draw attention to it. Maybe he wouldn't notice my funky mood. There'd be plenty of other people for him to pay attention to.

And hey. Maybe this would help me be less nervous to meet his parents. The thought of it had had me dizzy with nerves before we'd had to cancel on Christmas Eve. Now, I felt all but numb.

We loaded into his SUV and he smiled over at me once or twice as we drove up the winding mountain road to a gorgeous log-cabin style home.

"Here we are," he said, genuinely smiling.

I liked that about him so much. He didn't shy away from expressing his joy, and his family gave him so much of it. Well, maybe other than Leo, who seemed to make him want to pull his hair out.

Then I remembered, meeting the parents was stressful. I wanted them to like me, wanted them to accept me so that Liam felt good about dating me. Especially someone like him who clearly valued his parents' opinion.

"You okay in there?" He leaned over to find my eyes and capture my attention.

"Of course. I'm just a little nervous. This is kind of a big deal, right?" I tugged my gloves further onto my fingers.

"I suppose it is. But I don't want you to feel pressure here. If it's easier, think of yourself meeting the local business owners and part of the founding families of Silverton. It doesn't have to be as my girlfriend."

"*Founding families?* Wait, do I know this?"

"I think so," he said with a quirk of his mouth. "My grandfather married Elke Meier, my grandmother. Her family had been here since the 1920s and were one of the founding families of Silverton. They'd immigrated and kept moving west, along with a small batch of others who, like idiots, settled themselves way up here out of the way of most industry. Except silver, of course."

I nodded. "Of course."

"The silver rush didn't last long but it put Silverton on the map for a bit. After that, they lived small town life until my grandfather came back from the war, married my grandma, and two generations later, here I am."

"And your mom? Is her family from here?" I wondered.

"Her family was one of the founding families, yes. But her mother's generation moved away. She was lured back by William Morrison, Jr., and the rest is history." He grinned at me. "Plus, you know the Saints are practically considered founders. Tilda got here only about a decade after my Grandpa Will opened the mountain. She came with her daughter, of course, and because she was a busybody, had to have a project, as she supposedly called it. The inn was that project."

I loved hearing about Tilda. She was such an enigma to me when I thought about my mother and grandmother. "And her daughter, my aunt, went into ranching, I guess."

"Exactly. And now you have Wyatt killing the boutique beef industry, and his brothers are all going to end up sticking around too, I'd bet. Once they're done with their exploits."

I shook my head. "So I'm doomed to belong here, I guess."

He put a hand behind my head and pulled me closer, those blue-bird sky eyes boring into mine. "Guess so."

While the Morrison house looked quaint by virtue of the fact it had a log cabin and stone feel in the front, it was actually huge. Not in a pretentious or even a very polished way, but it felt absolutely warm and welcoming. Yet another example of how lovely Liam's childhood must have been, and somehow just putting that together made me even more nervous.

No one greeted us at the door. Liam let himself in and urged me on behind him, which was exactly where I stayed. I tried not to cower, but I'd had more than one flash of meeting Mrs. Umbridge, Preston's mother, and that had gone about as well as stone soup for dinner. It had been awful—I'd left feeling smashed like a mosquito, and Preston's only encouragement had been that I'd *figure out a way to make myself more likeable.*

I shook it off as we approached the kitchen and sounds of chatter and laughter skipped down the hallway to us. Liam led me with a hand on my back—we'd shucked coats when we came in and hung them in the closet right inside the front entryway.

Before we entered the kitchen, his voice was in my ear. "You'll do great. I'm so glad you're here."

And then, we were in the kitchen, which looked like a bomb had gone off.

Leo chopped something on a cutting board in the corner.

"Wells!" she said, dropped the knife, and came directly over to greet me with a giant hug.

"Hey Wells," came Danny's deep voice from somewhere I couldn't see.

"Oh, finally! *Finally* we meet!" A tiny dark-haired woman approached me, silver streaking her hair throughout and swirling back into a demure chignon. She held out her hands and took both of mine. "I'm so glad you're here, Wells."

I swallowed back an irritating gush of emotion—I'd never been greeted like this. "Thank you, Mrs. Morrison. I'm so glad to be here."

"No. No, call me Alice, please," she insisted.

"What can we do? What's left?" Liam asked, moving to the sink and washing his hands. I followed his lead.

"Nothing, honey. You and Wells relax, or you can show her around. We're ten minutes from eating. Da's out getting a bit more firewood—"

"You're letting him do that by himself? How long has he been gone?"

"You have to let him do some things. He's not going to have a heart attack if he exerts himself. He's had surgery and he's on medicine, honey. Don't treat him like an invalid. Aging is hard enough."

She moved on almost immediately, whirling around the kitchen checking timers, peeking in ovens, glancing at Leo's handiwork with the chef's knife.

"Okay then. I guess I'll give you the tour," Liam's voice grunted out, mildly defeated.

He guided me to a set of stairs, but I put a hand on his arm. "If you want to go help your dad, please do. I'll be okay here."

His blue eyes softened, and that sight melted me just a little.

"Thanks. But Ma's right. If I hover over him, he'll be miserable. I just hate the thought of something happening to him again."

"I'm sure. Come on and show me the house, and it'll distract you. We don't want to be slowpokes."

He showed me the upstairs where their two bedrooms were—yes, just two. Leo had her own, and the boys all shared, two bunks and a single. I couldn't imagine how any of them crammed into those beds once they'd hit their teen growth spurts.

"How did the three of you live in this one room?" I asked, turning a slow circle.

The space was all made up, the three beds done in matching navy blue with red, green, and navy plaid sheets. There was one desk, and three dressers—two on one wall, and one crammed inside the smaller closet.

"We were almost never home. We spent most of our time at school, doing sports or whatever activity we had going on, and then we were at the lodge. If we weren't, we spent our time outside or in the living room. We pretty much only slept up here." He ran a hand over the top bunk.

"Were you on the top?" I wondered.

"No way. I was oldest—I had the solo single. Jamie was on bottom, and baby Danny was on top," he said, that familiar fondness in his voice as he spoke about his brothers.

"Isn't Danny only about five years younger than you?" I hadn't pinned down everyone's ages exactly, though I did know the birth order.

"Yeah. Actually more like four and a half. I turn thirty-one in January, and he's twenty-six now."

"What day in January?" I inspected the desk—clean but for a small organizer holding pens, a sticky note pad, and paperclips. On the notepad, I found a lightning bolt sketched in pen.

"Twenty-third," he answered. "When's your birthday?"

"It's January twenty-fifth."

"Really? We have birthdays two days apart? We'll have to celebrate together then," he suggested, his voice light and excited. Then all that lightness dropped and he added, "Unless you'd rather not. I don't mean to put any pressure on you or anything."

I took his hand and laced our fingers together. "I'd love to. And don't apologize every time you ask me to do something. It's okay to have expectations and make plans."

His brow furrowed. "I don't ever want you to feel... stuck. Trapped. Whatever the right word is."

My heart swelled at that consideration. He was so sweet, so thoughtful. So different from my past relationship. I needed to shut my ex—I'd been trying not to even think his jerky name—and that phone call out of my head.

I smoothed a hand over his beard, loving the prickly, rough texture against my palm. "Thank you. I don't feel that way at all."

He stepped closer, dipped his head down, and touched his lips to mine. Before we could deepen the kiss, we heard, "Soup's on! Come on down!" hollered from the kitchen a floor below.

That alone was a stark enough difference between my upbringing and his. During my childhood, dinner was at six, no variations unless we were eating out, hosting someone, or holding a social event. Even then, it was still almost always at six. We ate at a table, largely in silence, always miniscule portions of whatever the cook had made.

Liam squeezed my hand and smiled. "Let's go eat, and you can meet my da, assuming he hasn't keeled over while gathering firewood like a man half his age should be doing."

I was in danger of falling in love with Liam's family. When we'd come downstairs, William Morrison, Jr. had shaken my hand, cupping mine in both of his large, warm ones, and smiled with sparkling eyes so like all of his children, it had been astounding.

"Welcome, Wells. Glad to meet you." Then he pulled Liam in for a hug with a rough arm hooked around his neck. "And good to see you, Boy-o."

"Good to see you, Da. How's the heart?"

I ducked my head to hide my grin, knowing Liam was trying his best to seem casual and unconcerned, but it just wasn't in his nature. He was a doer, a fixer, and I was learning just how hard it was for him not to meddle in things and have his way when he thought he could help.

"Just fine, Leelee, just fine."

"*Leelee*?" I asked, my eyes wide.

Liam cleared his throat like he was embarrassed—not something I saw often.

"When he was little, Jamie couldn't say William, and for whatever reason, he refused to call me Will like my parents had assumed everyone would if we used a nickname. But Jamie called me *Leelee*, and in the end everyone acquiesced and I ended up going by Liam."

"I'm sure you've wondered what kind of crazy woman would name two of her children Liam and Leo, but that was never the plan. We named William after his father and Grandpa Will, and we named Leo *Leonie*, after my grandmother, who was French. The nicknames ruined everything," Alice Morrison clarified as she carted a giant roast to the table just off the kitchen.

Everyone grabbed a serving tray or dish, and we filled the table. We sat down to eat, each child evidently knowing exactly where to sit. Liam pulled out a chair next to his and across from Danny and Leo. Mr. Morrison found his place to my left. Liam helped me scoot the chair in, then sat to my right.

"I love all the names you chose. They're solid names, but have great nicknames too."

And they did—William was Liam, Jamieson was Jamie, Daniel was Danny, and Leonie was Leo—it was warm and friendly and comfortable, but they all still had those regal, special names of the family.

"Yeah, except old Jamieson Morrison..." Danny muttered to his plate.

"Hush, you," Alice said, eying her youngest son.

"What? It's a ridiculous name. What if he'd wanted to go by his full name? 'Hi, I'm Jamieson Morrison.' What *is* that?"

Alice straightened in her seat and gave her son a look I was certain he'd seen a hundred times before.

"It is a family name." Then she turned to me. "My grandfather was Jamieson, as was my father. We named Liam after his father and the men on that side, so it made sense to name Jamie for my family. It's inconvenient that it... sounds the way it does with Morrison, but we never have called him by Jamieson—he's always been our Jamie."

"Well... Jamie certainly fits him," I offered. It did. Impossible to think of him as anything else, never mind the repeating *sons* at the end of his full name.

Alice gave Danny a smug smile and he chuckled.

"What about your name, Wells?" Alice asked as she passed a basket piled with warm rolls.

I scooped a spoonful of green beans onto my plate, then handed them to Mr. Morrison.

"My full name is Serene Wellington Bryant," I started, wondering how to explain why I didn't go by my first name.

"That's lovely," Alice said.

"I think Wells fits you way better than *Serene*," Leo said as she lifted a thin slice of roast beef to her plate.

"I always thought so too. My cousins—the Saints— dubbed me Wells when I visited them around my fifth birthday one year. I loved that they called me Wells, and that I got to be one of them—one of their Ws."

I smiled at the memory of how happy I'd felt. Being an only child was a lonesome proposition, and being a fourth in their rough and tumble threesome had been a dream come true.

"They are sweet boys," Alice said, but Leo snickered as she loaded a glop of mashed potatoes onto to her plate and then dumped gravy over everything.

"My mother was always mildly horrified by my insistence at introducing myself as Wells. I'd given up on it until I graduated high school, actually, and then reverted to it, much to their dismay."

My stomach churned as I thought of the dynamic between the three of us—my parents and me. It'd always been distant, practical.

I'd needed them to keep me alive, then to pay for things. But I didn't need them anymore. I was certain that irked them, maybe niggled a bit, but I was also certain that they were probably happier without me to worry about. Once they got over the embarrassment of my breaking the engagement with an Umbridge, *God forbid*, they'd ascend back to their place at the table, heads held high, and they could forget about me as they'd preferred to do all along.

"I like Wells too." Liam squeezed my thigh under the table with his warm hand.

After that, the conversation bounced around between reporting on Alice's parents, who were nestled into their retirement community in Arizona, and how much snow we'd had. I noticed they all seemed to tiptoe around the financial state of the resort, or really any business-focused topics.

I wasn't sure what I expected, but I had expected Liam to report on the Bauer Group, or something along those lines. Maybe he'd already done that—the Morrisons had met Jonas and Karla, so of course, they'd likely covered everything then.

But part of me wondered if everyone was leaving it to Liam. Even his parents, as kind and warm and lovely as they were, didn't want the worry. Danny certainly didn't. His interest lay in skiing, and being on the mountain, and being in the snow, and skiing. As far as I could tell, he had no other interests, until he mentioned off-hand he'd started volunteering at the library.

"Really? What for?" Mr. Morrison asked, sounding entirely perplexed.

Danny shifted in his seat and scowled. "They needed help. I figured I'd help out when I had the time."

Leo glanced at him, her eyes squinted in suspicion. "But *why?*"

"Because. I wanted to help, and it's good to be there. I read to little kids. Why is that a problem?"

I'd never seen Danny anything but easy-breezy, so this show of frustration was notable.

"It's just... you don't usually do that kind of thing," Alice said gently, and I could see on her face she hoped the comment wouldn't hurt him.

He sat up, ran a hand through his hair. "Well, I'm doing it. So... yeah. Thanks for the support."

"It's great, Dan. I'm proud of you. I'm sure the... *kids* are really enjoying having you there," Liam said, and then I noticed he was biting his lip to keep from laughing.

No one else noticed, but Danny shot him a dirty look.

"I think they are, so yeah, thanks." Danny studiously buttered another roll.

"How's Bel doing these days, Leo?" Alice asked. "I was sad she didn't come for Christmas dinner."

Leo glanced at me, then turned a spare smile to her

mom. "She was sad to miss. But she and Gran were together at the community dinner, so they were fine."

"How is she?" Alice pressed.

Leo shoved a forkful of salad into her mouth and chewed slowly. I wondered why she needed the minute, why the stalling tactic.

"She's really excited about the new marketing plan she made up, and she got to present that. She's so talented. Good job to Liam for challenging her to get some new ideas going. I think she needed that."

Everyone else was busy clinking forks against plates, diving through the delicious dinner, but I saw the look on Leo's face as she returned her attention to her plate. She was worried about her friend, and she knew Bel better than anyone.

We chatted easily for the rest of dinner, Mr. Morrison sharing a few stories about their visit to Sedona and the rattlesnake they'd narrowly escaped on a path. He warned me that Liam was deathly afraid of snakes, so he wouldn't be any help if I ever happened to need it.

"Really? That's good to know. I wouldn't have thought you were afraid of much at all," I said to Liam who was scowling at his father.

"I will admit I'm deathly afraid of snakes. I had a few bad encounters as a child, and I just don't like 'em."

"As in, he screams and flat out *sprints* in the other direction if he sees one on a trail, or anywhere." Danny chuckled as he wiped his mouth with a cloth napkin.

I laughed along with the family, but set my hand on Liam's thigh, just to let him know I was there. I didn't care. I thought he was great.

In some ways, it was reassuring to discover Liam Morrison had a weakness, or at least, had a fear. He was fast becoming too good to be true, so at least his fear of snakes gave me something to file in the *less than perfect* category.

We said our farewells and before I knew it, we'd pulled into his garage, he'd clicked open the lock of his door, we'd hung our jackets on the coat rack, and he was pouring us glasses of wine and starting a fire.

As the flames came to life, I saw myself standing on the edge of something vast and yawning and overwhelming. The glow of the meal with Liam's lovely family had died out on the short, freezing ride home. And all I heard, instead of Liam's smooth, deep voice, or the low music that had started playing at some point, was Preston Umbridge's voice in my ear.

"I shudder to think what you'll do without me."

CHAPTER SIXTEEN

Liam

Somewhere between my parents' house and sitting in front of my fireplace, Wells had withdrawn inward. A bit like she'd been when she first arrived.

"Everything okay?" I asked, pushing strands of hair behind her ear.

We sat on giant pillows a few feet from the fireplace. The lights were low, some indistinct music lulling in the background, snow falling outside.

It was what I thought of as a completely romantic moment, except for the fact that my date wasn't in the same room as me but a thousand miles away.

I nudged her chin up, just the barest pressure underneath, and she lifted to meet my eyes. "You in there?"

She huffed out a small breath, took a sip of wine, and leaned to set down her glass. "Yes. I'm here."

"What's going on in your head?"

My pulse picked up as I fully realized she wasn't just spacing out, but upset. Or thinking. Or quite possibly about to let me down easy.

She sat up straight and crossed her legs into a tailor sit, her eyebrows knit together.

"Your family is amazing," she said, like it was bad news.

"That's bad?"

"No, not at all. They're wonderful." She smiled though her voice had hitched.

"Why does it sound like a bad thing, then?"

"Preston called earlier. The stuff he said—it reminded me of a lot of things. And then talking about my name, and my parents... I'm just feeling a lot of things, I guess. I'm sorry to put that on you. I don't mean to."

I shook my head, desperate for her to understand. "Wells, don't apologize. *Please.* I can take all of this stuff you're giving me, sharing with me, but I can't take you feeling guilty for it. I want to be this person for you, kind of desperately, and I don't want you to feel bad about sharing stuff that is real and hard. That's life."

She sat for another moment, on the verge of speaking, but made no sound. Then eventually, one side of her mouth pulled up into a small smile. "That's outer space stuff right there. The people in my life don't talk like that."

I chuckled. "I'm sorry that's been the case. But now, they do."

My gaze ran over her face, the curved brows, the dark lashes, the smooth cheeks, the dip and rise of her top lip. My focus ended up circling there on her plush lips, and just as my breathing changed, so did hers.

We met in the middle, her hands pulling me to her just as I leaned forward to get closer. She tilted her head and her lips parted just in time to greet mine, and when they did, my little universe exploded into sensation.

I'd wanted this time, just the two of us. Then I was worried she was upset, or even breaking up with me. But now, here we were, kissing like it was our last night on Earth.

Before long, I'd pulled her, or she'd crawled, or both, so we were lying side by side on the carpet, legs hooked together, clothes disheveled, fast on the way to the next and a very significant level of our relationship.

Somehow, I pulled back, pushing up on an elbow, checking her face for signs of... anything but *yes* and *more*.

"Are you good? Is this okay?" I asked, willing my breathing to slow.

She let out a breathy laugh. "Does it seem like I'm not?"

"No. Not at all. Or... it seems like you *are* good. But I, just, this is moving along, and we haven't talked explicitly about—"

"It's good, Liam. I'm good. I am right where I want to be," she said, and then pulled me into another kiss.

Later—much later—I watched her comb her fingers through her hair and wander to the bathroom. She chuckled at her reflection.

"What's funny?" I wondered, because there was nothing funny about how painfully attractive I found it to have her wandering around my place, comfortable, having spent the last few hours showing me just how comfortable she really was with me.

Let's say, the night had done nothing to calm my feelings for her. It'd confirmed them, and then thrown gasoline on what had already been a raging fire.

"I look like I've been... I don't know what." She turned to me and rubbed a hand over the skin below her mouth, which, in the light of the bathroom, I could see looked red.

"Ouch. I'm sorry."

"Don't be. It's just... I never realize it's happening. And then I get a look at myself and I know I've been kissing Liam Morrison." She chuckled again.

"I guess that's not all bad. But I could shave, if it'd help?"

I didn't like the idea that I hurt her by kissing her. Granted, it wasn't like I'd kissed her *once*. I'd kissed her for hours. But still.

"No, you couldn't. I'm sure you're handsome without a beard, but I'm partial to it," she said, wandering back to the bed and sitting on the edge.

We stared at each other, and I for one was fairly certain I looked like a lovesick fool, but she just looked... radiant, if I did say so myself.

She grazed her hand over my cheek. "I should get going."

"What? Why?" I pushed up to sitting.

"I need to help with breakfast tomorrow," she said, like that was a good enough excuse for her not to stay the night.

"It's a quarter mile down the road. Stay tonight, and we'll wake up early so you can get back down there in time to help. It's two in the morning now. Just stay." I patted the space next to me.

She looked longingly where my hand was, then back at me. "Are you sure?"

My smile broke out. "Am *I* sure? Yes. One hundred percent, sure that the sun will rise, and that I want you with me, in every way, whenever I can get you. So yes. Please. Stay—if *you* want."

"Okay. I'll stay. But we're both setting alarms."

Wells had a Spidey sense for her alarm, or at least she did this morning. She jumped up out of bed about twenty seconds before her six a.m. alarm went off. She shuffled to the bathroom and shut the door, then emerged a few minutes later, all clothes in place, hair pulled back, ready to go.

"You move fast," I croaked, impressed, because I moved in slow motion until I'd had coffee. The entire family did, except maybe Leo. She was like a person who'd been set on *fast forward* and the button had stuck.

"I hate being late, and I hate running behind. And I spent two years of my life doing absolutely nothing, so I kind of love having to be somewhere at a certain time."

I wondered what *doing nothing* meant, but now wasn't the time to ask.

She must have seen the question on my face.

"You can always ask me. I'm getting better at talking about it and not letting it ruin my whole day."

"I wondered what 'doing nothing' meant." I pulled myself upright and attempted to shake off the sleep still dragging at me.

"It means Preston didn't like me to work, or do much of anything. It was a great way to make me dependent on him and lose any sense of self-reliance." She sat on the bed and kissed my forehead. "I'm going. I'll talk to you later?"

"Yes, please."

Since she'd driven herself last night, she'd refused my

offer to take her back to the inn. That worked out well since I had plans this morning—the ski patrol supervisor wanted to talk with me about a few things. It was unusual for him to want to talk at this point in the year—usually, he'd need more time to adjust. He'd been with us for two decades, and I'd take his advice any time he offered it.

The rest of the day felt like a dream state. I walked around people smiling, waving, meeting, chatting, ducking into my office to answer e-mails, all the while thinking that if Wells would agree to let me wake up to her crazy jolt-awake at the crack of dawn every day, I'd do it in a heartbeat.

Rod Smith sat across from me looking relaxed and happy, his face wind-and-sun-burned all but where his goggles sat when he was on the slopes. Somehow even his helmet, which he wore religiously despite it being a new trend in the last decade or so, didn't keep him from looking like a perpetual 1990s ski bum.

Rod, like many of our employees, had been with us for decades. He was our Ski Patrol manager and had been the entire time we'd been here. His safety record and expertise at blasting for avalanches recommended him year after year, not that there'd been any competition. Add to that he was roundly respected by all the different patroller personalities, and he was the man in charge.

I was incredibly thankful to have him, and so thankful he kept coming back. He spent his summers in New Zealand skiing—he claimed he skied 360 days a year.

"I'm retiring."

I'd just taken a sip of my coffee and swallowed hard. *Ouch.*

I took a deep breath, let it out. "Any chance I can talk you into staying?"

I'd always wonder if I didn't ask, though Rob wasn't the kind of guy you talked into doing anything. He either wanted to do it and did it, or he didn't do it. Period.

"No. I'm with you 'til the end of this season, but after that, I'm out."

He had one of those rich, western voices, like Jeff Bridges or Sam Elliot—deep and gritty and sort of manly in a way that came from the gut. If he'd lived a century ago, he absolutely would have been a cowboy chasing down outlaws.

"Can I ask why?"

Not necessarily my business, but I'd known the man as long as I could remember. He'd often come to family dinner —had rarely had family around, and as far as I knew, had never married or had kids.

"Met a woman in New Zealand. She wants me there year-round." He crossed his arms over his chest and nodded like he could see this mysterious woman's logic.

"Wow. Giving up the three-sixty, huh?" I couldn't fault him if he had real motivation.

He unfolded his arms and leaned forward. "I've been waiting for an excuse to give it up for almost thirty years. Now I got it, I'm taking it."

That stunned me. I never would have thought Rod Smith was a romantic, but damn, here he was, changing his ways and everything.

"Understood. Who do you think can replace you?" I asked, because even though he'd be around for the rest of the year, ideally whoever took over would shadow him the rest of the season.

For whatever reason, Rod was giving me a look—a cross between irritated and disbelieving. "You kidding?"

"No. I want your recommendation, and I'd like you to do what you can to train him or her when you've got time this year so I'm not dealing with someone who's never managed the shifts and schedule like you have, let alone the blasting and other safety issues."

Why was that hard to understand?

"I'm asking you if you really don't know who should replace me," he said, looking highly skeptical.

I nodded. *Ah.* "I guess you mean Danny."

"Of course I mean Danny. He's been patrolling since the minute he qualified. He's a better skier than anyone out there, better instincts, loves the snow—he's it."

My turn to give him a look. Because sure, Danny was all those things, and more, but one thing he wasn't was someone who wanted any kind of responsibility. I'd asked him before if he'd want the job one day, or how he saw himself jumping into the family business. In the end, after lots of waffling and trying to evade the issue, he'd told me he didn't.

Just like that. He didn't want the stress of it, didn't want the pressure.

Good grief, could I understand that, but that wasn't the way life worked. You couldn't avoid responsibility, couldn't escape stress. Especially not when you were in your mid-twenties and your life had barely begun. Those things were better left for the retirement years.

"Honestly? Sure, he's qualified, but there's no way he'd take it."

Rod scooted forward in his seat, just a touch. He wasn't

someone to gesture or get passionate—even-keeled was his middle name. That little scoot told me this mattered to him.

"You're wrong, Liam. Your brother is ready. I've been having him do the schedule for the last few seasons. You know he's headed the avalanche team for years. He's already doing the work of the manager, he just doesn't realize it."

"I can see your point, but I just don't think he wants it. It's not even the work—you know better than I do that if he wants to do a job, he'll work his ass off until it's done and done well. But if he doesn't, no amount of bribery or cajoling will get him to do anything."

It drove me crazy, because in that regard, we were opposites.

I saw the validity in duty. He saw none. I found passion to be ideal, but not practical. He found it to be the only thing that motivated him.

"Hate to say this, but you're missing it. He's changed over the last year. I don't know why or how, but he's got you all fooled into thinking he's the same old Danny Morrison, charmer about town and perpetual seasonal employee of his family's business."

I internally inspected the statement. Had he changed? *Maybe.*

The only outward sign of it I could identify was first, him mentioning he was interested in the new librarian and then second, last night at dinner when he said he was volunteering at the library.

That was so far out of Danny's wheelhouse, it might have been a different continent. But those two things, even though I suspected they might be something to do with Bel —and I hated to admit that but it was true—they were signals that at the very least, he was trying something different in his approach to get her attention.

"Huh. I guess there are some things. But he sure doesn't seem to want me to know." I thought of his constant joking about how glad he was he didn't have the stress I did.

"You gotta ease into it, and I will too. But I think he's the guy. He'll make the transition flawless, and he'll manage your mountain and your patrollers well. It just makes sense." He stood and extended a hand, which I took.

"I'll think about it. Keep that between us for a bit, will you? Give me a few weeks to bring it up with him and deal with a few other variables I've got going."

I rounded my desk as he clomped out of my office in his ski boots.

"Will do," he tossed over his shoulder.

I watched the door swing shut and rounded back to my chair, where I slumped.

This is all I need. One more thing.

One more challenge to deal with in the mix of this whole mess.

The word *challenge* made me smile and think of Wells and send her a message like a lovesick fool that I was, telling her I was thinking about her and hoped her day was going well.

At no point had I played it cool with her. Sure, I didn't ask her out the second I saw her on the street and felt attraction like I hadn't in years. And no, I didn't as we became friends, but mostly it was because she'd put out the *no way* vibe pretty strongly there. She'd all but ignored the fact that I was a man, so I wasn't about to go charging in putting myself on the line.

But as I figured out where she was coming from, I got it.

And, even if I was reluctant to admit it, thanks to Leo, here we were.

Well, here I was, certain I'd fallen for her. Where she was with that, I wasn't sure. I knew she liked me a lot—that was clear. And she liked my family. And she liked Silverton. But... could she love me? Did she even want to love someone, after what she'd been through?

I let my head drop to my desk and stay for a few minutes while I regrouped. I had to get my head back in the game, work through the numbers and adjust a few things in the schedule. New Year's Eve and day were always big ones for us, and those were coming fast.

Finally, I jumped up, hopped around a few minutes to get the blood flowing, and sat down, tall and strong in my chair. I'd work through my e-mail, then review the accounts, then check in with the chef, and then call my parents and see if they really wanted to do dinner again tonight or if they wanted to see some of their friends.

And I would definitely not relive every moment of last night with Wells. Or wonder if she was doing the same thing. Or think about when we could do it all over again. Or pray that she wanted me even a fraction of how much I wanted her.

CHAPTER SEVENTEEN

Wells

Somehow, the overriding memory from the last twenty-four hours was not the call from my wretched ex-fiancé.

Nope.

It was dinner with Liam's family. Liam being so thoughtful as I talked through my thoughts after the dinner and mentioned Preston. Then Liam's kiss, touch, *everything*.

I'd never felt this all-consuming desire to think about someone all the time. Frankly, it proved a little unnerving. I'd even called my therapist, which she had kindly accepted between appointments, just to make sure I wasn't a crazy person.

I knew I wasn't. I knew what this was. And I didn't understand how it'd happened so fast, or what I was going to do about it.

Because the weird thing was, I didn't want to do anything about it but let things keep going, keep progressing, and see where it went. And I'd had some very specific thoughts about where I might like it to go when not talking myself out of it.

I kept waiting to feel myself throw on the brakes. Where was that voice of reason to chime in and say I was an idiot and needed to slow things down and this couldn't possibly be right?

But the thing was, I'd already made the stupid mistake. And not like there'd been only one mistake—if only that were true—rather, I wasn't going into this blindly. I wasn't being naïve. I knew who Liam was, and I liked it.

I knew he wasn't perfect. He had a bit of a hero complex, which might extend to me in some ways. He tended to take on the family's burden, maybe even to the point of a little martyrdom, except when he realized it and reined it in.

Oh, and he was afraid of snakes.

Those were human flaws, things within the realm of normal and loveable. Not things that would ultimately drive him to use, control, or manipulate me into doing whatever he wanted at every turn, and that was essential.

So when I got his text asking how I was doing, I let the butterflies have free reign. I let 'em flap around while rainbows shot out my eyeballs and I embraced it. I'd met his parents. We'd spent the night together. It was getting serious, and that felt good.

By the time I was ready to head to dinner with Leo and Bel for our girls' night Christmas get-together, or whatever we were calling it, I was so far down the rabbit hole of my relationship with Liam, I'd actually thought *Leo could be my sister one day.*

Yep! My mind had run away with itself, and walking into a dinner with Bel and Leo, if I didn't want to tell them all of those things and more, was a bad idea. I needed to lock that down, at least a bit, or they'd have me spilling my guts all over the table.

As I bundled up, pulling on my heaviest boots because the night was cold and it would only get colder as the evening wore on, I heard a knock at my door. I grabbed my coat, my stomach flipping at the thought it might be Liam, but I opened the door to find my giant cousin Wyatt.

"Merry belated Christmas." He reached an arm out to pull me into a side hug.

"Merry Christmas. Did you guys do okay during the big dump? I couldn't believe how fast it came down."

I'd wondered if they needed anything. The narrow roads up to his land were low on the priority list for the county plows.

"We did fine. I'm just down here for a few things and figured I'd stop in and say hi, see how the season's going."

He hooked his fingers through the belt loops of his jeans, and I pressed my lips closed to keep from laughing at what a perfect cowboy he was.

"I'm good. I opened the west wing of the inn before the holiday, so we've got twenty rooms."

It felt so good to say that. We weren't full tonight, but we would be by end of day tomorrow, and we had been for much of December. And *full* was ten more rooms than it had been any other year, so I was pretty darn proud of that.

Wyatt beamed at me, and for not the first time since I'd seen him as an adult, I thought about how ruggedly hand- some he was. He was just exactly what you'd think of when you pictured a husky mountain cowboy, if you ever thought of that sort of thing. Some local woman should snatch him up.

"That's fantastic, Wells. I'm proud of you. Are you still thinking you want to build on the gap-land?"

We e-mailed or texted every few weeks since I didn't see him, and I was trying to cultivate better relationships with my cousins since they were the only worthwhile family I had left.

The gap-land he referred to was the space behind the inn, the area between the pine forest and where the ground sloped up steeply and turned into Morrison land. Apparently, the town had always called it the gap-land.

"Yes. Not any time soon, but seeing how well this has done, it'd be amazing. Ideally maybe two years? But we've got to see numbers tick up for everyone around here before I can get the kind of loan I need, I'm guessing."

He nodded.

"You're probably right. But that's good thinking." His eyes shifted to one side. "Nobody else has asked after it?"

"No. Plus, even if they did, I wouldn't sell it now."

I pulled my hat on my head as we walked through Reception. I waved to Tala who merely grunted in response, somehow seeing my wave without ever lifting her head from her book.

"Thanks for swinging by. I'm meeting Bel and Leo for dinner." I wrapped my scarf around my face, so only my eyes were uncovered.

Wyatt zipped up his heavy Carhart jacket and hunched against the gust of wind that blew. "I'll walk you in, if you want. I parked in town."

I took his arm and we plodded slowly down the path. The snow had been piling up, slowly but steadily, even on the walkways. This one was harder to plow, as Liam had mentioned those months ago before I'd ever thought of snow.

"You're pretty good friends with Leo Morrison, right?" he asked, sounding all kinds of casual.

"I am. She and Bel are my best friends—probably the best friends I've ever had. I'll never be able to thank them for taking me in. Why?"

We stopped in front of *Basta*, the Italian restaurant where I was meeting the girls.

"I... I just wondered." He shifted from one foot to the other.

Riiiiight.

I smirked. "You like her?"

Wearing only a cowboy hat and his Carhart jacket, I could see his face and the blush that crept in.

"She's smart. Pretty. Seems tough. If I ever do find a wife, it's gotta be someone who can handle me."

I grinned at him and tapped the brim of his hat so it slid down a bit. He cinched it back up and gave me a look.

"I won't say a word, but if you stand here talking to me for another minute, I bet she'll—"

"Who'll what?" Leo said, bounding up next to me and throwing an arm around me. "Hi, Wyatt."

Wyatt cleared his throat, tipped his hat. "Hi, Leo."

I could have died from the cuteness of Wyatt, my big, tough, rancher cousin, blushing like a schoolgirl and clamming up in front of Leo.

"You aren't joining us, are you, Wyatt? I'm afraid tonight is a ladies-only event." Leo smiled playfully.

"No, uh, I was just walking Wells. I wouldn't intrude. I'm heading back to the ranch soon anyway," he stammered.

"Okay, good. But maybe next time you're down here,

have Wells let us know and we'll all catch up. I never do see you anymore."

Leo hit him with a smile so spectacular, I thought Wyatt might have been paralyzed by it, but Leo didn't notice as she greeted Bel, who'd just walked up.

I patted Wyatt on the shoulder, and he tipped his hat with a "Hey, Bel" and "See you soon, Wells," and then he was off.

Now I had more than one thing I wasn't going to talk to Leo and Bel about.

"Is Wyatt shy? I don't remember him being shy when we were growing up," Leo said as she stuffed her napkin in her lap.

"He's not shy around everyone, Leo."

Bel raised an eyebrow at me. I gave her a slight shake of my head to tell her not to say anything.

"I know. You think he's shy around me because he likes me or something, but that's nonsense. That's not how guys are with me." She didn't bother looking up from her menu as she said it.

"What on Earth are you talking about?" I asked.

"Yeah, what *are* you talking about? Guys trip all over themselves around you. You intimidate them out of their minds, for one," Bel said, staring Leo down until the stubborn girl finally looked up at us.

"I know they're intimidated. But they don't talk to me. So even if they think I'm pretty or whatever, they don't actually do anything about it. And if someone's intimidated by me, they probably won't like being with me very much anyway, so it's easier on all of us if I go on being intimidating, and they go on being intimidated and find some other milk-bread sweety they can stand themselves around."

She gave us a *see, I'm right, as always* look and then closed her menu.

Bel let out a sigh that sounded like it'd been pent-up a while. "I love that this is your excuse to never to talk to men. Sometimes, men don't talk to you because they're intimidated, sure. But there are other reasons. Plus, I think more men would get over their intimidation factor if you didn't generally seem so uninterested in them altogether."

The way she said it told me Bel and Leo had this conversation often.

"Again, it's not my fault if they're not brave enough to approach frightening old me," she said, the sarcasm oozing.

"I don't think Wyatt's scared, or even intimidated, for the record. He mentioned he likes that you're tough, as a matter of fact. I think he wasn't entirely ready to talk to you, and for a man who lives in an even more isolated set up than we do, I imagine he might need to gear up for such things."

I did my best not to make him sound like a hermit. He wasn't, of course—he lived up there with farmhands and other staff, plus a brother or two whenever they rotated through for a visit, though they hadn't been back to town while I'd been here.

"I know. That's why I said you should let us know next time he's here. I just gave him the go ahead. Now it's not my problem if he fails to take it." She ran a finger along the tight braid that held back the front of her hair and snaked down behind her left ear.

Bel and I looked at each other, then both burst out laughing.

"I wish I had your confidence. *Good Lord*, how I wish I did," Bel said.

We paused and ordered, but Leo wasn't done.

"Bel, you *should* have the confidence I have. You should have *all* of the confidence. You've had guys declaring their love and devotion to you since third grade. What more do you need?"

I held my breath, wondering if that was too sharp a question for Bel right now, only a few days after Jamie had been in town.

"Third grade love declarations don't count," she said lightly, but I saw as she sobered, especially when Leo said, "But older ones do."

Bel nodded reluctantly. "They do. But, nonsensical as it is, that doesn't give me confidence."

The waiter brought drinks, and we all praised his timely arrival and the change of subject that the wine and the toasting brought with it.

"I want to take a minute to thank you both for being so welcoming. And Leo, thanks for being so pushy about us getting together. I don't know how much longer it would have taken me to make friends, but I am so glad I met you both."

We all raised our glasses, took a drink.

"Thank you, Bel, for being the best friend a girl could have. And thank you, Wells, for accepting my pushiness even though you haven't had a lifetime to become inured to it like this one has." She nodded to Bel. "To meaningful friendship."

"I shouldn't have gone last," Bel said with a shy chuckle. "Okay. To friends who stand by you, old or new, even when things aren't perfect, or you're to blame, or you're the messed up one, or you're the jerk. To friends who love you through all of it."

We all raised our glasses, chimed them together, and

drank deep this time. I was certain, by the shine of both their eyes, I wasn't the only one feeling a little emotional at that one.

The food arrived and we dug in. As was her way, after she'd shoveled in half her meal, Leo sat back and began an interrogation, but not one I expected.

"Can we talk about my big brother?"

"Uh, sure. What about him?" I asked, not unwilling to share details of our relationship but not sure exactly how much would be okay with Liam, or me for that matter.

"I want to know where we are with the resort, with Bauer Group, with investors... I can't get him to tell me anything." She stabbed some chicken a little too hard, and her fork screeched against her plate.

"He updates me every now and then. Honestly, I think he's really hopeful Jonas and Karla will take you guys on and turn things around. I don't know about investors or anything else, though. Thanks to the season and snow over Christmas, yesterday was the longest we've had together."

I took a drink of wine in hopes she might not notice the blush that even thinking about yesterday brought out in me.

"Well, what did you talk about last night?" Leo pressed.

"Uh, the family, and just, how different your family is from mine," I said slowly.

"But that couldn't have taken too long. You didn't talk about the plan? Or—"

"Leo, give it a rest. I think it's safe to say Liam and Wells didn't talk about the lodge last night. It's this thing couples do—they talk about all kinds of things, not just work."

Bel widened her eyes at me like she was trying, and I nodded in thanks.

"Ohhhh. You guys did it."

I burst out laughing, flames shooting up my neck and

face, and Bel swatted her friend on the arm. "Leo! You don't just *say* that!"

"What? That's all I needed to know. It makes much more sense why Liam didn't talk about work," Leo said, totally oblivious to why it was entirely unacceptable to be so direct about someone *else's* intimate moments.

Bel put her hands to her temples and rubbed. "I don't even know what to say."

Leo, as usual, did. "When you do talk to him again, please tell him he needs to let me in the loop. I have a bad feeling about this whole thing, and I want him to... I don't know. Listen to me."

That pricked my curiosity. "You have a bad feeling? How so?"

She wrinkled her nose. "Jonas Bauer. I don't like him."

Bel ducked her head, but I turned to Leo. "Why do you say that?"

She pursed her lips, casually deciding how to put it, but something in her posture didn't fit with that move. "He just gives me a weird vibe. I don't know how else to put it."

Alarm spiked. "Leo, did he do something to you? Or say something?"

"No, definitely not. No. I'm sorry. I didn't mean to give that impression. No. I just... I don't like how closed off he is. He's hard to read, and seems sort of... I don't know. *Secretive.*" She set her fork and knife on one end of her plate, signaling she'd finished.

"I guess I can see why you'd think that. I met Jonas and Karla before I ever moved here, and I've always had positive interactions with them. They're excellent at what they do, and based on what I know about them, if they end up taking you guys on for this year, you'll benefit from it. It could really turn things around for Silver Ridge, and maybe even Silverton as a whole."

It was no surprise Leo didn't like Jonas's tight-lipped approach. It was exactly the opposite of her usual way with things—get it out in the open and then deal with it. That just wasn't Jonas, nor Karla, and she'd have to live with that if they were going to work together.

Which reminded me, I should ask Liam about whether he'd had any news to that effect.

The waiter brought a slice of cheesecake to share, which we tried to wave off, but he insisted. Since it was just one, we all managed to stuff a few more bites into our mouths.

"Oh my goodness, this is so good. This has to be one of Sadie's," Leo said with a groan.

"It is. She's been selling them to *Basta* for years. I just never have room for dessert." Bel sighed in a similar state of ecstasy.

"I still haven't met her. I wish I could so I could thank her." I closed my eyes and let the sweet, creamy flavor drown my senses.

"You won't. She's not exactly a shut-in, but yeah... I wouldn't anticipate ever meeting her," Bel said as she took another bite.

"She's our age, you know." Leo set her fork down and stretched back in her seat.

"*Really?* I imagined her much older. Maybe in her fifties, for some reason." I'd imagined a sweet middle-aged woman slaving away in the back of the bakery early mornings.

"Nope. She's late twenties. She went to school with us for a few years, then was home schooled, but went out to New York and did culinary school and everything. She's legit." Bel gulped down water, then pushed her plate and glass away. "Okay, I cannot consume one more bite of anything or I will pop."

Leo rubbed her flat belly. "I love being this full," she said almost dreamily.

"Of course you do. I bet you only feel full right after a meal—you have the metabolism of a jack rabbit." Bel shot her an annoyed look.

"Oh, whatever. You have a perfect little body. Don't be jealous that I get hunger-induced rage five times a day unless I eat every two hours," Leo joked.

After paying, we all filed out onto the chilly street. We'd opted against Christmas presents on the promise we'd schedule a spa day when the season ended and work let up. Even *Rise and Shine* was extra busy since so many tourists were in town.

"Okay, well, let's get together next week again, yeah? Wells, do you have people coming in Wednesday?" Leo asked, ever the planner.

"No. No arrivals until Thursday evening, so I'd be good for afternoon coffee." I was already looking forward to it.

"Just come on over—you know where to find me." Bel waved before she headed off in the direction of her house.

Leo stepped down off the curb, then turned back and leveled me with her bright blue Morrison eyes before I could brace for it. "Oh, and Wells, you better tell my brother you're in love with him soon, or I'll have to tell him myself."

The next chance for any real time with Liam, it had been almost a week. It was a new year, but apparently, it hadn't brought good tidings.

"We're sitting there in the meeting, right? We're in the conference room, Bauer and Ritter up on the screen, and they can see all of us—fancy shit, right? And I am watching as Leo is *yelling* at Jonas Bauer. *Yelling.* Like literally hurling insults at him about everything from his suit to his haircut, all because he suggested we needed an outside investor."

Liam paced the floor, back and forth like a restless bull. The language alone told me he was keyed up and distraught.

I didn't know what to say, and he clearly needed to vent, so I waited.

"So then, he says he *insists* we get an outside investor. He says he thinks he has someone in mind. He says the bank failed us, but The Bauer Group can see the potential, wanted to take the project, but in order to do that, we would need to agree that a primary part of their revitalization plan would be to first and foremost seek out a substantial investor. *None of this is news!*"

He pulled his hands through his hair one way, then the other, leaving it wild and on end. He was about a week overdue for a haircut again and completely adorable, but very upset, so I shouldn't have been noticing such things.

"At dinner last week, Leo asked me what the latest was and said you hadn't been telling her what was going on." I didn't want to sound accusatory, but wondered if she might have felt totally blindsided by the meeting.

"Oh, that is a frozen pile of horse crap. She has been invited to every meeting. I have asked for her opinion *countless* times at this point, and she has refused to say a word. Even Jamie and Danny have commented on how odd she's been about it. But then, she shows up today, ready with her flaming arrows, insults the very man I've been groveling to in order to get him to take us on, and I don't know what to do. I literally have no idea how to handle her right now."

He was still pacing around in my room, back and forth around my bed in the cramped space.

"What did you do during the meeting?"

"I asked her to leave," he said, his voice low, steady, and full.

So full of emotion, I couldn't identify them all.

"Oh, yikes."

"Yeah. I don't know what I should have done, but I know by the death-glare she sent me as she stood up, all cool and calm, that I had not done the right thing in her opinion." He shook his head and swiped a hand over his face again.

"I'm impressed she went quietly."

His laugh sounded bare, tight. "She didn't. When she got to the door, she marched back, slammed her hands on the conference table, and said to me, 'If you care about this family, about the legacy of this place, and about your relationship with me, you will not allow this man to come into our company, dismantle it, sell it off for parts, and leave us with nothing.'"

Liam took a long breath, then continued. "Then she turned to the camera, looked right into it and said, 'And if you had any integrity at all, you wouldn't be trying to destroy what my family has built over nearly sixty years just for profit. You should be ashamed of yourself.' And then, she stormed out, slamming the door the best she could, though that door has a pressure release on it so it does the slow-close thing. I'm sure that just pissed her off even more."

His hands ran through his hair again, and he stopped,

his shoulders dropped, and he let his head fall back so he stared at the ceiling. "I don't know what to do."

I moved to him, held him by the waist, my hands pressing into his firm sides. "You do."

His blue, bloodshot eyes found mine. "I do, but... Leo's going to hate me. And I hate that I've had to beg Bauer to take us. Not literally, but I feel like I've been walking on eggshells, just waiting for them to see what I see. Shouldn't they have seen it the minute they got here? If they want the job, shouldn't they have taken it and run?"

I reached up and smoothed a hand over his wrinkled forehead. He was hot, energy and stress rolling off him, and he felt physically, notably *hot*.

"I don't think that's the way they do things. They're extremely thorough because when they take on a project, they do succeed. So if it's yes from them, I think you can relax a little. And if the investor is the only way, which it sounds like it is, then Leo will see that eventually. She's not going to hate you when she realizes you love this place as much as she does and want it to be a success."

I dragged him with me to my dresser and handed him a bottle of water.

He took it wordlessly and gulped down the entire thing.

"When was the last time you ate? Or slept?" I asked, unable to ignore the toll the stress was taking on him.

His eyes were reddened from lack of sleep, the circles under them dark and bruised-looking. He was sallow instead of that vibrant reddish tint he had that brought his pale Irish skin to life. He seemed thin, though I wasn't sure.

He scrubbed a hand over his face. "I'll sleep tonight. I've got to run over some things, maybe track down Leo... I don't know. I'm sorry. I shouldn't have come here and dumped this all on you, but I had to let it out. Danny's nowhere to be found after the meeting, I don't want my parents to worry... I've got to call Bauer back and confirm. I told him I'd be in touch later today, so I better go get it done."

I put my hands on his shoulders. "You're doing what you can. That's all anyone can ask."

"Thanks." He trudged to the door and pulled it open.

"Liam, I—" I cut myself off. Now wasn't the time.

He turned back, his eyes weary and sad. "Yeah?"

I smiled. "I'll be thinking of you."

CHAPTER EIGHTEEN

Liam

Bad to worse. That's how it felt things were going lately. Anything other than me and Wells, that is.

She was great. She'd been reassuring and on my side, which was amazing. Not that I wanted her on my side and *not* on Leo's, but what a relief that she heard my perspective and saw that Leo's response was off.

I knew my sister didn't want investors, but she didn't understand we had no choice. Absolutely no choice at this point. If Bauer thought he could find someone, we had to take that chance, or we wouldn't just lose part of this place—we'd lose all of it. That was a major reason we'd hired him from the beginning, but clearly she'd missed that.

The walk back to the lodge had been clarifying. The January day was gray and cold, one of those days that would end with flat light everywhere and lots of work for the patrollers. You could tell it was coming hours away when you lived this life.

I dialed Bauer first. I knew this was right, and I knew I had to deal with Leo, but I needed to lock this in first.

"Good to hear from you, Mr. Morrison," Bauer answered, his voice crisp.

I pushed down the wash of nerves. We were at this guy's mercy, and I felt that more distinctly than I ever had before. "I apologize for the delay. Obviously, we see the necessity of an investor. The bank was option one, but you make a clear argument for an investor, and it sounds like your group prefers that to a bank loan."

"It isn't *preferred*, but it is in no way the end of the world. I'm concerned that your family isn't in agreement with this."

One thing he'd made clear—when he dealt with family businesses like ours, he insisted on unanimity of involved parties. He'd given no reasons for this, but I wondered if he'd had bad experiences with the family business dynamic.

I appreciated that. No one wanted a hostile takeover. But as Leo had demonstrated, any hostility was coming from her.

I cleared my throat as quietly as I could. "My sister is fearful of what an outside investor would do. She doesn't understand the full scope of our financial situation, but I don't think she'll be a concern in the long run."

Bauer was silent for a beat. Then, "Your sister does not strike me as a woman who would appreciate being spoken for."

"Ultimately, Leo will fall in line. Don't worry about her," I insisted, frustration with my sister and the whole damned situation roiling in my gut.

Quiet once more, Bauer didn't mention anything about

Leo again. He did mention he thought I needed to create a larger write-up for our vision. He and Ms. Ritter would be in touch with a suggested outline in the next day or so. He'd like to get the funding in place before season's end so we could, ideally, get another lift or two in this summer.

Talk of adding lifts made my heart beat faster, especially with a timeline of this summer. That was amazing. We'd known for at least a decade where new lifts would go and in what order. They were part of the necessary infrastructure of a mountain that turned it into a *resort* rather than simply a lodge at the base of a great mountain.

I hung up the phone and sat back in my desk chair, wishing there was more natural light and I didn't have to rely on the fluorescents hanging over head drilling my headache deeper into my skull.

Now to find Leo.

At five o'clock, all the kids from the *kinderschule*, our kids ski program and daycare, were gone. It'd taken four visits to earn even a glance from Leo, and once I had, I'd known she wouldn't talk to me until she was done with work.

Leo did a lot around the resort. She'd held almost every job, trained in every department, but her real passion was running the kids' program. She wanted to run a ski team eventually, which I loved her for. She headed up the whole ski education program, the *kinderschule*, and this year also supervised the ticketing office since our manager there was on maternity leave.

Leo was impressive, and I knew she wanted the best for this place. Nothing in me could believe she wanted anything but success for the lodge, the mountain, the community, the family. But what she didn't have was perspective, and I needed a way to get it to her.

The last childcare worker left the room, and the door slowly swung shut.

Leo leaned back against a set of cabinets and crossed her arms and legs. "I hope you're not here expecting to convince me of your position. If Jonas Bauer himself can't do it, I'm sure you can't."

"When did you talk to Bauer?" I asked, stepping farther into the room.

"When he called my cell phone yesterday afternoon. I assumed you'd put him up to it." She raised one eyebrow, asking the question.

"I didn't. I thought the best strategy was to give you some time, especially after you virtually threatened Bauer. I never would have suggested he contact you, plus I have a feeling no one puts Bauer up to anything."

I was shocked. I wouldn't have thought he had any way *to* contact Leo, but I was sure her information was listed somewhere on the website or maybe even in all the paperwork I'd handed over in the last few months.

"Well, he did. And he talked a good game. He was all understanding and approachable and reasonable. But ultimately, the problem is still there, no matter how palatable he tries to make it with his accent and his fancy language."

She scrubbed a disinfectant wipe across the countertop that had a sink and drying rack with a surprising amount of aggression.

"At this point, I'm not trying to convince you. I want you to understand and feel good about what's happening, but the bottom line is this—we have no other options."

She physically bristled, the tension shooting up her spine, and she whipped around to me. "How is that possible? We've always had other options before now, and we haven't always used loans from banks. There are federal and state grants. There are non-profits to talk to—tons right here in Utah. How can you say there's no other option?"

I ran my hands through my hair, took a breath, tried to calm the frustration I knew was building to a dangerous point. "*Leo*. I'm not ignoring those things, but they are not the answers to this problem. Most of those are five thousand here, two thousand there. We're talking hundreds of thousands of dollars we need to get this place where it needs to be."

She crossed her arms, her jaw set. "I refuse to believe that we're in this crisis all of a sudden. It doesn't make sense."

A bitter laugh escaped. "Of course it does. Silverton has less draw now than it did a decade ago. We're all but off the map for tourists, and our lodge and lifts are aged. We don't have new entry gates, we don't have the latest *anything*, and fickle as they are, people want that. It doesn't matter that we have the best mountain and the best snow if people don't ski it."

I could see her running through rebuttals, her face hard. All her fury was releasing on me, though it wasn't my fault. At least not entirely.

"Bringing in an investor is going to edge us out. It's always been a family business, and it always will be. I can't stand by and let you sell off pieces of this place just so you can put in shiny new lifts."

"That's what you think I'm doing? Trying to make it look good for no reason? My God, Leo, you are so far out of touch, it's insane. I'm trying to keep this place *open*. If we don't get an investor in here with deep pockets, maybe a few, we're done for. We won't even have time to let Bauer work his magic and revitalize, nor will any of our efforts to get the state to push more advertising our way put a dent in the problem. We will *close our doors* in less than two years if we can't turn things around!"

She paled, and I didn't stop.

"I have been looking at every angle and every option for *years*. We're coming to this point because it was an inevitability, and the *only* thing we can do is follow Bauer's advice, get investors in here who'll see the potential and get on board, and change things. Otherwise, you might as well shelve those dreams of a ski team and a full kinder school and everything else you have in mind, because *it will no longer exist*."

Leo's face could be wiped of all emotion in a way none of the rest of us could manage. That's what she was doing now—locking it away.

But then, red shot to her cheeks, and she seethed at me. "I don't know what you've been doing these last few years since Da put you on as manager, but looks to me like you've done a piss-poor job of managing things if we've come to this crisis point under your watch."

I shook my head at her, disappointed, exhausted, and *done*. "I—"

"I don't care, Liam. I don't care. I don't want to hear your sob story. If this is your best, you've failed. And if you sell us out to some fancy foreign investor just to cover up your own mistakes, you better find yourself a new last name because you'll be no brother of mine."

She threw down the wipe she'd been clutching and barged past me before I could respond.

～

I'd gone back to the office and tried to channel my frustration with Leo and the whole busted up situation into work. Bauer's assistant had sent over a list of things for me to get together, much of which I had ready from the bank loan application. But beyond that, he wanted to sweeten the deal, so I was sifting through all of the things he thought we'd need to do to get the right person.

A vise clenched my chest. The list was long. Proposals for new restaurants, space for building lodging for guests, outlines for adult and child ski education program build outs, marketing strategies for longer term... so much work. So many things. And he wanted them all *now*.

I appreciated his sense of urgency. After all, we wanted this money in soon, so we could put it to good use. He wanted to start this summer and see some of the fruits within the next season or two. But the constant push to pull brilliance out of my butt, when all I really wanted to do was hang with my friend John and make great beer and sell it to people who liked beer, was becoming harder to embrace.

And, speak of the devil, the time had come to check out and meet him for a drink at *Craic*. As I walked past the inn, I messaged Wells and told her I was walking by and it was killing me not to come find her and kiss her. She suggested I stop by on the way home for just that purpose, and I happily agreed.

After that, I took the next three minutes of my frigid walk to get my head right. John was rightfully frustrated. I didn't know how to do much other than appease him and assure him that by summer, I was hoping the situation would be dramatically different.

I strolled up right on time and John was already there waiting. His family was universally punctual. Even for mountainfolk and people who lived in a small town who you'd assume might be a little more casual about things, their internal clock was known to run ten minutes fast.

"Hey man, good to see you." I approached his high-top table and shrugged out of my jacket.

"You too. It's a rare thing these days." He stood to shake my hand and pull me into a one-armed hug.

He still wore a charcoal suit, dark blue shirt, and subtle tie. His hair was already mostly gray, but since it'd been blond as we'd grown up, you didn't realize it was gray until light hit it and that silvery glint shone back.

"Much to my dismay, that's true."

We both sat and Mallory, our waitress, appeared instantly. "What can I get you two tonight?"

Her eyes wandered over John's face, suit, and back to his eyes before briefly acknowledging me. Mallory had gone to school with us, like most younger people in the town, but she'd been a few grades behind us. She always looked at John like that, and John always seemed to miss it.

"Chips and salsa, and I'll have our pilsner," John said, and by *our* he actually meant it. The one he and I brewed and sold together.

"Same for me, and I'll take the porter." She knew I was requesting our beer too. They sold a decent selection of local Utah brews. Ours was the most local, but only bottled. Just the thought made me restless, as usual.

"How's it going at the lodge?" John asked, easing us into what we really needed to talk about, no doubt.

I gave him a placid smile. "Mostly terrible."

We both chuckled, and then I elaborated.

"It's okay. I think these consultants are going to make a difference, but I feel like my back's against the wall with them and with the family. I won't be surprised when everything takes a dive and I end up with a defunct non-resort hanging on my guilty conscience for years to come."

"So stress with a large side order of self-pity, huh?"

I nodded reluctantly. "I'll admit, I'm wallowing a bit. I just had it out with Leo, and I don't know how to fix that."

Mal returned with our beers and two baskets towering with chips and small bowls of salsa, and we both took a drink.

"Leo's always been her own woman. And she's always been a hothead. I don't think there's much you can do to *fix* that. If you're doing the best you can in this situation, then that's all you can ask of yourself."

"It's true. And I am. But it doesn't mean I can't whine about it to my best friend."

"You can always whine to me, buddy. I just didn't realize we were throwing a pity party here. I thought we were making plans."

He eyed me as he took another drink, and I scrambled to figure out how I'd deal with this. Another person I would probably be letting down today.

"So..." John said after I didn't say anything.

"I'm doing what I can. When the season's over, it should lighten up. We're looking for investors, and that will make a huge difference. I'm hoping before next season, I can be transitioning with someone."

I hated it. I hated saying it because I knew it was unlikely everything I wanted to happen in the next year would.

John nodded repeatedly in shallow movements, like he had to do that to absorb the situation. It was a familiar action, and one I knew meant he was sorting through his thoughts about what I'd said before he'd respond. He was extremely even-keeled—one of many things that made him an excellent business partner.

"I can't keep doing it like this, Liam," he said, his voice low and clear.

I stifled a frustrated groan. "I know, man. I know. Honestly, I can't either. I feel like I'm about to burst. At the same time, I don't feel like I have any other options but to get this wrapped up—there's no one else to step up, and you know I can't just leave."

"I know."

We sat a moment, eating chips, sipping beer, eyes shifting from one big screen TV to another, each plastered with various European league soccer game replays.

I leaned against the tabletop with my elbows and rolled my beer back and forth on its bottom edge. "I know I've been saying that for years."

"You have."

And for John, that was a lot.

He was slow to accuse or criticize, but it was true, and somehow hearing him confirm that I'd been *saying* I'd make a change but had failed to do anything about it made the circumstances sting all the more.

"I don't want to sound like a broken record, but I do think what's happening now is different and is going somewhere. And if it does work, we'll have a chance of attracting someone who'd manage the place far better than me." Just the thought sent a potent mix of hope and anxiety twisting in my stomach.

"And if it doesn't work?" John asked, ever the one to voice the thing I didn't want him to, if necessary.

"Then I'm out of a job anyway, because we'll be prepping to close up shop. I'm telling you, even six months from now, I should have a real sense of when I'm done—maybe even a final out date."

John took another drink and watched a replay of a goal, then turned back to me. "I can't wait six months, Li. I need something concrete. I want to be done at the firm this summer, and I need to do it with you, or I need to find something elsewhere."

Whoa.

"What do you mean *something elsewhere?*"

John pursed his lips, a sign of his disappointment which hit me in the gut. "I mean I'm done this summer. I gave my dad and brother notice. They want to hire someone else and it's all the better if that person gets going sooner than later. I want to brew beer. I want to do that with you, like we've dreamed about for years. But I need to go at it full throttle. I've got savings, but I'm old enough that I can't just sit around. I have to make something happen, and soon, or I'll never be in a place to have a wife and a family I can support."

I wished he wasn't making sense, but of course he was. And I got that. John had wanted to brew for longer than I'd known I wanted to help. He'd been homebrewing since high school. He'd apprenticed at local places even while in law school—he'd stretched himself thin as paper to pursue both law and his passion, and he'd done it.

And I'd been the reason we'd delayed.

I'd been the one putting him off. I'd come back from my time in the Army believing I'd interim-manage. Then Da had his heart attack, and we put finding someone new on hold a bit, and then it became clear we couldn't get someone decent in because things weren't going well.

And that whole time, John had been waiting. He'd been

cranking out amazing beer at a tiny level, lapping up the scraps I was willing to give my time, energy, and money.

"I know I haven't been fair to you—"

"It's not about fair, Liam. And this isn't something else to guilt yourself over. This isn't a problem you need to solve. I know you're stuck, and you're doing right by your family, and I admire and respect that."

He held my eyes with his, a stern look on his face. I searched for something to say, but he kept talking.

"I don't want this to sound like an ultimatum. Working with you is by far my choice. But if you're tied up here for another few years—if you won't have even a bit more to give, then at the very least I need to get someone else involved. And at most, I need to look at other options entirely."

Oh, but that hurt. I knew it wasn't an ultimatum, and yet it *was*. He wasn't trying to be a jerk about it, but it felt like he was stabbing me in the kidneys with that thought— bringing someone else into *our* brewery, or leaving altogether. Both made me want to spit and yell.

"I get it. I wish I didn't and could be pissed with you, but I get it, and I'm sorry I don't have a better answer. Depending on how this investor thing goes, I could see a real change. I'm hoping for it. But I won't know for a bit."

I shoved a chip into my mouth, stopping the next words on my tongue, which were absolutely me begging him to hang on a while longer and not abandon the dream.

"I can wait a while. Not forever, but I can wait a while."

After that, we sat and crunched on the best fresh tortilla chips in the country, sipped great local beer, and talked only occasionally. We understood the situation, and each other.

As usual, now it was up to me to make something happen.

CHAPTER NINETEEN

Wells

It was late by the time Liam knocked on my door. I wished I was snuggled in the cabin across the field, though that would mean more work for him to get to me. But then at least, we'd have space and privacy, and a fire to curl up next to.

In my tiny room at the inn, we had barely any space except on the bed. And I didn't mind being on the bed with Liam, but I anticipated him needing more time to vent or process, and that might be tough in these cramped quarters.

A light double tap on my door arrived at nine o'clock.

"Wells, you in there?" Liam's muffled voice came.

I hopped up and opened the door. It was dumb how happy I got just seeing him. Even his message earlier had had me fluttering around all giddy and happy.

He looked so handsome. His dark beard was on the long side, like his hair which curled a bit at his collar.

Something about those little wisps of hair that should be trimmed made me feel like gushing—completely endearing.

Blue blazed out of those dark-rimmed eyes, offset all the more by slightly cold-reddened cheeks and dark hair.

From his unzipped jacket, I could see his long-sleeved shirt, no tie, and dark jeans with heavy snow boots insulating his feet.

"Hi." A thrill of joy and excitement bounced through me at seeing him.

He shook his head without speaking, a glint in his eye at the sight of me, and stepped through the doorway. He pushed the door closed behind him as he set his hands on either side of my waist and paced us back until the backs of my legs met the bed. He stepped closer as I tumbled back into the fluff of the comforter, and he leaned down, smashing against me, his arms rising to bracket my head as he brought his face an inch from mine.

Then he leaned down just as I raised my chin, and our lips met. It felt like relief and excitement all balled into one moment, then another. He broke the kiss, and when he pulled back, I was certain I had a hazy, hungry look on my face.

"Hi," he said, his eyes smiling.

"Good to feel you—I mean see you," I said, chuckling. Both were true, after all.

His broad smile looked perfect. "Likewise."

He pushed off me and sat down on the bed next to me.

I sat up so I could look him in the eye. "How'd it go with John?"

He scrubbed his face with his hands and scratched at his cheek. "About like I expected. He's ready to focus on the brewery. He's told his family he's leaving the firm, and they're going to hire someone in the summer. So that's his short timeline."

I laid a hand on his back and smoothed over the wide shoulders and down his long spine. He rumbled a sound of pleasure which had me smiling. I loved touching him, being near him.

"Is that something you can do? Is that realistic?" I asked, hoping it didn't sound like I didn't believe in him.

His smile was thin. "I don't know. I mean I definitely can't be *done* by this summer. But if we find the right person —if I can put together this portfolio the way Bauer wants and get someone great in here, who believes in the mountain and the lodge..." His shoulder slumped. "Short answer —I don't know."

"Tell me about what Bauer's asking for now."

"He's got a whole list of things he wants me to outline. Some of it I'd already done for them in the process of trying to get a consultant to take us on, but it's a lot more. It's a cross between a bank loan application and a vacation brochure. He wants the place to appeal to investors, and we've obviously got shortfalls or we wouldn't be where we are now."

He let out a slow breath and leaned back into the hand still making small circles around his back.

"I'm sorry. I know you're exhausted. Did you talk to Leo?"

His head dropped, and I didn't have to see his face to know it hadn't gone well.

"I'm sorry. She'll come around."

He rested his forehead on my shoulder, and that sweet, raw move just melted me. His voice was gruff when he spoke again.

"I don't know that she will. That's not really her style."

"Maybe not, but she loves the lodge, and she loves you. She's not going to resist doing something if it's right for the lodge and the family."

He rolled his head side to side as he said, "I wish I felt confident that was true."

I put two fingers under his chin and urged his head up so I could see those bright blue eyes. "You guys will be okay at the end of this."

"We will. Somehow."

That thought lined his brow, and I could almost hear the afterthought—that *he* would be the one to sort it out and fix everything.

"And if the lodge closes, which I don't think is going to happen, but if it does—that's not all on you."

I held his attention right where I held his head in my hand, my fingers grazing the side of his bearded face.

He huffed a breath, and a smile slowly crept over his face as his eyes searched mine. "Thank you."

"You don't have to thank me for saying something true." I planted a soft kiss on his lips, because being this close and *not* doing that was becoming impossible.

Before I knew what he was doing, he fell back on the bed, then pulled me down too, not that it took much convincing.

"Can I just stay here for a few minutes?" he asked, his arm around my shoulders pulling me close so my head could rest on his chest.

"Of course. You can stay 'til morning." A little drumbeat of anticipation picked up in my throat.

"I wish. But I'm actually going to go back to the office and work another few hours. Bauer wants this portfolio by end of day Friday, and I have a week's worth of work to do on it in the next three days."

He tucked his head to mine so I could feel his breath in my hair.

I wanted to reach up and tell him to stay. I wanted him to stop taking everything so squarely on his own shoulders and let someone help him, or just ease off the pressure. But I also knew this was him, and part of what I loved about him was that insistence on taking care of things, even if it drove me mad.

"All right. Just let me know when you have to go."

I continued to see Liam basically only in passing. We'd wanted to do something for our birthdays since they were so close, an excuse to carve out time together, but we were both swamped. It'd been a week since he'd stopped by and we'd snuggled together after talking.

He slowed things down for me in the best way. Preston had made me feel anxious all the time—I was doing too much, or too little, or not quite the right thing.

With Liam, we just... spent time together. We talked about what was going on in our lives, whether the picture was pretty or not. He saw me in ratty jeans or sweatpants more often than he did coordinated outfits and makeup, and he still seemed to like me.

Part of me remained baffled by that, even though all the logical parts of me knew that's how it was supposed to be. You weren't supposed to tiptoe around your significant other. You weren't supposed to feel like you had to earn your lover's love every day. That's a gift, and because it's a gift, you enjoy it, embrace it, and stay mindful of that person, but you don't turn yourself inside out to make him happy.

Liam made me happy, even when he was spiraling into his savior complex and overwhelmed by his situation. He made me want to comfort him and care for him.

He made me want to love him.

Well, I already did love him. But I wasn't running scared.

And this was the surprise. I hadn't expected to feel so much for him so soon. But I did. I'd known it for weeks now, but each interaction drilled it home, and I'd felt it welling up in me every time we were alone together. I wanted to tell him, and soon enough I'd end up blurting it out. But I didn't want that time to come in a moment when we were only seeing each other in passing.

So I was going to tell him I loved him when we got together to celebrate our birthdays next Tuesday. We both had busy weeks, then my weekend was slammed, so Tuesday it would have to be. He was putting the finishing touches on the details of his portfolio after lots of interaction from Bauer, and I knew he would finish it well.

I was meeting Bel and Leo for dinner again. I had a break in new arrivals, though I'd had weekends at capacity and also, happily, many weekdays at capacity. I'd heard things in town were going well too. I couldn't compare to seasons past, but a full inn, especially now that it was bigger by almost double, was a good sign in my book.

Before I made it to *Basta*, our destination for the night since Leo was demanding Italian food and none of us would argue *Basta*'s brilliance or appeal after our last glorious meal, I saw Liam shuffling down the street, shoulders hunched and collar pulled tight, lost in his own world.

Normally, he greeted everyone he passed, acting as a kind of honorary mayor of the town. He was charming, good-looking, and he seemed to enjoy it. But lately, whenever I'd seen him, he'd been inside himself.

"Liam? You okay?" I asked, setting a hand on his arm and startling him out of his focus.

"Wells, hi," he said, then leaned in to kiss my cheek. "Sorry, I'm scrambling to get back. I was going to grab some takeout from *Basta* but the place is slammed. I had to get out of the office."

"Everything okay?" I asked, noting his eyes looked darker than usual. The sun had set hours ago so it was dark, though we were under a streetlight and little flecks of snow shimmered down on top of us where we stood.

"I don't know." He let out a breath it seemed he'd been holding a while. "Bauer's not happy with the portfolio. He wants land. He wants hotel plans. He wants it to be a resort—one an investor can sink his teeth into. I get it, but we don't have it. We don't have the space. The forest would have to be cleared on the east side, and we don't want to encroach there anyway. Plus part of that is county property. Your land is to our southwest, and west is down... I'm not sure where I'm supposed to come up with it."

"That makes no sense. You guys are focused on the mountain—the skiing. Why the sudden emphasis on the land and the hotel?" That wasn't something I'd heard him mention before. Not specifically anyway.

"Bauer says it's what'll appeal to the kind of investor we want to attract. He says we've got to have the potential for growth, and the only way to do that in a place like this that takes so long to get to is to keep people here in rooms for days at a time."

"That does make sense. But isn't having other properties, like the inn, going to do that? And there are quite a few rental apartments coming available now that that's a popular thing."

Bel had even talked about converting the basement of her house to a small apartment she could rent out on sites like VacayStay.

"Evidently not. I don't know. I'm sorry, I'm scattered, and I've got a call with Bauer tomorrow to clarify some of this. Apparently, he's got someone who's interested and specifically asked about buildable land, both for rooms and for the lodge at base and midmountain. So we've got details to hammer through." He gripped his cap and scrubbed it around on his head, then let his gloved hand drop.

"I'm sorry. That's... frustrating." I wished I had some way to help—some smart thing to say to ease his mind or make the situation better.

"Don't be sorry. I'm glad we ran into each other." He ducked his head and kissed me softly. He backed away slowly, his eyes glittering in the lamplight. "I like you, Wells Bryant."

I grinned. "I like you, Liam Morrison. Even when you're stressed out and brain-fried."

He chuckled at that. "Well that's good news, because that's about all I am lately."

"Well, if it isn't the conquering hero, my big brother," Leo's voice cut in from behind me.

"Leo."

Clearly, they hadn't made peace. I wondered what dinner had in store for me and Bel—would it be Leo complaining about Liam? I wasn't up for that and said a silent prayer she wasn't either.

"We better go, Wells. Bel's already inside. I saw you down here and thought I'd come grab you." Leo turned and disappeared back down the sidewalk to the restaurant.

"I'll talk to you soon, okay? Let me know how it goes tomorrow, and I'll check in too. A week from today, we'll be having our birthday dinner and we'll have the whole night to ourselves." I hoped that bright spot would help him in some way.

"I can't wait."

~

We'd kept it surface level until the waiter left with our orders.

"Let me say now, I won't take sides. I've told Liam my opinion and I'll tell you, too. But I can't sit here and listen to you tell me anything negative about him." Okay, so that had come out a little strong.

Leo's eyes flared. "Okay. Good to know. Say your piece and we'll move on."

"He's doing the best he can. He thinks this is the right move, and based on what I know, he's right."

I watched Leo's face carefully, but she didn't betray her thoughts at all.

Leo was one of those people who was extremely expressive and very *out there* with her emotions if she wanted to be. If she didn't, then you'd have no idea what she was thinking.

"Good to know. And so we're clear, I disagree. I think he's going to end up selling off the lodge and everything my grandfather dreamed of building piece by piece until nothing's left. I think he'll do whatever he thinks he has to in order to get what he wants."

She stayed cool. Nothing of that fiery Leo I was used to shone through. If nothing else, that was the surprise.

Before I could stop myself, I asked, "What do you think he wants?"

She pursed her lips, then blew out a breath. "I think he wants to be the guy to save the day. In this case, he wants to save the family, maybe the town. It's not all bad, but I think he's scared of failing and can't see the whole picture."

"And you can, Leo?"

She looked at me then, with a ripple of something I couldn't recognize crossing her face just before she glanced away and took a drink.

Bel set her hands on the table. "Okay. That's done. Now what?"

I sat back, thankful for her intervention, but couldn't ignore the feeling in my gut that Leo had a point. Was she right about his blindness? I didn't think so, though most of my information had come from him.

But I trusted Liam to do what was right. He wasn't flawless, but he wasn't running around with bad intentions either.

Leo's mouth twitched. "Now we talk about you, Bel."

Bel's eyes shuttered. "There are much more interesting things to discuss than me."

"Never," Leo said sharply, and we all laughed.

"Seriously, I have nothing to report. I finished the ad campaign for the lodge for this season and sketched out some things going forward for summer and the anniversary. I'd love to do more marketing work, so I'm working on a website and looking at freelancing. But I like the coffee shop. Oh, and I think Gran has a boyfriend."

"A boyfriend? At, what, eighty-five?" I asked.

Bel's face lit up as she told us more.

"He's eighty-six. They've known each other for years, I guess. But the day she moved into the community, he started trying to sit by her and talk with her every day." Her eyes softened and filled, but she took a moment before she spoke. "He's really sweet to her."

"I'm glad, Bel. Gran's got game—I'm not surprised," Leo said.

I'd learned that for Bel, little was more important to her than her gran. Really, nothing was. Her parents were removed, and though Jamie was important in some sense, I wasn't sure it was in a positive way. She'd given up much of her life for Gran, and even in the six months we'd been friends, I knew she didn't regret it.

The joy she had for her Gran's love life was precious. But now that I was looking at life through the lens of having a healthy and satisfying relationship, I couldn't help but want that for my friends.

"It's great," Bel agreed.

Leo's whole demeanor changed then—just the oddest thing. She started to say something, but stopped.

Bel saw it and gave her a tight-lipped smile. "I know, Leo. I heard Grandpa Will talking about it yesterday."

"I should have told you when I found out. I just didn't want..." Leo trailed off.

Bel turned to me. "Jamie's coming back in March. For a while, sounds like."

Ah. No wonder. Leo wasn't delicate about anything but this one subject with her friend, and she wasn't always that way to begin with.

"Oh," was all I could say.

"It'll be fine. I'm busy. I'm guessing he'll be up at the lodge with Liam or... whatever."

She really did seem fine—wasn't looking thrown by it. Maybe because it was still over a month away, but I wondered if the other shoe would drop here. Even the *mention* of Jamie at other times was something that'd set her on edge, the color draining from her cheeks.

"He'll be busy. I think he's supposed to be writing a new album and told his manager the only way he'd do it by their deadline was if they left him alone and he did it here," Leo explained.

Jamie was a big deal—huge, but not surprising that he'd want to come here and step so far out of the limelight. Though, come to think of it, he wasn't all that big on the limelight, from what I'd seen in the past. He wasn't someone constantly showing up at parties or in the tabloids, though that's probably why when he *did* step out with someone, it made front page news.

He'd dated Whit Grantham, the country star, last year at some point. Maybe they were still together—who knew. I wasn't up on my celebrity gossip these days.

"He—that's good." Bel nodded.

I saw it then. That well of emotion that ran deep in her when it came to him.

"Ladies, your dinner is served." The waiter set our dishes down one by one.

"So, Wells, what are you and Liam doing for your birthdays?" Bel asked around a bite of penne fra diavolo. For as sweet and mild as she seemed, the woman loved spice.

"We're going to dinner Tuesday. He's swamped this week, and I have a big group coming in tomorrow, so we're putting it off a while longer. It's been a while since I've celebrated a birthday, so I'm excited," I said, happily digging into my spaghetti carbonara.

I only looked up when I realized the table had gone silent. When I did, they were both looking at me.

"Why haven't you celebrated?" Leo asked with narrowed eyes.

I waved my fork as I finished chewing the bite in my mouth. "Preston wasn't big on birthdays. And I wasn't great at ignoring that and doing what I wanted."

"I have a feeling that's putting it mildly."

"You're right. It was a bad situation. Birthdays were just one more thing he could control. But that's done, and I get to celebrate with Liam, a man I—"

Leo straightened. "A man you...."

"Care deeply about and enjoy a great deal," I said, then smiled at Bel as Leo rolled her eyes.

"I'm glad. You'll have to tell us how it goes." Bel smiled at me, then sent a pointed look at Leo.

And from there, we moved on, but I had the pleasant juxtaposition of last year and this year in my mind. Preston was sure to remind me birthdays weren't something to celebrate. *"Why should we make a big deal about you getting older? Who wants to celebrate that?"* The unspoken insinuation was I shouldn't be glad about it. I should be concerned, be doing whatever I could to counteract the entropy life was wearing on me.

I didn't feel bound to that in any way this year. I didn't feel anxious, other than anticipation. I couldn't wait to have uninterrupted time with Liam, who'd said, "Of course we'll celebrate. We get another year in this life—what's better than that?"

CHAPTER TWENTY

Liam

This was it. All my work had been sent off to Bauer early this morning, and in an hour, I'd be sitting down to a video conference to see what he thought. His investor was eager to get the ball rolling too, so had blocked out his morning to review the portfolio and confer with him. Then Bauer would relay the results to me.

God, please let it be good news. I'd found myself chanting this prayer all day, begging for this to be the end of the desperation.

But some part of me knew I wasn't heading for the easy answer. Bauer would have news, but it wouldn't be a simple yes. It was never simple, not in real life, and I was bracing for it.

At the same time, my rational side was fleeing. I could feel it, a feeling I'd only felt one other time, during a deployment while on active duty. I'd been awake for more than twenty-four hours at the time, and had the sense I wasn't sure everything I was doing was right, or real, or mattered. And *that* freaked me out. Fortunately, I'd had a smart commander who'd pulled me out and made me sleep rather than take watch, and we all survived.

This wasn't the same—of course, this wasn't war. And I wasn't under *that* kind of pressure—I wasn't worrying about keeping men alive in the night, eking out another day without casualties during the fighting season in Afghanistan.

But I felt the same wildness, the same sense of surreality. I was exhausted, stretched thin by stress, lack of nutrition, lack of sleep. I'd let it all pile up on my shoulders and like an idiot, I'd let it stay there.

And now, I had to deal with it. I had to finish well, at least this part well, but... could I?

I debated trying to take a power nap, but couldn't sleep. A to-do list a mile long waited for me, and I could barely make out my own handwriting on my calendar. I needed to start digitizing my stuff. I needed to get more organized.

I needed to get a life made up of more than lists and organization and stress.

The thing was, I had it. I had that life, and I wanted *more* of it. If anything, getting close with Wells had made that all the clearer. I wanted less stress, more passion, less monotony, more challenge. Yes, what I'd been doing these last few years had been a challenge, but a challenge for someone else's dream. It's remarkably hard to take satisfaction in toil when it's not toiling for your own crop.

"Dude, what are you doing?" Danny's voice came from the doorway of my office.

I groaned unintelligibly.

A faint chuckle and footsteps came, then the sound of his body hitting the chair across from me. "Go ahead, then."

I raised my head, not having realized I'd let it fall to rest on my desk in the first place. "I'm smoked. I've gotta get my act together for this meeting, and I'm just..."

I felt my eyes glaze over again.

"You're in bad shape. Here's what we're going to do. First, you need to go shower. Make it a cold one—quick and dirty, in and out. Put on fresh clothes. I'll go grab you a few shots of espresso in the caf and meet you back here in ten minutes. Then you're going to talk through everything you need to say to Bauer, and then you're going to do it again. Then you're going to go outside and stare at our mountain for five minutes, and then we're going to go into that meeting and you're going to kill it."

I blinked at him, absorbing the fact that my little ski bum of a brother had just crafted a plan—any kind of plan— for *my* success.

He clapped his hands in front of my face. "What are you doing, man? *Go.*"

Forty-five minutes later, I'd followed Danny's directions to a T. I'd showered in bitterly cold water, dressed in a suit instead of my usual jeans and a button-up, taken the espresso and a banana he'd forced me to eat, and we'd rehearsed all the points I might need to make if Bauer found fault in any given part of my portfolio. Of course Bauer finding fault would really mean the investor had, which raised the stakes.

I banished that thought. Now wasn't the time to drum up more nerves. The time had come to focus.

"You're prepared. You've done what you could, and now we see how things fall," Danny said, still completely nonchalant even as he'd taken the reins from me.

"Easy for you to say. You're not the one who'll be blamed for losing the place when it goes under in eighteen months," I grumbled.

He stood up and leaned on his hands against my desk. "It'll be just as much my fault as yours, brother. You've done the work while I ran around not taking responsibility. I get that, and I'm sorry for it. I can't change the way I've been for... well, for most of my life. All I can say is I'll step up if we get to keep this place long enough for me to do so. You can share the burden, if you can figure out how."

Where was this months ago? And for that matter, who was this version of Danny?

"What brought this about?" I asked, sure I sounded completely baffled by his speech, but I couldn't hide that. If that hurt him, sorry, but I couldn't help that this was anti-thetical to who he'd been.

He sat in his chair and leaned back. "A lot. I've been changing, but I haven't been letting you or hardly anyone see. But I get that I've set myself on the sidelines, and I'm done. If I care about something, I'm going to work hard to keep it. And so this is me officially saying I care about the lodge, and the mountain, and I want to work with you to keep it."

I scrubbed my hand over my beard. "Dan, man, I wish you'd come to this revelation a few months ago. *Years* ago, even."

"I know. Crap timing, but there it is. So tell me what to do."

"You've done it, for today. Now go into that meeting and help me keep it together, and hopefully we'll be walking out of there and popping champagne because we've got good news. And if not, help me figure out plan D."

"Plan B?"

"No. At this point, we're at plan D. Or maybe F. I don't know. Whatever it is, we'll work on that if we need to."

I felt it then—my determination that had been lagging and weak snapped into place.

"That sounds like you're planning on this going wrong." Danny folded his arms and eyed me.

I stood up, a burst of energy, or caffeine, hitting me in that moment. "You know, you're right. We're going in there, and we're going to make this happen, whatever it takes. We're coming out of there with an investor and our mountain taken care of."

Danny's smile was bright. "Let's do this."

Leo slipped in last minute. I felt my eye twitch, but gave her a nod in welcome, determined to be the bigger man/sibling.

Danny had been an incredible support in the last hour, and even though it was about as eleventh-hour as he could get, it proved valuable to me. If Leo could get on board, maybe we'd have a chance at dealing with this problem if this whole thing with Bauer fell apart.

But it wouldn't. It wasn't going to fall apart. Danny and I had decided we'd do what it took to get this thing nailed down, and as long as Bauer had even remotely good news, we'd push it through. We could be flexible. We could bend in places and get this investor locked in.

The conference started and Bauer appeared in front of us in his usual full dark suit, white shirt, and no tie, sitting at a circular glass table, Ms. Ritter to his right, and his admin to his left—notably beautiful women, if one were noting such things.

Leo's back was stick straight. I figured we were all mastering our posture with this meeting.

"Good to see you, Mr. Bauer. Ms. Ritter. Ms. Smart," I greeted.

"Mr. Morrison. Mr. Morrison," Bauer said to me and Danny as he reached for a folder on the table. Then his eyes shot to Leo. "Ms. Morrison."

Leo didn't acknowledge his greeting. *Great.* That's all we needed. The volcano in the room piping away, gearing up for a late-game explosion. Though she didn't seem particularly volatile today... she seemed thoughtful.

After a few more greetings from Danny and Ms. Ritter, we commenced.

"The investor we've found is extremely interested. He's practically ready to sign. He pointed out a few things here and there, but if we can address them, I'm guessing he's in for the full proposed amount."

I sat back, stunned. This was better than I could have imagined.

"That's great news." Danny slapped me on the back.

"Yes, great. Let's dive into those questions or issues he has so we can get it tied up," I said, all too eager to see an investor's name on a contract.

We'd have an endless list of things to hash out before that—particularly the level of control the investor would have.

Some of that was outlined in the portfolio, as Bauer had advised, but he'd specifically suggested we keep some of it vague to allow for negotiations at the time of signing.

Based on where we were, and the news he'd just given, the man knew his stuff. I'd known it. I'd been told. Even

Wells had assured me he had an impeccable reputation in Colorado. But I'd been doubting everything, including Bauer, despite Wells' opinion and his resume. This was good.

We talked through a few small things—negligible. Things we could manage, or change, or could give on. Even Leo was nodding here and there in approval of the suggested change.

"And finally, the land," Bauer said, rimless glasses perched on his nose as he tapped at his computer.

"Land?" I asked, feeling my stomach line with lead, my pulse pick up.

"The only parcel of land you've listed as a possible buildable stretch is one that would need to be cleared. The investor is concerned about the growth potential as it presents higher costs and a slower timeline." He looked right into the video camera and pulled his glasses off as though we needed him to do that in order to see him better. "The investor requests land alternatives."

There it was.

There it is.

What I'd been dreading—this very section. This very item. This issue, which I couldn't get around.

"We can't change the mountain, or the fact that the buildable land has a forest on it. It's part of what makes the area so beautiful." As though Danny's sweet, naïve logic would matter.

"Indeed," Ms. Ritter agreed genially. She'd been on board with Silver Ridge for a while now and had been largely positive. Evidently, this was Bauer's show today, so her input had been minimal.

"Danny's right. There's not much we can do about this—"

"If that's true, I'm afraid there might be a risk to the investor's interest," Bauer cut in.

"We've got it outlined there—it only creates a few months' extra work. In the long term, that's not untenable," I argued, hoping he'd agree though I knew he wouldn't since obviously the investor found it problematic.

"There is more land. I've seen it." Bauer's voice emerged sharp, though as calm as ever.

"Where are you thinking, Jonas?" Ms. Ritter asked him. She wasn't clued into his perspective on this, and that comment showed.

But Bauer didn't betray any sense of agitation. He looked into the camera. "On the southwest side of the property, there is space. Not the base—below where the lodge and gondola meet. It's ideal for a hotel."

My pulse pounded in my throat, in my head. That was Wells' land. There was no way to get it.

"That's Wells Bryant's land," Leo said, her voice granite.

"Indeed. But from what I understand, you are quite close with Ms. Bryant, and she might be given to negotiating, for the right price." Bauer's eyes moved from Leo's glare to me.

Wrong. All of this was wrong. In no way could the future of my family's legacy, of my town's livelihood, rest on land inherited by a woman who hadn't stepped foot in Silverton before this year. Land I'd intended to acquire all along.

"That's Wells' land, and it's got nothing to do with us," Leo said.

Danny was moving his head, trying to catch her eye, likely to stave off another yelling departure. My mind was a rush of thoughts, a jumbled wreck, but before I thought better of it, I said, "I could probably talk to her. We're close. I—I could talk to her."

If the room hadn't been silent before, it was now. Leo's head snapped to me and I saw the fire in her eyes, the fury in her pinched lips and the set of her jaw.

Bauer let us hang there for a moment, glancing between me and Leo before responding. "Good. Then we'll move forward on that contingency, and I'll push the paperwork through the investor's office as quickly as I can. I'll send over the documents for your review as well."

He was all business, wrapping up, and likely completely unaware that he'd tossed a grenade into our conference room and instead of jumping on it myself, I'd tossed it to Wells, unbeknownst to her.

The Bauer Group said their goodbyes, and the screen went dark.

"You're even worse than I thought," Leo said, quiet and firm, as she left.

I sat there, staring at the screen for a while before Danny got up and left without a word. Maybe he didn't have anything to say. Maybe he couldn't stand to speak to me.

What should I have done? Let the whole deal fall apart?

I'd done what I'd set out to do—I'd secured our investor. That it hadn't been as clean-cut as I wanted, I couldn't control. Bauer was good at this, and he knew what he wanted, how to get it for the investor, and he'd done it.

But he was working for us—he was doing what we'd asked him, and he was good. I could tell. I could feel it.

But as I left the conference room and walked back to my house, I felt it. I knew what I'd done.

How am I going to tell Wells? How am I going to convince her to sell me that land?

She wanted to build on that land. But she didn't have the capital, or even the knowledge, as far as I knew. Maybe we could team up; we could do it together. It could be a joint venture. Or maybe... maybe she'd be happy to sell it, once she knew who it was going to and that it'd benefit the town, even bring more people to her business if the hotel was full.

If you think that makes sense, you're an idiot.

I argued with myself all the way back to the house, through shoving a peanut butter and jelly sandwich in my face to calm my jittering nerves.

I wasn't sitting there at the bar in my kitchen, shoving a stale PB&J down my throat because I was upset. My hand wasn't visibly shaking because I'd just made the biggest mistake of my life, probably.

No. Had to be that espresso.

CHAPTER TWENTY-ONE

Wells

Liam was surprisingly tight-lipped about how his meeting had gone. When I'd messaged him to check how things went with his big meeting last night after I'd gotten in bed, he'd sent me a few short sentences.

"Went well. Will fill you in tomorrow night. Sleep well."

He'd been running on fumes lately, and I knew that, so I couldn't blame him. And I didn't think too much about it, though it had been less warm than our usual exchanges. Usually, he let simple chats like that slide into some flirting or sweet mentions of how he'd been thinking of me or hoped I was doing well, just thoughtful things like that.

But I couldn't blame him for being a little short on the words at this point in his long day. He'd been working non-stop—one reason we were both so eager for our date tonight.

The last few days had been moving like sloths were at the wheel.

I was taking a break for some afternoon coffee, a quick breath of fresh air to pop in and say hi to Bel before I went back to the inn to wrap up business and officially take off for at least twelve hours.

I was already vibrating with excitement. No doubt a cappuccino was unnecessary, but I was restless.

"Wells, how's it going?" Wyatt's deep voice came from across the street just as I stepped up to the bright entrance of the shop.

He jogged over to meet me.

"Hey, cousin. I'm good. It's great to see you," I said, that warm sense of comfort he brought with him everywhere he went shrouding me as he bent down to hug me.

"Just in town for some errands today. You?" he asked as he stepped back and surveyed me.

"Grabbing coffee. You want some?" I asked and nodded toward the door.

"Sure." He held the door open for me. He was old-fashioned and thoughtful that way. I wondered, if he ever went out with Leo, if she'd let him do that for her or not.

I was surprised to see the table where the veterans normally gathered around this time every day was empty.

"Where are the guys?" I asked Bel as we approached the counter.

She handed a customer his coffee and smiled at me. "Hey, Wells. Hi, Wyatt. Good to see you."

She turned on her lovely smile and I didn't have to look to know Wyatt was charmed. Everyone was charmed by Bel.

"So? Where are the vets?" I asked, a surprising disappointment settling in me.

I always enjoyed catching them in action, greeting them, stealing a few moments to chat with Grandpa Will. Anyone who was close to Liam held an allure for me, but Grandpa Will was a legend in many senses—it felt special to have his attention.

"They've started having breakfast on Tuesdays. Sadie's got some new breakfast dishes that one of them had and raved about, so now they do breakfast Tuesday and Thursday and coffee the rest of the days," Bel explained. "What can I get for you?"

I ordered my cappuccino and offered to buy Wyatt's coffee.

"Absolutely not. I'll buy yours."

"So old-fashioned," Leo said from behind us, and Wyatt visibly jumped, then blushed furiously.

"Not all that. Just aware that Wells here is working hard to build a business where I've established mine. Plus, I'm older." His eyes darted to Leo, then me, then back to Leo.

"Well, all right then. Go ahead and order yours so I can order mine," she said, and even though Leo was upfront, her level of impatience was surprising.

Wyatt turned to Bel and I heard him mumble "Large black coffee please, Bel," as I turned to Leo.

"What's wrong?" I asked, eyeing her more closely and noting the redness in her cheeks, the slightly wild flare to her eyes.

"I need to talk to you." Her voice held more urgency than I'd ever heard.

"Is everything okay?"

"No. Which is why I need to talk to you." She pressed her lips firmly together.

"Okay, go for it."

"I need some water, and I'll come sit with you." She

dropped her voice and looked to her left at a table of tourists. "I don't think we want this to be too public."

Bel said my name quietly, handed me a bright blue mug and saucer with snow-capped mountains drizzled into the foam of the drink. I resisted the frantic feeling in my chest, refused to wonder what had Leo so off-kilter, and joined Wyatt at a table near the door, away from the tourists. He nodded at me as I sat down.

Leo arrived soon after.

"You want to wait 'til later?" she asked, clearly irritated with Wyatt's presence.

"We were going to have coffee—can you go ahead and tell me?" I scooted my chair closer to the table and cupped the rounded mug in both my hands.

Leo glanced at Wyatt. "None of this goes anywhere, got it?"

He agreed with a nod. "Understood."

She sipped her water, glanced out the window to the street, then centered her bright blue Morrison eyes on me. "The meeting with Bauer went well, until it didn't. He put pressure on us for more land and asked about the land to the southwest."

I straightened in my seat. "That's my land."

She nodded slowly, jaw tight. "Yep. But Liam suggested he might be able to get you to sell it to him."

I swallowed and set down the mug. "What?"

"He said he was close to you. Could probably make it happen." Her lips flattened into an invisible line.

"I—we've never talked about that," I said, my voice shaken. My heart was pounding now, but all I heard was a slow rush in my ears.

"I'm surprised. He told me over a year ago he wanted to

approach Grandma about selling it to him," Wyatt said, assessing my response from his seat.

"No. No, he's never..."

Wyatt shrugged. "I don't know what to tell you, Wells. He's always wanted that land. Now it sounds like he plans to get it."

Hours later, I sat in the cabin. I'd excused myself from the table at *Rise and Shine*, burst out the door holding my winter jacket and scarf, and mechanically layered myself with my clothes as I walked back to the inn.

I'd told Anthony I was done for the day. I'd planned to help him with our version of happy hour—beer, wine, and enough food to make it legal in the eyes of the state—then go change, but I couldn't think of anything.

Nothing.

I trampled down the path to the cottage, the one I'd lovingly restored all these months. The roof still needed work so I couldn't live there until things thawed and they could reroof, but they'd covered it and sealed it well enough to keep the work I'd done on the inside safe, and Liam and I had agreed we'd spend the night there.

Before I knew what Liam was.

Before I'd figured out I was an idiot, *yet again*, and had let a man use me for his own purposes.

The thought rang hollow in my heart, but my head couldn't ignore the facts.

Wyatt said he'd wanted the land for a year—maybe longer, who knew.

Leo said he'd told Bauer he could get it.

My fists clenched so hard, my nails left crescent indentations in my palm. Good that I'd forgotten my gloves, so my hands were numb. Part of me wished the nails would pierce the skin and draw blood to better show my rage.

That's what I felt.

Blinding, engulfing *rage*.

How could I have done this again? How could I fall for this prince charming swill? Why did I ever let myself care about this man who I knew would do anything to keep his family's legacy afloat, no matter how many icebergs threatened to sink it?

After an hour staring out at nothing, the shadow of Silver Ridge in the corner of my eye, I made my way inside. I showered, changed into the little black dress I'd planned on. It didn't make sense for me to change, or bother, because as soon as he showed up, I'd kick him out.

The old Wells in me wanted to text him, tell him I was sick, couldn't see him. She wanted to avoid the situation, curl up and wallow in the hurt, anger, disappointment.

The new Wells, the one that'd been shoved around for far too long, said it was *enough*. This was ending tonight, and there would be no question as to who the land belonged to and who it would stay with.

And there'd be no question Liam Morrison and I were done for good.

I'd been staring in the mirror for a few minutes when Liam's knock came. Not exactly in a trance, but my mind was blank. My rage had distilled into focus—get through this face to face, say my piece, and say goodbye. I knew the aftermath would be ugly, so I'd let myself go through the motions of getting ready—shower, dress, hair, makeup. It had calmed me and also felt like a kind of armor.

I smoothed down the dress and clacked across the wood floor of the cottage to the door.

When I swung it open, a handsome, miserable Liam stared back at me. His beard and hair were trimmed. Under his jacket, now unzipped, his shirt was a deep blue that made his eyes look endless. He wore black slacks and nice shoes and a belt. He was all dressed up for me.

My stupid heart gave a double beat at the sight of him, but I locked it down with a grit of my teeth.

"Hi."

The black smudges under his eyes revealed maybe he hadn't slept like a baby after his choice to betray me yesterday. *Maybe.*

I stepped back without a word and let him walk past me. He set a bag of takeout on a small eating nook at the back.

He turned to face me, not moving to touch me, and I was startled by the look on his face.

"I need to talk with you."

So he wasn't going to pretend it hadn't happened. That was something.

Or he knows Leo told you.

"Okay." I crossed my arms, still standing a few feet from him.

"The meeting with Bauer... it didn't go as planned."

I wondered whether that was true. Whether he'd somehow known the Bauer Group's chosen investor would push for land and that he'd need me to get it, or if he was simply disappointed it'd happened in that way and not on his own terms.

I didn't respond. I wasn't giving him anything—he'd taken enough.

He pulled in a breath. "They wanted land. I'd proposed clearing behind the lodge and to the north, had hoped that'd be sufficient. But the investor didn't like the time delay clearing would cause. They wanted the land southwest of the lodge."

"My land."

He nodded. "Your land."

"And?"

"And I led them to believe I could get it."

The room was silent but for the racing of my heart. I hadn't expected him to lay it out like that—to not soften what he'd done.

"Why?"

"Because it was clear that if I hadn't, the investor would have walked. Bauer made it clear the land was a deal breaker, and I didn't want the deal to break. You know I've been—"

"I know," I said, my voice low, shaken. I didn't need him to remind me how important this deal was to him. That wasn't the issue.

He stood there, his shoulders slightly hunched, his brow pinched. Finally, he spoke again. "I'm sorry I said it."

I jerked. "Why?"

"Because I shouldn't have. I shouldn't have made them think I could use our relationship to get your land. Or that I *would*. I was backed into a corner and did the only thing I could think of, but it was the wrong thing. I know that."

My heart begged me to listen. It urged me to notice that desperate, regretful look, that pleading shade in his voice.

My mind told me what I knew—he was still trying to make it happen. Even now, in this room, he was still working me. Trying to make it seem like he hadn't meant to hurt me, maybe assuming that if I felt sorry enough for him, if I let myself cave to the compassion and love I had for him, that he *had* to know I had for him, then I'd offer up the land, offer to sell, and solve all his problems.

My voice and words were sharp when I spoke. "You've always wanted the land."

"True. I'd planned to talk to Tilda about it a year ago. And I'd planned to talk to you about it when we met," he admitted.

Something about hearing him say it felt like a knife in my belly, threatening to rip me open.

"But you didn't. You never did. This was a better way for you to get what you wanted." My hands shook with anger now.

"What? No. I saw how much this place meant to you. And even after that, I admit, I thought maybe you'd sell the land and focus here and not on that parcel, but then you told me your dream of expanding, using that land, and I knew I couldn't ask you to sell. I knew you wouldn't."

His eyes were bright, almost shocked.

Like he wanted me to believe he was innocent, a well-meaning Captain America just like everyone in town thought he was.

"Of course you didn't ask outright. Where's the fun in that? I'd tell you no, and there'd be no further discussion. But this way... *This way*, you get to seem like the guy who needs saving, you get to wrap me up in sweet gestures and your nice family and your perfect little town and make me think you care about me, just to then come ask this *one little thing* of me."

I was nearly spitting. The rage had returned, but

watching him react to me, the shock and hurt on *his* face, had my own heart throbbing, aching in response.

Stupid, feckless heart.

"No. No—that's not what... Wells, *no*."

He stepped toward me, but I stepped back. I didn't want his hands on me, didn't want anything of him near me.

"You should go. We're done here."

The tears weren't far off. I didn't want to cry a single one for him, but my mind was all cymbals crashing, my blood surging to every part, dizzying me with the emotions of the day.

"No. Wells, please. Talk to me. This isn't me manipulating you. I didn't have some master plan to fall in love with you and use our relationship to get a piece of land. This is insane."

He ran a hand through his hair, eyes searching the room for who knew what.

"Is it?" I walked to the door and opened it.

I heard him let loose a breath, then grab his coat and plod after me. He stopped on the threshold.

"I know I messed up. I'm sorry. I can't go back and change what I said, but I will make this right. I hope you'll get to a place where you can remember I'm *me*, and not *him*."

He slid his arms into the jacket and jogged down the stairs, then began the slow walk back to the inn on a packed snowy path, somehow not faltering even in his dress shoes.

~

Hours later, I hadn't let the tears fall. All I felt was angry.

He was blaming me for this. Ultimately, that's what he

was doing. He said he was sorry, but that didn't fix anything. That did *nothing*, in the long run.

And that parting shot—that he hoped I could remember he was him, and not Preston.

How dare he?

How dare he accuse me of forgetting who he was? I knew him. Or I'd thought I did. What I did know? He was a man who'd do anything to save the day, and sure enough, he'd done it. When the hard moment had come, he'd sacrificed our relationship in order to secure his family's business an investor.

"I didn't have some master plan to fall in love with you and use our relationship to get a piece of land."

How dare he slip that in, too? He tells me for the first time he loves me in that context? Just another way of manipulating me. Of making me feel like I should bend, like I was in the wrong.

I sat there on the bed, still in my dress, the smell of cold Italian takeout stale in the room, and shut my eyes against the sweep of sadness that threatened to gut me.

I knew better than that. I knew there was nothing wrong in seeing this situation for what it was—he'd been positioning me to be useful to him when he'd need me. Well, the time had come, but it was a bit too soon. I wasn't so far gone on him I couldn't say no, or couldn't recognize the problem.

That he'd apologized and said he'd make it right didn't matter. That he *was* a different person from Preston, and as far as I knew hadn't done anything else to manipulate me, didn't compute. All I could see was that he'd wanted that land for a year, and I'd waltzed in, a willing target for his charm and smile and too-long hair curling over his collar.

What a fool.

CHAPTER TWENTY-TWO

Liam

As though I needed help confirming that my blurting out that I could leverage my relationship with Wells to get her land wasn't the dumbest thing I'd ever done, she'd helped clarify things.

She thought this had been my game all along.

To what? Charm her, date her, and steal her land? I had no way of doing that in the first place. I wouldn't have thought I'd end up dating her based on her reaction to me the first month we'd known each other, let alone that I'd fall in love with her, want her with every part of me.

Damn it.

It was too late to call Bauer, but as soon as I hoofed it back to the lodge, I e-mailed him and asked for a meeting the next day. I had one thing left to do, and it had to be done quickly.

The other question was how she'd found out, but I

didn't really have to ask that question. Leo had probably run right to her and told her.

I couldn't blame my sister—not entirely. I just wished she had a little more faith in me. Did she really believe I meant it? Did she think I thought I could finagle the land from Wells if Wells didn't want to sell it? Had she met the woman?

But the worst part of all this? A not-small part of me had felt confident that Wells would be angry with me, but also that she would listen. And she would see I was sorry, that I was miserable with what I'd done, and that I didn't want to continue with that plan if it meant sacrificing what she and I had.

But she clearly didn't have qualms about that. She thought she knew what kind of man I was, and it wasn't a pretty picture. That stung.

More than stung—a punch to the gut.

The maddening thing was, I couldn't fully deny it. I *had* wanted that land. I'd introduced myself to her with the purpose of ultimately asking her if she was going to sell. I soon learned that wasn't going to be an option, and once I untied my tongue and remembered how to talk after meeting her, we'd become friends.

I knew much of her response was because of her history. But I couldn't blame it all on that. Some of it was my piss-poor choices the last few days, and I could own up to that.

What I couldn't accept was that we were outright done. She hadn't given me a chance—hadn't let herself remember who I was, and who I wasn't. I prayed, with time, she would.

For now, it was time to track down Bauer. By the time I woke this morning, I knew I had to clarify that I didn't think I'd get the land—that I had no intention of trying to. But of course, I couldn't get to Bauer—he was flying transatlantic for something and was out all day—wouldn't be available until tomorrow.

So I e-mailed him again. Said we needed to talk—that I could keep it short, but that I had to talk to him.

And I paced. And waited. And pulled my hair out strand by strand at my desk, letting the weight of my idiocy sink in.

I could defend the choice with thoughts of my desperation, my loyalty to my family, my thinking it was just talk and not that meaningful for me to say I would use my relationship with her, but the truth was, none of those things made it okay. Perhaps human, but still a mistake, and one I had to make right.

The reality that this move—my taking back what I said —could both ruin this investor's interest and my relationship with Bauer, came second only to my concern that Wells might not, in the end, forgive me.

I dragged myself to bed after sending the e-mail and woke feeling exhausted—the restless five hours I'd gotten having done nothing to quell the anxiety, the sadness, the general sense that I'd failed everyone I cared about.

The interminable hours of the morning crept by. Danny stopped by for just a minute, but kept his visit short. He knew what was wrong, and I was sure he didn't need to guess it hadn't gone over well with Wells. Maybe he'd seen Leo; maybe they'd talked about it—or maybe he was intuitive enough to know not to ask.

Whatever the case, I was relieved to see him, and relieved when he left. I wished Leo would come and talk to me—give me a chance to explain what'd been going through my head and what I planned to do about it. But she wouldn't. She'd shun me for a while before she came to skewer me, and I'd be ready by then.

At one that afternoon, Bauer called.

"I understand you need to speak with me," he said, all inflection absent.

"Yes. I need to clarify that I have no intention of using my relationship with Wells Bryant to get the land we discussed. She has plans for it, will not sell, and I will not exploit our situation to that end."

Bauer was silent on the other end, as he often was when absorbing something, not unlike John.

I cleared my throat. "I understand this may drastically change the investor's interest, but if that's the case, then we'll look elsewhere."

An unusual show of exhaustion from Bauer, a sigh broke over the sound. "I am certain this will change the situation. I will be in touch soon—after my meetings here—with any possible alternatives."

"I'll look forward to that."

It was a surprisingly calm, normal discussion. Bauer could understate, so perhaps his certainty this would change things meant he wouldn't touch Silver Ridge with a ten-foot pole nor would anyone else, but it almost sounded like he'd approved of what I'd said. That didn't make any sense whatsoever, but the best I could hope for was Bauer sticking with us and finding someone else.

So that's what I'd hope for.

The week dragged on with a vengeance. By Friday, I called Bauer's office to learn when he'd return to the states so I'd have a better sense of when I might hear from him. The not knowing all this time had started to further chip away at my ability to sleep or eat or do anything.

I'd done what I could to fix the mistake I'd made regarding the land, and soon, I'd track down Wells and we'd have it out. Or I hoped we would.

I hadn't seen her since Tuesday night. I hadn't expected to, but I had gone to *Rise and Shine* for coffee and some bread once, just to get out of the office, and I'd hoped to see her.

No such luck. And probably for the best because seeing her in public after the events of Tuesday wasn't exactly ideal.

Part of me wanted to stomp through the door at the inn and demand she sit down and talk with me. Listen to me. *Me.* Because so much of her hurt was coming from her past, not from what had actually happened. I knew if she could separate out what I'd done, what an idiot I'd admittedly been, we could get past this.

But I was also angry with her for that—for conflating this situation with what she'd been through. That wasn't fair to her, even though her shutting me out and refusing to see my perspective, my penitence, wasn't fair to me.

So I was waiting. I thought maybe if I got things resolved with Bauer, I'd feel more level-headed and could approach her more calmly. Or maybe she'd come to me.

I doubted that. But still. Maybe she would.

Sunday evening, still dressed in her ski boots and snow pants after an extended private lesson with a wealthy client who only took lessons with her, Leo knocked on my front door. I'd ducked out of the office early since it was a Sunday and I'd been working all hours every day anyway.

"How'd it go?" I asked, hoping we could slide into the

larger conversation after some business-focused pleasantries.

"Well enough."

"Did he hit on you?" The guy wasn't old, though he was definitely a decade Leo's senior at least, but the way he looked at her... it was intense.

I'd asked her a year ago when he started taking lessons if he ever did anything inappropriate or if he made her uncomfortable, but she'd said no, they got along fine, and he took instruction well.

"I always feel like he's... never mind. That's not why I'm here." She stepped through the door and kept walking, straight to the kitchen, while I shut the door.

"I figured not." I moved to get her a glass for water. "Go ahead. Let me have it."

She slumped onto a bar stool and dragged the glass over the granite bar top to rest in front of her. She stared into the crystal water—exceptional since it came from a mountain spring purified locally—and then took several long drinks.

She set the glass down. "You're an idiot."

I couldn't help the half-smile that pulled at my mouth. "I know."

"You never should have said anything. You should have told him, in the moment, it wasn't a possibility. You're not the kind of jerk who would do something like this, and I don't know where—"

"Before you get too wound up, let me say I've already contacted Bauer and told him the land isn't an option, that I shouldn't have said anything. I've also apologized to Wells and told her I was going to make it right, though that was before I'd been able to get in touch with Bauer and actually *do* anything. And finally, I know it was stupid. It lacked integrity in a way that makes me want to punch myself, and

I hate myself for ever saying it, and then for not taking it back right away."

Leo's eyes widened, and she jerked back just a bit. "Wow. Okay. That was a far more thorough response than I was expecting."

I chuckled at her shock. "What were you expecting?"

Her eyes searched the kitchen, then landed on me. "I don't know. Something a little more diplomatic, a little more *I did what had to be done.*"

"I didn't. I did something stupid and desperate and wrong. But not irrevocable, and not something that I can't atone for by changing my tune, which I've done." I leaned my forearms on the counter across from her.

"Always Captain America, aren't you?" she said, but without her usual irritation or bite.

"I'm just trying to figure out what to do. It hasn't been easy," I said, feeling a slice of hurt at the way she'd been so antagonistic through this process.

Her lips thinned into a frown.

"I know." She let loose a sigh. "I do know that, Liam. And I'm not trying to fight you on everything. I just happen to disagree with every decision you've made in the last six months or so, and I can't not voice that."

"Oh, just the last six months?"

A corner of her mouth quirked up. "Well, at *least* the last six months."

"I wouldn't want you to stop voicing your opinion. It's valuable. You know your stuff, and you care about the lodge. But I know my stuff too, and I'm looking at it from as many angles as I can."

"I didn't come here to get into this." She ducked her head and unzipped her fleece halfway, then pulled the zipper back up.

"Why did you come?"

"I came to say I'm sorry I told Wells. I'm sure that… messed some things up for you. And I am sorry about that, because I do think you're good for each other." She pulled on one of the long braids that snaked over her shoulder.

"Yeah, that was pretty crappy," I said, running a hand through my hair. "It's not that I wasn't going to tell her. I was. But I think she spent the time between when you told her and when I saw her Tuesday night figuring out all the ways I'd betrayed her and spent our relationship manipulating her to get this land. I hope you know, that's not why I was ever with her, or why—"

"I know that, Liam. I know I don't give you much credit, but I do know you're not like that. And not like the guy before you." Her eyes darkened a bit.

It wasn't a surprise Wells had told Leo, and probably Bel too, about Preston. I was glad she had their support.

"When did you tell her?" I asked, needing to know how long it took for the thing I'd done to turn into poison in her mind.

Leo tugged that pigtail again but looked upset. "She was getting coffee with Wyatt that afternoon. I saw her—I'd been looking for her once my afternoon lesson ended early —and blurted it out, right in front of Wyatt."

"Damn, Leo. You really went for it," I said quietly, feeling extremely angry but also knowing it wasn't her fault. Not truly.

She nodded. "I did. And I'm sorry. I should have circled back to talk to you—to make sure you were going to tell her, and talk to Bauer, and I didn't do that. I'm sorry."

"Thanks. I'm sorry I railroaded in and said something so stupid—that I didn't stand up to Bauer and just tell him no, even if it meant losing the investor."

Leo stood. "Will we lose him now?"

"Yes. And probably any interest the Bauer Group had in us right along with him," I admitted, despite the seemingly positive conversation I'd had with Bauer just days ago.

It hadn't seemed dire, but I'd settled into the reality that it wasn't going to turn out. We didn't have what he or any investor he dug up wanted.

Leo's jaw clenched, a look of sheer determination on her face when she said, "I don't know about that."

"We'll see soon enough. I'm pretty sure he'll contact me by Tuesday and we'll have a better sense of what's coming—or not coming."

Leo looked at me, then around the room, then back to me, her eyes slightly squinted. I knew that look—her *don't mess with me* look.

"Let me know what you hear."

With that, she was gone—back out the door, no coat since she'd come without one, and I was left to think about her exit.

Relief flooded in knowing we'd made peace—at least a tentative one. I was sure she wouldn't want another investor in the same way she hadn't wanted this one, but maybe she saw that we could find someone who wouldn't ask us to change everything—who wouldn't ask us to compromise so much of our family's legacy and the history of the place in favor of shiny and new.

At least one small thing in my life was repaired—my relationship with my sister. In part. We wouldn't ever be close, not in the way me and Jamie, or she and Danny were, but we were family, and it felt a little more like it now.

～

No word from Wells. I'd texted a few times over the last week—it'd been a week since it'd all blown up. I'd kept it simple—saying I wanted to talk with her when she was ready. That when she was, I'd need her to tell me, because I wasn't going to force it.

It sounded very noble, but it was hardly that. Also not easy. She lived a little over ten minutes away from me on foot, and we lived in the same town with a population of a few thousand. We were bound to run into each other, and if I saw her, I wasn't about to turn the other way.

I was getting the sense that desperation would be the new theme of my life. First desperate to save the lodge, and now that that had turned into a daily endeavor, desperate to see the woman I loved. To touch her. To kiss her. To get to be with her without this giant festering *issue* between us.

No luck. Not a word. Not a whisper from Leo or Bel, not a text, nothing.

I'd nearly picked up my phone to call her, was about to make the call, but my office phone rang instead.

"Hello?"

"Mr. Morrison. Jonas Bauer. Do you have a moment?"

His voice had this soft but firm quality to it that felt unnerving, especially over the phone. Even though the tone gave nothing away, the disembodied voice amped up my anxiety.

I'd been expecting the call, and even still, I was here, steadying myself before I replied, "Of course."

"Good. The news is as you expected, I imagine—the previous investor is uninterested in your property without the possibility of a faster build-out on the Bryant land. He has withdrawn his interest officially."

I took that blow, knowing it was coming, but it still hurt.

Still felt like I'd taken a shoulder to the sternum in a game of basketball.

"I understand."

"Good. I have secured another interested party, though this investor will require a more hands-on approach."

Something in his tone, or maybe simply that phase *hands-on*, had my hackles raising. "What does that mean?"

"I have been given to understand that you do not plan to hold the position of general manager indefinitely. Is that correct?"

How did he know that? I hadn't mentioned it, at least not formally, and Bauer wasn't exactly the chatty kind. But maybe it'd been obvious by the way I was so eager to get the changes made, though even if I didn't want this to be my life indefinitely, one couldn't blame me for wanting the business to grow and flourish rather than fizzle and die out on my watch.

"I don't know where this is going. But you're right—I have another business venture I plan to transition to full time as soon as the lodge is doing better and we've hired someone competent."

More than competent, I hoped, but at this point, I wasn't going to set the bar too high, as long as things were going well.

"The new investor stipulates being a voting party in the process to decide the general manager when you vacate the position, and he requires an in-house entity to oversee his interests."

"I—how would that work?"

"If all parties involved are amenable, I would recommend that *I* be the liaison between you and the investor," Bauer said, more emphasis in his tone than I'd ever heard.

"Wouldn't that be a conflict? You're our contractor, but

you'd be reporting to the investor. Sounds messy." And we didn't need more complications.

"I have anticipated the concern by suggesting that, if you accept the investor's proposed changes and schedule, you would terminate our contract, since we will have done everything we set out to do—namely, securing the funding to revitalize the resort. At that time, I would come oversee the construction and other changes under contract with the investor—so my presence would be at no cost to you."

Was it that simple? I wasn't sure.

"I'm not opposed to this, but I'd like my lawyer to look over the new contract and also see a formalized plan for what your role would be. I hadn't thought this kind of management was in your wheelhouse, but I'm happy for you to manage anything in the project, as long as it falls in line with the family's agreement."

"I assure you, Mr. Morrison, that I am fully capable of project management of this kind. I have overseen no fewer than twenty hotel restorations and dozens of resort revital- izations. I know what I'm looking at, what to ask for, and how to get the job done to make everyone happy."

It was the first and only time he'd touted his own skill— usually, his reputation preceded him. In this case, it did too —I just hadn't realized his transition to an in-person role during construction and expansion was a possibility.

"Good to hear."

"If there are no other immediate questions, I'll work to draw up all official paperwork this week and get it over to you. We'd like to start construction before June, which means we have an inordinate amount of work to do to get bids and contracts in place by that time."

He'd pushed to start this summer, and I'd believed we could do it.

Now that it was February and I was staring down another eight weeks of the season, at least, before things quieted and I could focus all of my attention on this, it felt impossible.

"Mr. Morrison?"

I must have been quiet for too long. "Yes, sorry. I'm here. I'm concerned about the timeline."

"Leave it to me. I know your location is a challenge, but that won't stop us. I have contacts at almost every major lift builder in the western United States, and they'll all eagerly take my call."

There was that arrogance, or at least confidence, again.

"Okay. I'm sure we'll need those connections."

"If there's nothing else, we'll speak again soon," he said, curt but not discourteous.

I hung up the phone and sat back in my chair.

Jonas Bauer had indeed saved the day. And now, he was going to be prowling around with his stern mask in place, likely terrorizing the children of Silverton and barking orders at the pitiable contractors who sign up to build out the first phase of our lodge's revitalization.

Scratch that.

Our resort.

Another piece had fallen into place, and it looked hopeful. At the very least, it wasn't calling me to compromise myself and my relationship with Wells.

And that was the last piece, the one I was least certain and most determined about.

CHAPTER TWENTY-THREE

Wells

I'd been avoiding everyone for ten days, and I knew my time was up. I'd known since Liam had messaged me and said I'd have to come to him. A good gesture, but an annoying one considering it left it up to *me* to forgive him and come tell him so.

The anger had shifted to annoyance. How dare he *message* me? How dare he not come groveling at my feet, begging for forgiveness?

But that was sort of what he'd done the first night, in the moment—he'd made no defense of himself. He'd done nothing to get me to see his side other than speak honestly.

He hadn't twisted my arm, hadn't tried to hurt me to make me see his side. Hadn't given me backhanded complements to shift the sand under my feet.

He deserved my forgiveness, and in truth, he already had it. But I didn't know how to get from here to there—I didn't know how to get from holing up in the inn and hiding to walking that quarter mile up the hill to his house near the lodge and starting the conversation.

It was Leo who came and burst my bubble. She arrived Monday morning, her morning off, and demanded to speak with me.

A small part of me felt sure she had more bad news—that version of me who was still waiting for Liam to turn out like Preston, though I knew full well he was nothing like him.

"You need to forgive my brother." She leaned against the closed door of my room, her arms crossed, long braids running over each shoulder and hanging by her ribs.

I whipped my head to her. "What? You were the one who told me he'd betrayed me."

"I might have been, but I'm also the one telling you to forgive him. He made a mistake, he's sorry for it, and he's fixing it the best he can." Her voice rang with impatience.

"It's not that simple," I mumbled, turning away from her to look out at the swirling snow tapping the glass of the window.

"The thing is, though—it is. And if you choose not to, then it's on you. He made a mistake, but he's admitted it, and he's fixing it. If you choose not to forgive him for being human, then you don't deserve him." She uncrossed her arms and turned for the door.

"That's—that's not fair. I didn't start this. You never go to bat for him—why now?"

"Because he's my brother. He's a good man, and he loves you, and you love him. Don't be an idiot and let pride or fear stand in your way. Forgive him and move on with your lives," she said, a weary look on her face I'd never seen before.

Before I found the words to respond, she was gone.

And I was left with the truth of it—I loved Liam. That's why it'd hurt so much—to know he'd always wanted the land. To know he'd even consider suggesting he could sway me into letting him buy the land—for wanting anything more than me and my happiness, if I was honest.

That was the ugly truth—I hated he'd put me up on the chopping block, and yet what I hated about that moment was also something I loved about him: he was unwavering and dedicated and wanted to do the right thing. It'd led him astray this time, but he'd somehow fixed it. I didn't know what that meant, but it filled me with hope.

That conversation had played over and over again for three days. After my Friday check ins, I decided it was time. No more waiting, no more letting life happen to me.

I was about to happen to life.

I knocked on the door, my heart in my throat. Such an odd phrase, but so true—all I could think was I didn't want to be at odds anymore. I didn't want to feel hurt and angry at him, or at me.

Because in the end, as I was so expert at doing, I'd become furious with myself for shutting him out and for forgetting who he was.

"Wells, hi." Liam pulled the door wide once he saw me, his posture straightening.

"Hi. Mind if I come in?" I asked, even as he gestured for me to do so.

"I—I'm glad to see you." He closed the door, took my coat and hung it on the hook, and followed after me.

I went to the living room, where he'd obviously been.

The TV was on but the volume low, the fireplace flickering with a dancing flames, and his computer sat on the coffee table, displaying a spreadsheet.

"I'm sorry to interrupt your work. I don't have to stay long."

"Don't worry about it. I'm glad you're here," he said quickly, sitting on the couch and nodding to the spot next to him. "Please."

I sat there for a moment, gathering my courage. I'd felt nothing but the clarity that I needed to come, and it had to be tonight, as I left the inn. But now that I was here, in his house, for the first time since our relationship had taken a more serious turn the last time I was here after Christmas, nerves snapped through me.

"We should talk," I said lamely, like that needed saying.

"We should." He nodded, swallowed. "I want you to know I made it clear to Bauer I am not going to make any attempt to buy that land at any point, regardless of our relationship."

Something in my chest eased, but my pulse raced. "What'd he say?"

"We lost the original investor, but I'm sure you won't be surprised to find that he's dug someone else up who will take the original plan with only a few stipulations."

He laced his fingers together in his lap and I wished they were fitted with mine.

"That sounds like good news, overall."

He nodded. "It is. It's better than I could have hoped for. I was sure he'd bail on us altogether after my idiot move in the meeting, but it was strange. Almost like he was relieved I'd refused to do anything about the land."

A smile pulled at one corner of my mouth. "I think maybe he has a soft spot for me. He's a shark with business, and he's consummately professional so he wouldn't let this feelings sabotage something beneficial for you. But I wouldn't be surprised if he was hoping I'd get to keep the land."

"Why would he put the pressure on to use our relationship in the first place? Why not refuse on our behalf?"

I could understand his frustration. He'd been through a lot these last few weeks, and if Bauer had simply told the original investor the land wasn't an option, as Liam had originally said it wasn't, then none of this would have happened.

"I don't know. But I'm sure he had a reason," I said, feeling unconcerned about Bauer's role in this. We needed to clear the air between *us*. "I'm glad you clarified with him, and I'm so glad he was able to find someone else."

"Me too." He looked down at his hands, cleared his throat, and looked up at me, his bright blue eyes piercing, even in the firelight. "I shouldn't have said it. I certainly never meant it. I hope someday you can find a way to forgive me."

I inched closer to him on the couch, drawn by his genuine apology, by his willingness to accept that he'd made a mistake. But before I satisfied the need that had been growing by the minute since he'd left the cottage over a week ago, I had to take responsibility for mine.

"I'm sorry too. I didn't give you any credit—I jumped to the worst possible conclusion, which was aided by Leo and Wyatt, but that's ultimately still on me. I should have called you right away, asked you to clarify, asked you what happened with you wanting the land before Tilda passed."

"I should have told you right away. I know waiting until we met that night didn't help—it'd been a full day since the meeting, and I'm sure it seemed like I was keeping it from you rather than being transparent."

He reached to grab my hand, which I gladly gave him.

"It didn't help, but I shouldn't have assumed the worst. And I'm most sorry for that—for taking my experience with Preston and putting it on you when you didn't do anything other than make a mistake. It was wrong, and it was stupid," I said, and smiled at his sheepish look. "But it wasn't this nefarious, manipulative plan you'd had in place since meeting me. That's right where my mind went, and where it stayed, and when you came that night, it was all I could think about."

His eyes were sad, his brows knitted together in frustration and concern, but I went on.

"I spent so long looking the other way, making excuses for the things Preston did... I was afraid to give you the benefit of the doubt because I'd been doing that for so long that it blinded me. But in this case, you deserved that, and I hurt you *and* me by not giving it."

I squeezed his hand and searched his handsome face.

"I'm sorry I did it. If I'd just kept my mouth shut, or stuck to what I knew was right, it never would have been an issue," he said, the misery on his face clear.

"No more of that, okay? You made a mistake, but you did what you could to fix it, and everything's fine. I made a mistake too, and now I'm here, asking for you to forgive me for failing to trust you."

"I forgive you, no question."

His hands moved to my forearms, gripping me reassuringly for emphasis.

"I forgive you, no question," I repeated, smiling at him.

His features calmed, his mouth answering my smile. "I missed you. These last ten days have felt like a month."

He tugged gently so I slid across the leather cushion.

I wrapped my arms around his neck, leaning closer. "I missed you too."

Our lips met in a sweet, long-awaited kiss, each of us letting out relieved breaths in the breaks between kisses.

His hand threaded into my hair, one hand behind my back crushing me to him, and I pulled him close, hands roaming his muscular arms and back, before he pulled away.

"I love you, Wells. I hope it doesn't freak you out for me to say that. I know it's soon—"

"I love you too," I said, an out-of-control smile taking over my face.

Liam closed his eyes as though to let that sink in, then pulled me to him and didn't let me go for a long, long time.

We'd been inseparable for the weeks since making up other than when work demanded we return to real life, but I'd promised the girls we'd meet and catch up.

"I'll see you later?" Liam asked as he pulled me into a hug.

"Yes. Just for a minute though—I have some people checking in tonight and Anthony can't be there. I thought you were busy too." I tucked my face into his warm neck as a gust of wind raced down the street.

He backed me up against the nearest wall between storefronts and shielded me against the wind, then spoke low and soft into my ear. "I do. I'm meeting John so I can give him the good news that I'll be part time with him this summer and hopefully full time at the brewery by fall. But anytime I'm not with you I'm thinking about when I will be again, so I figured I'd spare myself the angst and ask now."

He nuzzled his beard into the soft skin behind my ear and I pushed him back before we ended up making a scene right there on the street. "I'm glad you have good news for him. And I'm certainly happy you're so desperate for me you can't wait until you see me again."

We chuckled together, the sound of his rich laugh sending a shiver through me. He leaned back and tilted my chin up so we were eye to eye, his bright blues mesmerizing.

He cleared his throat, his brow creasing a bit. "You have no idea. Wells, you have—"

"All right, that's about enough of that. I do believe it is noon and therefore I get custody." Leo walked *right* up to us to cut Liam off.

Liam scowled. "I'm saying something important, Leo."

Leo returned the look effortlessly. "That's nice. But save it. You've been monopolizing her and my job as her friend is to remind her there's a life outside of *you*."

My turn to scoff. "I admit to being a bit wrapped up in your brother, but I've also been extremely busy with work."

Leo smiled sweetly. "Of course, my friend. Of course. Now say goodbye to this one," she nodded to Liam, "and let's find Bel."

Leo turned her back as Liam shook his head. He leaned in for a quick kiss. "I'll see you later."

"Ok." I smiled as he wandered away, very much appreciating the view and the warm glowing feeling filling my chest when I thought of how much we had in front of us— hopefully a lifetime.

"So you're in love with my brother, huh?" Leo said as though she hadn't known nearly as long as I had, slinging an arm around me as we walked to meet Bel.

"Sure am," I said, laughing.

"And when will you officially be my sister?" She grinned like it was nothing at all.

"We're a ways from that, okay? I'm still getting my head on straight, and we haven't even known each other a year yet."

Despite myself, I could feel the blush covering my cheeks, though it probably just looked like wind burn, very much the mode around town these days.

"Sure, sure. The hearts of women all over Silverton will break when you lock down Captain America, and he'll be that much closer to living his dream life," she teased.

"Who's living his dream life?" Bel asked as she walked up, looking exceptionally put together for someone who had on a giant puff coat, beanie, sunglasses, snow boots, and snow pants.

"Liam. Once he marries Wells," Leo said, again, like talking about her brother marrying me wasn't a big deal that I'd need to talk to him about before I go chatting around town about it.

Bel just chuckled, then ducked her chin into her coat to avoid the chill wind that pushed past us.

"Most eligible bachelor, off the market." She snapped, a fakely reluctant cluck following it.

"I'm done with this wind. Let's get inside." Leo jerked her head toward the sign for *Guac* and we hustled down the street.

"I gather we're always in for more winter, even in March?" I asked, not all that surprised since we were high in the mountains and spring snow was common in Colorado too.

"Yes. We'll probably close early April, but it might last through until May, depending on spring snow. Fortunately, the spring run-off happens fast and by early June, we're all wildflowers and sunburns." Leo smiled, the conviction of her love for this place clear, even in her discussion of the weather.

"Bel," a deep voice said, and Bel stiffened, eyes wide, face immediately pale.

Leo stepped in. "Jam! I thought you got in later?"

She moved to stand in front of Bel and hugged her older brother.

Jamie kissed Leo's cheek, a gesture I wouldn't have anticipated, but his eyes didn't leave Bel's face.

"Hi," he said, breathless if I had to describe it.

Bel nodded to him, and her eyes fluttered. "Hi."

"Well, we've only got so long for lunch. I'll see you tonight for dinner at Ma and Da's, right Jamie?" Leo said as she patted his arm, nodded for me to follow her, and pushed Bel in the other direction.

Jamie must have left, and I never saw who he was with, though it wasn't Liam or I would have noticed that.

"I guess he's back for his writing time?" I asked quietly as we shimmied into a booth in the restaurant, Leo on the end by Bel and me across from them.

"Yep. Went to collect his Oscar with Whit, and a few days later, here he is."

"You say that so casually," I marveled.

"He doesn't make a big deal of it. Plus Whit is super down to earth. I got to meet her last year when I visited him in California and they were dating..." Her voice trailed off when she realized the terrible timing with a small wince. "Anyway, yeah, he's back for... a while."

"So what's everyone ordering?" Bel said, a smile pasted to her face.

"Chimichanga for me." Maybe talking about food

would move things along, away from that awkward encounter, away from the hundred questions still on my tongue.

Someday, Bel would have to deal with Jamie. Someday, Leo would find her own Captain America, as she teased Liam. And someday, maybe, I'd be a Morrison too.

The End. (For now.)

~

Thank you for reading Liam and Wells's story! I hope you loved them as much as I did. The Silver Ridge Resort Series continues with Jamie and Bel's story—grab it today!

If you're curious to learn more about Wells' cousin Wyatt, he'll be starring in Almost Perfect, the first book in the Back to Silver Ridge Series!

~

The new OCONUS Bonus Series

Sweet Military Romance Overseas

The Problem with Planning Love, Book 1

Livie Anderson's got a plan for her life and she's on track for her next step. The last three years traveling Europe and working on a US Army base helped her experience all the adventure she wanted before she settles down in one place and stops the nomadic life. Now, her deadline to return home and start a family is fast approaching and there's a wrench in her perfect plans. Colonel Eric Wolfe came into her life and it's getting hard to picture leaving this world behind—but the Army life is the opposite of what she's always planned for.

Eric can't deny his interest in Livie, which is monumental in itself considering his total disinterest in everyone since his divorce three years ago. Despite his efforts to remain just friends, he can't resist Livie's pull—her joy, love for life, and genuine way of dealing with people. But he can't see a way to be with her without subjecting her to the military life that ruined his first marriage, and Livie's leaving anyway, so why can't he bring himself to let go?

Their lives are too different, and their plans don't match. They definitely shouldn't date, and they certainly shouldn't develop feelings. Too bad neither one of them can seem to stay away.

Finding Happiness in a Hoax, Book 2

Learning to Fight after Flight, Book 3

The Bright Side of Brooding, Book 4

Holding On to Hope, Book 5

ACKNOWLEDGMENTS

Thank you to all the readers and friends who've supported this series—I'll admit I was nervous to step outside of the Rambler world (and truth, am eager to get back to military romance when SRR is complete). Thanks to the many people who influenced the naming and shaping of my fictional little Silverton. It's purely fictional, but is an amalgamation of places I love in Utah.

Thanks to God, creator of the mountains I love so well!

As always, thanks to Jamie, whose friendship and support provide me wisdom and sanity daily. This is so much more fun with you!

Thank you to Christy and Emma for being Beta readers again for this book—your insights and notes have helped tremendously and I can't tell you how valuable it is to have your help!

Thanks to Zee Monadee for your incredible editing skills and love for this book! I can't thank you enough for your careful reading and suggestions.

To Meme Hernandez, thank you for your hard work and creative genius on the cover. Thank you for your patience with me as we worked to find the right look for the series and especially this first book!

To my family, who continues to cheer me on, and especially to Matthew, who always inspires me, but did so particularly by mentioning the amazing men of the 10th Mountain Division and their influence on US ski culture.

Though that's hardly in the book itself, it's a large part of the way I think of the town and the first generations who lived there. Thanks to my third and surprise baby, who has kept me company during the formation of this book—from my writing retreat weekend during which I wrote about a third of the book just after we found out about you, to these last days before we meet as I type up last thoughts and tuck it away to publish in a few months—like your brother and sister, you've already taught me much about love.

Thanks again to everyone who has taken time to read the book—what a gift! I hope you enjoyed. Please take a few minutes to post a review as this is immeasurably helpful! Thank you for your support.

ABOUT THE AUTHOR

Claire Cain lives to eat and drink her way around the globe with her traveling soldier and three kids, but is perhaps even happier hunkered down at home in a pair of sweatpants and slippers using any free moment she has to read and cook. Or talk—she really likes to talk. She has become an expert at packing too many dishes in too few cabinets and making houses into homes from Utah to Germany and many places in between. She's a proud Army wife and is frankly just really happy to be here.

You can also join Claire's facebook reader group for exclusive content and fun: https://www.facebook.com/groups/clairecain/

Website: http://www.clairecainwriter.com

E-mail: Claire@ClaireCainWriter.com

Newsletter sign-up for new releases, exclusives, and freebies: http://www.clairecainwriter.com/newsletter

SNEAK PEEK: SECOND CHANCE AT SILVER RIDGE

Can't wait to see more of Liam and Wells and find out what happens between Jamie and Bel? Read on for a sneak peek of Second Chance at Silver Ridge, available now!

~

Bel

Not shockingly, the walk into town was quiet. Neither of us attempted conversation, which I found to be both annoying and a relief.

I couldn't have him in my house, so we walked to *Rise and Shine*. I waved to Hailey who worked afternoons and found a seat by the window so I'd have somewhere else to look while we talked.

"What can I get you?" Jamie stood by the table, towering over it and me.

"Nothing, thanks. You go ahead."

He didn't even nod, then turned and walked to the counter. I could hear the tones of his voice and Hailey's, but did my best not to concentrate on them. I didn't need that voice in my head more than it would be by the end of this sham of a meeting.

While he ordered, I focused on pulling up the small ads I'd been making and a few of the larger poster-sized campaign items. Liam had loved them when I brought him the idea last summer—vintage ski posters to help promote the mountain and the town.

"That one looks familiar." Jamie sat and slid his chair in, then leaned closer to my computer screen. I held my breath, intent on not knowing if he still smelled the same. It should've been easy to block out his scent in a coffee house with fresh baked goods only feet away, but my stupid mind hungered for anything it could get from this man.

So I held my breath.

We sat on opposite sides of the small two-person table with the computer between us. Just like it had been years ago when he'd taken me to dinner, the space was too small. His ridiculously long legs bumped mine under the table and I tried to ignore the fact that it was the first physical contact we'd had since we'd kissed—if we could call it simply a kiss —nearly a decade ago.

"I pulled it from the archives. This is one of the origi-nals from the first few campaigns in the 1960s, I think."

His gaze turned to me and pulled me in. I met his eyes and the drop and spark in my stomach made me huff.

"That's a great idea. I can see why Liam wanted you for the job."

I opened my mouth, but no sound came out right then. Hearing anything nice from him felt precious and dangerous to me, even something as ordinary as that.

Why is he complimenting me?

A shadow crossed his brutally handsome face. "Listen, before we go any further with this—"

"No. Nothing personal," I rasped, barely capable of speech after meeting his light-socket eyes.

He clenched his jaw. "At some point, we need to have a conversation."

That low voice just loud enough for me to hear had me swallowing hard, working to summon speech. "I guess so. But not now. Let's just get through what Liam asked for and then we can be done."

So we did. I showed him everything I'd worked on and explained what media packages we had in place with different outlets. I told him what Jonas's goals were for the summer season while they pumped in money to build three new lifts and survey land for a hotel property. I explained what a big deal the sixtieth anniversary celebration was and all the places we'd start advertising it online and around the state.

"I know I'm just a musician, but over the years I have gained some experience with events and advertising. I've been in a lot of strategy meetings, watched a lot of albums and tours launch..." If he meant to be self-deprecating, he'd missed. You can't look like Jamie Morrison—pardon, Jamie *Morris*—and be anything but arrogant.

"I'm sure. That's great. I'm not saying I don't need help, but it might be a bit different than what you're used to." I waited for him to get that point, but he didn't seem to.

He shook his head, brows furrowing in frustration with my dismissal, no doubt. "Really, Bel, I can help. One thing I was thinking is the way they do festivals in the UK—"

I tsked, impatience rising. "Jamie, not to belabor this point, but that was different."

"Because it's music and not a ski resort?" His frown was deep and his face looked so... disappointed. With me?

I exhaled my frustration. "No. Well, yes, actually. But

with all of that stuff, they're advertising *you*. And *you* are this rare, special thing people wait all their lives to see in person. You're their favorite concert or their dream night out or their most-played album. You're not a floundering ski resort in a remote town with minimal capital and lots of hopes and dreams."

He brought his coffee mug to his lips and squinted toward the door. Was he not going to acknowledge all of that? Was he really *that* stubborn?

But then, he gently set the mug down and revealed his weapon—perhaps second only to his voice.

The smile.

The man didn't smile often, but when he did, *ouch*. Walking on glass with bare feet kind of business to my heart.

Had I seen him smile since we'd been friends? No, not even in photos online when he popped up unbidden in a headline somewhere. That smile with his sharp white teeth and perfect lips, his dark stubble dusting his jaw.

Heartache. Heartburn. Heartmelt.

As stupid as it made me, that's what I felt. Not broken, but a real pulse, a pang that shot through me with longing and nostalgia and sadness and hope.

I swallowed that down with a gulp from my water bottle, then tucked it back in my purse. "Why are you smiling?"

"I didn't know you think of me as a *rare, special thing*. But that's good to know." Those Morrison blues downright twinkled.

My cheeks burned and I clamped my mouth shut as I saw the teasing gleam enter his eye. He wasn't allowed to tease me or make a joke like that. That wasn't what this was.

I shut the computer lid, grabbed my purse, and headed

for the door before it all came roaring out. He'd followed right behind me, much faster at stemming my retreat than I would have guessed. Before he could touch me—and it looked like he might've, if I hadn't nearly leapt through the coffee shop's door, I met his eyes one last time.

"Trust me, Jamie. I don't."

Jamie and Bel are out now! Don't miss a thing—sign up for new release alerts and exclusives at http://www.clairecainwriter.com/newsletter.

9 781954 005044